Between Lions and Lambs

N. T. McQueen

To my beautiful wife,

who is the true model of faith

Between Lions and Lambs

Between lions and lambs

1973

Though he stood illuminated in white light, he was surrounded by darkness. He gazed into the sea of faces forever expanding into the darkness in front of him; faces and torsos climbing the giant walls and flooding the space of the stadium like a swarm of singing locusts. The fruit of his labor sang before him and he clutched the cross that hung about his neck, concealed under clothes.

The choir sang behind him, bellowing the glory among a score of finely tuned voices of all octaves and styles. The piano and guitar's gospel groove energized the song like a melodious engine.

Upon the platform, he stood in his finest black suit, pressed and immaculate with shoes that shone like the idiom claimed. His slick black hair glistened atop his slender frame. The stage was ordained with the most sparkling of golden ornamentation: a large golden cross imbedded with jewels, a pulpit made of dark and glossy wood, banners hung from lights and uttered exclamations of rejoice and exhortations. Fellow ministers stood to his left, clapping out of rhythm, singing, weeping, raising hands and speaking in bizarre tongues; vocally and physically worshipping for all the Lord has done in their lives. The sound seemed to envelope him in a surreal dream. Witnessing in a vision how He is walking and talking alongside them in the garden the song spoke of.

He raised both his hands toward the sky, eyes closed, swaying softly left to right, portraying an absorption of the presence of God. He listened to the crowd's tangle of voices as if a wave was ebbed and flowed over him. The ministers' mouths scrambled under some invisible force. The words battled back and forth among choir and crowd in a swell of sounds and moans and invectives. The chorus bobbed and swelled once again as the choir ends in unison with the band's engine. A great applause propelled toward the stage, the clapping hands bringing a visual life to the great sea before his eyes. He claps as he walks to the decadent podium with the gold crucifix. He placed his skinny hands at either side of the stand; his worn leather Bible displayed before him, marked and tagged with notes for the evening's sermon. The uproarious applause continued as a man, dressed in modest attire with his wavy brown hair, approached from the side of the stage and comes to his side in the spotlight.

"They're in place on the bottom floor. Two guys and an old woman," he said into the preacher's ear with a grim voice, the warm breath tickling the canal of his ear. "You give the signal and they'll be ready and then say the diseases and they'll come up at the right time. Just like we've been practicing. We paid them pretty good so they shouldn't be like the last ones."

"I sure as hell hope not," the pastor threatened jokingly, patting the man on his broad shoulder. He smiled those white teeth with the wide gap. The man's eyes were heavy and he could smell the faint, familiar odor before he exited to the side of the stage. The pastor opened his arms, holding them out to the thousands of believers in a hushed gesture and warm embrace. The crowd simmered to a murmur as he began a prayer in anticipation of his words, of God's words; his strong, congenial voice both demanding attention yet draped in tenderness and compassion as it echoed through the monitors. He noted the placement of the cameras before he began.

"Lord Jesus, we are here. We stand before You as humble men, women and children begging you for a glimpse of Your glorious Spirit. We are here with open hearts, open ears and open souls, standing at the doorway to Your kingdom, knocking on heaven's door for the gifts you have promised. The divine gifts we long to taste of from your bountiful table, Lord God. We pray tonight, Jesus, for the anointing of the Holy Ghost. Baptize us in Holy Fire, Christ Jesus. Light this building ablaze with your spirit. With your love. With your power. With your awesome light, God. Come down, Lord Jesus, come down and bathe us in Your presence and mighty grace. Wash us clean of our iniquities and sin! Redeem us of our pains and burdens. We worship you, Lord. We praise you! We glorify with our tongues and gifts and songs! O King of Kings, glory be Your name. Walk with us, Jesus. Walk with us tonight in this garden of desperate souls searching for Your divine fruit. And all God's people said..."

The voices, half bemoaning in desperation and ignited with passion, proclaimed an amen that shook the foundation of the immense walls. He brought his hands down and placed them on the sides of the podium. He took one hand and ran it across his slicked black hair.

"Does anyone feel the Holy Ghost tonight?"

Fervent echoes of agreement and snaps of gunfire clapping penetrated the thick, warm air. The massive building coming to life before his commands. He jolted with his arms outstretched with divine appointment.

"Glory to God, hallelujah. Please be seated this evenin'."

He made note of the camera's positions, making sure to avoid gazing into it directly as instructed. He placed his shaky hands on his Bible. His father's Bible. He surveyed the sea, then he began:

"Brothers and sisters, do you know why you're here today? Do you know why you have ended up here, in this place, in the presence of the Most High at this meeting? It is not a coincidence. No, it is not by chance. No, no, no. It is ordained and decided by the Lord God of Heaven and Earth that you be here today. That you be here and receive what God wants you to receive. To be here and receive what He has promised to bless you with. It is written that faith as a mustard seed will blossom into bountiful fruit. Thus sayeth the Lord, I urge you to listen tonight! When I was a young boy, when I was travelling the roads of this country, runnin' from God and all else, I met a man. Now, this man had lost his right hand in the second war and wandered the streets and alleys of this world. He was a battered and broken man who had seen his share of hardships. I befriended this strange man, not knowing what God was about to do. Now, listen here closely. I had never known this man before nor seen him in my years on this earth. And when I met him on that road, he looked at me with this puzzled look. Like he was shocked to see me though I'd never met him 'fore in my life. Now, he looked at me and I at him and he said, 'Are you the one God has sent to heal me?' I says no, sir, I don't believe I am but he wouldn't take no for an answer. So I asked him why he thought it was me that God had sent and he said God had told him in a dream. Listen close now, brothers and sisters The Holy Spirit is movin'. I kept fightin with him sayin' no, I ain't the one but he kept nudging me and I heard a still small voice in my ears saying, 'Touch his hand'. I said no way, I ain't touchin' his hand. Ain't it funny how we fight with God? But that voice kept urgin' me, over and over. I didn't know it then but the Holy Spirit was touchin' my heart. Can I hear an Amen? Hallelujah! Finally, I gave in to the will of God and touched this man's hand who I had never met before in young life. Now, I won't lie to you, brothers and sisters. I swear by the power of Jesus Christ, the Son of the Living God who died on Calvary, a jolt of electricity shot through my body and into that man and before my eyes, his lost hand was found, praise God, in heaven's name. Hallelujah! It was restored through faith in Jesus Christ-uh! Do you know why you are here tonight? Do you know why you are here? You are here because the Lord God of Heaven and Earth has placed you here tonight-uh! In this very place-uh! Every single person here tonight, black and white, young and old, man and woman and dearest child, has come to ask God for a washin' of their spirit in the blood of the lamb. You are in the presence of the Almighty, Jehovah, the King of Kings, the Alpha and Omega! God is here to-night to cleanse you of sin and restore you. Take away the sexual immorality, the carnal lusts, the drugs and drink that have saturated your lives with Satan's instruments.

"Now, you may say, Pastor, how can God save me from my sin? You may say, I've sinned too much to be saved. I am beyond salvation. Well, brothers and sisters, if He can create the heavens and the earth in seven days, then He can certainly save your soul-uh! Nothin' is too big for God. I'll tell you right now how to do it. It's a simple step that any of God's children can take. It's easy. One easy step you have to take to be saved. You ready now?" He leaves an anticipatory pause lingering above the audience. "Believe," he whispers. "Believe in the healing power of Christ Jesus. If you believe in Jesus Christ, the Bible says that as the soil makes the sprout come up and a garden causes seeds to grow, so the Sovereign Lord, the King of Kings-uh, Jehovah God, the Alpha and Omega, the Ruler of Heaven and Earth-uh, will make righteousness and praise-uh spring up, up before all the nations. Our righteousness must shine out like the dawn-uh! Our salvation must be as a blazing torch for Jesus' name-uh! If you believe, let me hear your faith with a shout of praise tonight!"

The audience erupted as if to battle, rattling the foundation of the building; the response escalating to a point of complete control. He held his hands up, as if to hush the spiritually riotous young and old believers.

"Stand with me and give God the praise, hallelujah Jesus! Praise God! God is here tonight, you know. Waiting on you.

He wants to enter this place and touch your needs and purify the black spots of your hearts. But he can't do it unless you give. Give of your mind, your heart, your soul, your time, and your tithe. Just as the Lord taketh, he can also give. If you give to the Lord, He will give to you. Just like any transaction. The Salvation Station. But give with a glad heart and He will fill your cup with the healing power of the Holy Ghost."

He paused. The crowd restless for the movement of the Holy Ghost. Closing his eyes, he bowed his head forward and the piano began to play again; a soft and placid soundtrack.

"Yes, Jesus. Yes, God. The Lord is speaking to me right now...there's someone here with...I believe it's...I believe it's...deafness. Yes, Lord. Deafness. Come forward now, in the name of Jesus and be healed. You know who you are."

From the bottom floor of the sea, a young pale man with brown hair and mendicant clothing wandered forward down the open aisle. His arms outstretched to the altar. The faces of the aisle passed unaware to him, some with hands raised, eyes closed, and others dealing with their own skepticism. He arrived at the stage and the man and two other pastors escorted him up the steps to the platform. The preacher met the young man to the left of the large stage, bringing the microphone with him.

"Hello, son. Can you hear me?"

The man stood reticent, dazzled by the brilliance of the spotlights and the millions of eyes watching his every move.

"Son?" He said as he snapped his fingers in front of him. The man caught sight and focused facing the preacher.

"Can you hear me?"

The young man shook his head.

"How did ya know to come up here, son?"

The man pointed to his lips.

The pastor leaned in close to the man's ear away from the crowd and whispered, "When I scream be healed, take a fall. The boys will catch ya."

The crowd, unaware of the exchange, continued to watch with alacrity. He faced the crowd and asked, "Do you believe that when two or more are gathered, the Lord will be there also?"

The crowd cheered back and the prophet placed his hands over the young man's ears and prayed feverishly, "In Jesus name, I command this spirit of deafness to be cast out. Lord, restore this man's hearing. Habolla santa yehova. Heal this man, God. In the name of Jesus Christ, the Son of God, be healed!"

He shook the man as he prayed. The young man simulating the touch of God with inconceivable veracity. As cued, the young man fell back into the arms of the pastors; igniting ooh's and aah's among the spectators. The organ continued its soothing and inviting song. They laid him supine on the stage and began waving their arms in thanks and glory.

"Praise, Jesus."

"Hallelujah to the Lord God Almighty."

After a short moment, they helped the young man back to his feet. The pastor came to his side and asked him, "Son, can you hear me?"

A smile indescribable graced the young man's face as he fervently nodded his head. His arms in the air, "I can hear! God, has healed me!" Tears began to career down his cheeks in utter euphoria. Even the preacher felt the authenticity.

"The Lord is good! He is in this place, tonight. Come and receive the miraculous healings He has in store for you. Thank you, Jesus!"

The sonic sound emerging from the inspired and panicked crowd almost caused actual deafness in the young man. The choir resumed their stance and began to sing joyfully as ushers passed the offering plates through the rows of distracted believers. Each reaching mindless in their pockets and purses; each row overflowing the buckets before they reached the end.

The healer sung along with heaviness inside like a boulder being placed on his spirit, slowly pressuring his soul. The words of the hymn pierced his side and he shook it off. He glanced over at the man, his friend, and saw the same heaviness in his posture. He resolved to continue on and deal with his conscience another time.

He motioned to the choir and musicians to lower the volume. He spoke into the microphone, "God has given me another vision. I...I see an older woman. Perhaps, sixty or seventy years old. The Lord is showing me a...a...tumor, yes, a tumor in her chest. It is cancerous and she knows it. Are you here, ma'am? Come forward, please."

A hunched woman, heavy and slow with a round face stood and made her way to the aisle as her white skirt shuffled with her jittery step. Two pastors met her at the end of the row and gently ushered her to the platform. With an empathetic smile, he grasped her hands and held them close.

"What's your name?"

"Rose."

"Rose is a beautiful name. Do you believe in the healing power of Jesus Christ?"

"Yes, sir, I do."

"Can you show me where the tumor is?"

She pointed to the center of her floral blouse.

"May I place my hand over your chest so you can receive the healing power of Jesus Christ and be baptized in the Holy Ghost?"

She nodded.

He leaned close to her line ridden face and whispered, "Just fall back when I say be healed. The boys will catch you."

"I'm not falling back. Do you know how old I am?"

He froze a moment, unsuspecting of this insurrection. The music soft and ethereal.

"If you fall, it'll be more convincing. They won't let you get hurt."

"Ain't happening," she stubbornly replied.

He began to feel panicky, wondering if the audience noticed the hesitation.

"Fine. Don't fall. I need to place my hand on your chest though."

She closed her eyes and lifted her hands. He placed his hand over her sternum. He heard her softly but sternly warn, "Be careful with those hands, preach." He paused and then placed his hand over her worn chest, praying, "Lord, heal your child of this affliction. Just as you made the lame to walk and the blind to see and the deaf to hear, release this woman from the bondage of sickness. In Jesus precious name I command you, be healed!"

He slightly pushed her chest, catching the unsuspecting woman to totter backward but not fall. Her eyes opened briefly and glared at the pastor who glared back and shouted in tongues. She resumed her scene and began to praise and sing to the heavens. Then she opened her eyes wide and proclaimed, "The tumor is gone. I can't feel it! I can't feel it! The Lord has delivered me! Hallelujah!"

"Hallelujah to the King of Kings! Praise be to Jehovah! The Holy Ghost is here right now, calling your name!" he hollered to the masses. The crowd grew agitated with the Spirit, the moans and cries of laudation swirled around the room and into the ears of every person in the place like pouring water over rocks. The choir, with passion and voice, began again.

He breathed out a sigh, relieved that Rose hadn't pulled a stunt like previous miracles. Everyone sang again, some in tongues and others in sobs, some with shouts and others with laughter. He had discovered this spiritual pandemonium produced the highest amount of donations than any other time of the service.

The man motioned for the pastor to join him at the side of the stage, clapping his hands to the rhythm. He leaned in close to his ear with his back to the congregation. The pastor spoke first.

"Goddamn, that last one was feisty. Don't bring her back."

"Boss, I can't do this," the man's soft tone was strong and concerned, nervy.

"You're being crazy. We ain't gonna get caught."

"It's not right. It feels wrong."

"It ain't wrong. They need this."

The man looked out to the massive crowd and asked, "Is this about money?"

"Money? How can you say that after what I've done for ya?" The pastor's southern twang sharp.

"Then for what? For what? I need to know." The song filled the air around them like a squall, booming.

"See those people out there? Those thousands of people in here and the millions on the other side of that camera? I can bring God to them. I am the intercessor. The mediator. I am the prophet. All their life they been waiting to hear from above and nothin' is all they received. You know that. But because of me, they have something to live for. Something to hope in. For the first time in their lives, they have faith in something other than death and taxes. Do you want to be the one to take that away from them?"

"But we're robbing them and they don't even know it."

"We ain't robbin' em…"

"Yes, we are!" he snapped.

"Shut up!" Beads of perspiration crowned his forehead. "Just sing and let it go."

He smiled and began clapping his hands, singing and smiling and praising as he stared at his friend. "Just let it go," he mouthed.

The pastor looked into his friend's eyes and saw the eyes of his brother. He focused his attention toward the crowd, turning his back and resuming his place at the center of the stage. The man turned and walked with his clenched hands toward the darkened side of the stage and disappeared. The pastor lifted his hands. The congregation was still.

"The Lord is speakin' to me, brothers and sisters. He is here. Jesus Christ said that I am the resurrection and the light. No one comes to the Father except through me. Can I hear an amen?"

"Amen!"

"Now…a voice is tellin' me there is a boy. A sick boy. A dying boy who needs the touch of the healing powers of the Holy Ghost. If you are here, come forward and receive the gift of healing."

He scanned the audience, searching for the last performer to arrive. He saw movement and noticed, under the glare of the bright lights, a young father carrying his son in his arms. He searched for the man at the edge of the stage and saw nothing. The two other pastors met the family at the stage and brought them forward. These were not the actors. His mind raced and tried to improvise. The father and son stood before him, smiling blankly as their smiles shone of hope and faith.

"W-What is your name, sir?"

"Tomas", the father responded. His accent strong and difficult as the tears garbled his words. He stood tall and dressed well in his cheap clothes.

"My son name is Gabriel," he added, looking down to his gaunt child. The boy's eyes were slits hovering over blackened bags. His arms and legs feebly grasped his father's strong shoulders. The pastor looked down at the sick child and his heart pounded. His mind spun and his flair stalled as the choir hummed. He placed his hands over the child's heart and asked, "What is wrong with the boy?"

"His heart is bery bad. The doctors say he no live."

The pastor placed an empathetic hand on the father's shoulder. A father with such care and love that it seemed foreign and uncomfortable to him, even to the touch.

"Sir, do you believe in the healing powers of Jesus Christ, the Son of the living God?"

He nodded emphatically. "Si. Yes. Yes."

The pastor, out of desperation, began to pray with sincerity for the sick child.

"Lord, we pray to You tonight. We pray that You deliver this child from sickness and restore his heart, Jesus. Make his heart new once again. We proclaim Your name, God, and we love and honor You. Just as You created a new covenant with us, create a new heart in this blessed child. Heal him, in the name of the Father, the Son, and the Holy Ghost."

His words began to flow again louder and louder.

"Jesus, You are the same today and forever! Create in us clean hearts and wash us of our sins! Esobobo hiya kokriah ibida. Devil, I call your name. I call you out of this child of God, in Jesus' name-uh! You have no power here today, Satan. This boy has been washed by the blood of the lamb. He has been washed by the blood that flowed on Calvary. In the name of Jesus Christ the Son of the Living God, I say, 'Be gone'!"

His tongues sputtered out of him wildly and he trembled as his hands clutched the heart of the child. The father's eyes gushed, dripping from his dark black mustache and dropping onto the boy's chest as his mouth never ceased to pray. The place stirred with a fire yet to be witnessed and he could feel it.

"In Jesus mighty name we pray, be healed! Hallelujah!"

The father stammered back as the pastor's voice blasted through the monitors. The boy trembled with the sudden movement and lifted his graceful hands in praise to God, muttering thanks in his native tongue. The pastor shouted out, "See, the child lifts his hands in praise of the King of Kings! Glory to God who was and is to come! You are all witnessing the healing touch of the Holy Ghost. He is here tonight, brothers and sisters, the Lion and the Lamb, the Prince of Peace is here to meet with you!"

He watched as the young father embraced his child. In his watery eyes, the unconditional love and faith in healing poured out upon his flesh and blood and he stood praising God fervent, reverent. The son in return embraced him in a familial joining that conveyed such pith that the pastor could hardly watch. He saw the hope he had falsely delivered reaped in the eyes of this broken family. He felt stained and alone and empty. Abandoned by God through his own machinations.

As he stood stationary before his credulous sheep, the shepherd felt a tugging at his heart and a shame nestled in, deep and rooted and black. He felt alone amongst thousands. A loved man with no one to love. He motioned upward for the choir to sing louder and louder but it only intensified the nauseating digging with each melodic decibel. Lines were forming down the cramped and cluttered aisles as believers filed toward the stage for prayer like a school of fish. He closed his eyes as perfidious tears formed in the corners. He surveyed the faces of the mass of believers. Their hands raised in worship and prayer, yearning for something they believed he could usher them into. Faces of broken men, women and children in their desperation for anything more. On the heads of each sobbing individual, the only face he could see was the red, blotched face of his father, laughing maniacally at the fruit of his loins.

Dead Men's Bones

"Lord, give me the strength to endure another day. By Your grace alone can I overcome the forces of darkness. Lead me in the path You have set before me and open my eyes to what is good and evil. May my life be a reflection of Your glory, grace and mercy. Amen."

I've said this prayer every morning for the past fifteen years and I have to ask myself why sometimes. I walk across the pink carpet, twirled with cream, floral designs to his door at the end of the hallway. Generic paintings line the walls and a musky smell of tobacco. There are only ten rooms on this floor because it has the most expensive rooms in the hotel. My shoes shush across the carpet like hesitant ships into a squall. An anxious feeling always catches me when I reach his door with my hand raised to knock at every hotel in every city. Not always but sometimes. I think it comes from the anticipation of the unexpected. I never know who or what I will find in his room but I do know I will have to take care of it. I will have to make it disappear.

I am a normal man in an abnormal position. With a position like his, it is imperative I exist. Not only to deter an inevitable destruction but to also fix what would seem unfixable. I'm what some might call a publicist but who I represent shouldn't need one. I'm more like a janitor. Of course, I wasn't always his janitor. There was a time when he didn't need one. But I guess we all need a janitor sometimes.

I arrive at the white door with the gold letters, I remind myself that I'm doing the right thing. I wrap my knuckles on the hollow white door and wait for an answer.

Nothing.

I knock once again, my gold wedding ring making a loud tap harmoniously with my fingers. "Boss?" I say to the door.

Still no answer.

I wait a moment and say to the door, "It's 9:50. You have to be at the convention center by 10:30 for a sound check and a run through of what's going on for tonight's meeting. I told you this last night. Open up."

I hear a mumbled gripe through the door and realize today is going to be one of those days. I reach into my pleated khaki's and pull out the key. I always have a key. It always saddens me when the key is in the lock despite my exhaustive experience. I slowly turn the gold door handle, entering the suite with trepidation. My breath chokes me a moment as I am witness to a familiar sight behind the swinging door.

I survey my employer's room and find affirmation of the significance of my position. Various clothes, both male and female, are strewn about the room like moss on boulders, including a red, lace brassiere dangling from the crystal chandelier as if to represent a flag of conquest. I see torn silk curtains across the wide glass windows, letting in slats of light from the new morning and accenting the overturned coffee table and countless wine bottles placed randomly throughout the excess. The pink carpet is littered with broken wine glasses, cigarette butts, and various types of food and stains including soup, a half of some pasta dish and what appears to be a mixture of vomit and wine. It smells of musky smoke and a concoction of spoiled food, hard liquors, and perfumes. Essentially, it smells like any other night. In the bathroom, I hear water running and look to see an oceanic puddle seeping onto the pink carpet, turning it dark. God knows how long it's been running. A scene as greedy as the grave.

Amidst this aftermath, I see the man, the source of my livelihood sprawled out on the king-sized bed, his thin and naked, aging body half covered by the silk sheets and two half naked women laying across his unconscious body in a licentious cross, crumpled into each other.

I stare at the evidence of his debauchery with hopeless eyes as he groggily revives from his late night. He opens his eyes, squinty and bloodshot, and looks at me with an incoherent smile. I hate to see his eyes this way. And sadly, they are always like this. In a mumble of burps and groans, he says, "Gerry, my friend, how's it do..." as his eyes roll and he slips back into unconsciousness.

I drop my gaze to the floor, fighting my heartache from coming out my eyes. I've tried not to care but I can't harden my heart that easy. I always break down at some point along the road even though it alleviates nothing inside me.

I compose myself and rub my palm across my head, back and forth. It's hard to tell whether God or Clemens has made my hair leave but, as I come closer to the median of my life, I can't help but lean toward the latter. I look at my boss, my friend, and see the gold crucifix dangling across his chest and wish that that gold piece meant something to him if it ever did. That gold cross that has been our lives. My eyes travel to the nightstand and see the black leather Bible open and surrounded by jewelry and crumbs, lit by the nightstand lamp that I assume has been on all night. The old Bible he once held with passion and eagerness; the source of his conviction surrounded by sin.

I walk over to the nightstand, the smell of rotting food and alcohol strengthening as I approach. I pick up the beaten Bible in my hands. The pages crinkle an old hymn to me, filled with nostalgia and moments of genuine faith and miracles along the way whatever way this road I'm on is going. I rub the thin pages between my fingers and look back at his face. It's a face I used to find familiar and inspiring but now, it is something foreign to me. An acquaintance I've known most my life. I don't know if it's the face itself or the man behind the face. I used to know a man I respected and I admired that had a face like his but the aging lines are brandings of so many hypocrisies that his features seem unintelligible. I don't think I know this face. Maybe I never knew it to begin with. Or maybe, I don't know my own.

I peer down at the book, noticing a faded, maroon blotch across the bottom of the pages. It's open to the book of Matthew, Chapter 28, verse 19 and Jesus' red words pop out at me from the pages like road flares burning blood. It commands, "Therefore, go and make disciples of all nations, baptizing them in the name of the Father and of the Son and of the Holy Spirit and teaching them to obey everything I have commanded you." The red words, written in blood, so innocent and penetrating, prick my conscience like cacti and I shut my eyes tightly for strength. When I open my eyes, the rest of the verse comes to me. "And surely I am with you always, to the very end of the age." Really? Is this what Jesus Christ died for? I can't help but wonder if He really is.

I close the book phlegmatically and toss it back on the nightstand, knocking over an ashtray onto the pink carpet, scattering ash and butts across the discarded remnants of last night's events. I watch it scatter in a transparent cloud as my mind goes back to that verse. "...teaching them to obey everything I have commanded" and my throat tickles with irony.

I chuckle not at God. Not at religion. Not at my boss and old friend, wasted and defiled. I don't even chuckle at myself but in a way, I am. I laugh at God's finest creation, man.

I spy a glass half-empty with vodka on the nightstand and toss it into my boss' face as he lays passed out on the bed. His head jumps forward and he lets out a hoot. The two harlots readjust their position and continue their post-inebriated sleep, twisted within the red sheets. He brings his hands to his face and gives it a slow rub, groaning. I stand over him, holding the glass in my hand and I say to him, "Come on,

Clemens. If you are late again, we might not be able to get this venue for next year. If we lose this venue then we lose a big audience. Is that what you want?"

He looks at me, his stubbly face upside down, and smiles revealing the gap between his two front teeth and the immaculate whiteness of his enamel. Thousands of dollars worth of dental work to create a flawless smile and he refused to part with the gap. Said it was his flair. I never understood that.

"Is it?" I repeat to him.

"Gerry, my friend", he answers in that lazy, country drawl, "do you think anybody is going to deny me anything? I'm a prophet of God. Everybody loves me. 'Ask and it shall be given unto you' as the Good Lord once spoketh."

He burst forth with a disturbing laugh. My heart feels like it is sliding down my chest and into a drain with each chortle. I look at him, wishing him to quit, but he keeps on laughing, absorbed in himself.

"Boss, why are you doing this?" I ask.

"Doing what?"

All of this, I think to myself. He looks at me with a soft grin. The veins in his dark eyes bright and red.

"Oh, come now, it's just some harmless fun. You think Christ was as square as you? Hell, he turned water into wine. I should know."

It's not just the drinking it's everything. You're going too far with it, Clemens, and I'm worried. I'm worried about the people out there looking to you for hope. I'm worried about the consequences not only for you, but for me. I can't keep all of this undercover anymore. Early on it worked but, now it's getting beyond the point of no return. I can't fix all your mistakes and I can't live with mine. This sounds great in my head but the thoughts never escape to daylight.

"Don't try to pass your fear onto me. I know what I'm doing," he says, trying to sit up. I just watch him labor to elevate himself. He squints and breathes out his foul heavy breath into the air. I can smell the stench from where I'm standing.

"Aren't you..." I begin to ask but then it dies out.

"Huh?" he says, rubbing his eyes. His gray and white hair, extending and curling like a colorless fire frozen in time. I stop and shrug it off as if I were saying nothing. Inside I'm burning but a captive to my insecurities.

Soon, he is rummaging through the mess on the floor, lifting bottles to snatch a last droplet of liquor, clearly dismissing anything I have to say. The women on the bed begin to stir and stretch as the sunlight arrives across their sleeping faces. Their nakedness becomes exposed and I turn my eyes away and pick up the phone to dial a cab.

"Is there anythin' to drink round here?" he asks to no one in particular. I watch him and can't help but wonder if there's a God at all and if so, why doesn't He care? Why not change this?

It takes twenty minutes before the cab arrives to take the two women back to wherever they came from which leaves us twenty minutes to get to the convention center in time. I escort them to the elevator and pay them their fee of three hundred dollars each and tip an extra one hundred for their silence.

"You got it preacher man," the tall brunette smirks with a wink as she slaps my backside. I jump at the gesture and they both giggle. Eyes hidden behind layers.

They step in as the doors close, waving flirty as they disappear. I have a nauseating sense of déjà vu. This scenario, this scene, where I fund the devil's work with God's money, is common practice, day in and day out. Only I know about what goes on behind Clemens' closed doors. If not, I haven't been doing my job. No other board member or associate pastor has a single inclination of the immorality I've witnessed on these tours. It's become worse since the camera crew started filming the revival meetings. Much worse. As for the women, they come only after really good revival services where the Spirit is moving.

When I get back up to the hotel suite, Clemens is not on the bed. The television set is on, tuned to last night's sermon, but there is no sound. The duplicitous man before me on the screen is not the man I know as he waves his arms elegantly and persuasively. I hear a retching sound coming from the bathroom and I walk over to see my employer, naked and pale, cradling the toilet bowl, sitting in a putrid mixture of toilet water and bile and booze. His forehead is christened with beads of sweat and I just shake my head and go to repair the chaos that has plagued this luxury suite, plagued our lives. Through years of experience, I find it best to leave him be when he's spooning the toilet after nights like this. His gold cross is dangling down from the rim of the toilet bowl, swaying above the remnants of his hypocrisy.

I begin the cleaning up as best I can, tossing bottles, trash, and food into a large plastic bag as occasional growls of discomfort and bitterness come from the bathroom. What a mess. The cost of this room just doubled. I scrub vomit stains from the carpet and wipe up God knows what from beside the bed. Shortly, I manage to upgrade the room from disaster to mess in a few minutes, now leaving us ten minutes to get out the door. I grab the large black duffle bag that has accompanied me for all these years, and unzip the largest compartment to stuff the plastic bag into it. I zip it up and place it on the disheveled bed. Back in the bathroom, Clemens is still hunched and attached to the side of the bowl.

"Alright, boss, let's get you dressed and some coffee in you so we can at least attempt to look like men of faith," I say as I put my arms under and hoist him up, shuffling baby steps to the bedroom. The sour stench hits me and I abruptly make an about face and head toward the shower stall.

"We have a busy day today and I need you to shape up. You have an interview this afternoon so, please, get yourself together by then, alright?" My voice sounds empty, rote, like there's no substance as I open the frosted glass of the shower door. Like these words are a script I've been rehearsing for the past two decades. A cycle that can't be broken. Useless words that fade into the air to be remembered by God alone and the speaker. The tiles inlaid in the shower have floral designs as well and I wonder why such an expensive room has such inexpensive taste. What are we paying for? I turn on the hot water and wait for it to warm. The pungent, lingering odor gives me a small nauseous feeling.

"I need a smoke," he pleads through his hands.

"You need a lot of things, Clemens."

"I just need a smoke is all."

I wait till I see the steam rising inside before I help my incapacitated employer get into the flow of water. Luckily, there's a small ledge he can sit on. I place him there as the water pours over his naked body, running down his face, chest, and all. He opens his mouth and lets the water overflow. I walk over to the large mirror at the sink and open the complimentary soap and shampoo.

A wave of depression washes over me as I help bathe this man, this man-child, whom I've spent more hours with than my own family, wash, shave and dress himself, regressing back to an infantile state. The man who rescued me from hell when I was twelve years old has now put me through it ten times over and I'm confused and, in a way, alone. Is this what God had intended in my salvation? Is this my purpose to uplift this façade? I feel disgusted with myself for enabling this downfall. It has only fed the beast, all this secrecy. But I'm pummeled with guilt over confronting him. How can I be the voice of truth? Do I tell this man of God what is righteous and just? He's the prophet, not me. I am just as much a sinner for not stopping what should have been stopped long ago, back when we started all of this. What makes my sin less than his? My heart breaks not only for Clemens, but for myself. I have wasted my life with nothing to show for it but good intentions.

I get him dressed in relatively good time. I sit him on the beige, floral couch and go to call Bill. He moans and slumps down, putting his forearm over his eyes as I face the desk.

"You put any thought into callin' Abigail?" I ask as I dial the numbers. He doesn't answer behind his slouch. I know he hears me it's just a matter if he wants to listen.

"I'd call her if I were you," I advise. My reasons don't make sense to me. It's all so futile with him. Nothing changes for the better.

"Not now, Gerald. For the love of Christ," he moans at me.

I get Bill on the third ring and tell him to meet us out front with the Cadillac in five minutes. I hang up and see Clemens still slouched, eyes covered, humming an old hymn he used to sing when we were ministering on the road long ago, when he first began evangelizing in small churches around the country. I remember that song well. It was after he found out his father had passed that he began singing it. That's when a lot of things began. I thought Clemens wouldn't care, would just shrug it off. I knew he hated his father but, when he heard the news, his eyes were hollow and mournful, like a buried love had been unearthed all too late. Maybe from guilt or regret or love. No one knows. Not even Clemens, I believe. He would never open up about it anyway, not even to me. Listening to him sing those words now, in that raspy broken voice, brings back nostalgia of a time when our mission was clear and true. Straight and narrow. After that phone call, he became everything he swore he'd never become.

As the words flow, I see a tear slide down his cheek from behind his covered eyes. Over all this time, I've seen him cry nearly every day over some of the most simple and irrelevant reasons imaginable. A dead bird, a crying child, spilled water. It's just something he does. No one knows why especially me. But the words seem haunting and authentic as he sings them.

1932

The boy awoke to the rumbling sound overhead. Small stones jittered to life on the damp mud at the force of its passing and his ears were blanketed with sound. The air was cold and dank under the bridge and condensation dripped from the steel beams stretching over the wide and fast river like tears. Through the slats, he could see the massive body and its infinite tail of cars loom faster toward its destination. The trellises shaking with the force of the thunder.

He sat up quickly at the start and covered his ears. The act did little but he liked to think he was being responsible. He looked out over the shallow mountains and noticed the sun had been up before him. The scream of the engine waned as the end car passed his place of rest and went across the river toward the north. He watched in longing as it left. Sitting up, he pulled his dismantling shoes off his feet and saw the bulbous blisters swollen and filled. They were sensitive to the touch but he welcomed the physical pain from the thirty-three miles walked last night from somewhere to here. He didn't care where he went as long as it was from where he'd been. He rubbed his face and picked at his gaping grin and sat a moment, procrastinating using his feet for anything. The new stubble surprised him and he puffed with a sense of boyish pride. He picked his pillow up from the damp pebbles and converted it back into a jacket. When on the road, necessities take on multiple purposes.

He carried an old sack made of a table cloth he had stolen from a family picnic and used it as a means to transport his exiguous valuables. It held a can opener, his father's Bible, two cans of baked beans, and a golden cross with a thin chain. Besides the clothes he wore, these had been his possessions since he had left.

The water's edge lay at the end of a sloping embankment thirty feet from the bridge's base. Knowing that he reeked of sweat and filth, he thought it best to wash himself and, gingerly, stood and hobbled carefully down to the shore. The water flowed slowly. He took off the jacket, his once-white shirt, and his trousers and stood naked save his long briefs. He watched the water flow and thought of his brother, noticing the ache of the memory still strong. The nausea returned but faded as it came. He stepped into the frigid water to his waist. The current pulling at him but not enough to sweep him away. On the riverbed, the round stones poked his tender soles. His skin rippled as he put his hands into the river and washed under his arms and other essentials, holding his breath as he bathed. The shadow of the bridge captured the chill of the morning as sunlight overcame all other areas. He wondered about his mother and sister and felt shame for leaving.

When he finished, he wobbly made his way out of the river, picked up his clothes, and headed up the slope to the base of the bridge. It wasn't until a few feet away he realized a shape stood at the base of the open cave. He startled back and survival kicked in. The ageless man stood in the darkest of the shadows and watched him with eyes that were unmistakably drowned in sorrow. Under his massive, brown, matted coat, he could see the man's almost skeletal frame. He wore no shirt and his pants had been cut just above the middle of his calf. The fray of the hem dangled lightly. He resembled a lost boy grown up.

"I ain't got no money," he informed, shivering and wet. He kept his clothes close to his chest. The water slid down his body, climbing over endless bumps of skin. The man just swayed back and forth, itching his thick beard. His face was covered with brown hair that eyes peered from making his nose the largest characteristic on his face.

"I said I ain't got no money," he repeated louder. The boy looked down at the shore, looking for the largest rock he could find. The man shook his head and mumbled, raising his hands, palms toward him in a surrendering gesture.

"Well, whatcha want then?" the boy asked. The man kept his eyes on him, only averting to look at the underbelly of the steel bridge and its intricate design as if he had never seen something so intriguing. Both not wanting trouble but wanting it simultaneously. They stood at a standstill. Neither knowing what the other wanted until the man finally spoke.

"What are you running from?" he asked in a gentle but pinched voice that seemed to flow directly from his sinuses. His bare feet were black and, by his stance, one could tell he had grown accustomed to being shoeless. His nails imbued with the remnants of countless paths.

"Who says I'm runnin'?" the boy responded, looking querulously at the man. His fingers and toes had lost their feeling yet stung and pricked with pain.

"You should get dressed," the man suggested and sat down on the concrete slab at the base of the bridge. The boy felt skeptical but knew he couldn't afford to get hypothermia. He put his clothes on quickly and rubbed his arms, hugging himself as he stepped over closer to the bearded man, examining his surroundings.

"How old are you?" the man asked as he looked up into the boy's face.

"Eighteen."

"Nope," the man said, shaking his head.

"Am too."

"You can't be no more than sixteen." He coughed a deep guttural cough. The sound thick and choked.

The boy looked at the man then out across the river and said, "Sixteen."

The man smiled. "I left when I was fourteen."

"Why'd you run?"

"Why does anybody run?"

The boy thought a moment. It was nice to talk with somebody foreign. Someone with no knowledge of the past or future. A companion to oblige his loneliness. "My daddy was a drunk."

The man looked up into the boy's face. "A mean one?"

The boy nodded.

"That's a good enough reason as any."

The boy shook his head in agreement.

"What's yer name?" the boy asked.

"A name means nothing."

"It may mean nothin' but ya still got one, don't ya?"

The dirty man raised his long, tattered face to the boy and smiled a humored smile.

"I'm called Righty," he said, nearly chuckling.

The boy extended his right hand to the man as his father had always taught him to. "Name's Ezekiel."

Righty looked at Ezekiel's hand and then into his eyes. From under his oversized sleeve, he produced a stump where his right hand should be. The scarified flesh pocked and coated. Ezekiel hesitated a moment and then slowly shook his invisible hand. Righty seemed to not fret. A silence lingered between them a moment as if the conversation had withered out. The cold air clung to the shadows like ice. Ezekiel rubbed his arms trying to warm himself from the bite of frigidity. Righty simply stared at the dark, grey and brown stones contemplatively. Righty smelled of dirt, musky sweat, and one's own filth; his mendicant clothing spotted and marked like a land map with the remains of substances only God could recall.

"Where ya from?" asked Ezekiel.

"Nowhere...Everywhere. It doesn't matter. I'm of the earth," he answered without looking up.

"Do ya have any family?"

"It wouldn't matter if I did."

Ezekiel scratched his scalp, trying to think of anything that would engage his new transient partner into talk. The man's voice distant and apathetic as if he could find no use in trivialities. Ezekiel avoided looking at his amputation for fear it may arouse some hidden anger that lay just beneath the surface. The isolation of the road had been what bit at Ezekiel most. The human-less silence, the lack of food, the cold, bed-less nights were peculiarly cathartic but he could never be free of the small haunt of loneliness.

"You haven't been doing this long," Righty said.

Ezekiel glanced from the corner of his eye over to the slouched, grimy man. "Doin' what?"

Righty looked with his head bowed and eyes up toward Ezekiel but not looking at him. "Don't do that."

Ezekiel looked puzzled. "Huh?"

"That," he answered sharply. "Stop doing that."

Ezekiel feigned confusion but became irritated and almost felt it worth the pain of isolation to leave.

"I said, you haven't been doing this long," he repeated, rubbing his crooked nose on his flag-like sleeve.

Ezekiel, staring, openly asked, "How you know that?"

"The water," Righty said.

"The water? The water tell ya that?" He chuckled.

Righty's concealed cheeks made what seemed to be a smile underneath the blanket of fur jutting limply from his face. "New guys always feel the need to bathe. To be clean. Even when it's too cold to be cleaning, they still have to do it. People always have to feel clean when nobody is really clean. Water won't do it."

"Oh," Ezekiel realized, surprised at the man's observation and slightly embarrassed. Righty continued, scratching the pink stump of his right arm inside his large jacket sleeve.

On his sole hand, the nails were long and mustard yellow and the cuticles caked, impacted underneath.

"What most people don't realize is that everybody is on the road somehow. Going from one spot to the next. They don't know where they're going, or what they're doing, but they're going somewhere. Roads are roads no matter how you travel them," he said wagging his accusing finger in front of himself. "People just don't see that. Just don't see it at all." Righty's face looked dejected at the thought as if his words were veracious to the point of burdening.

Ezekiel listened intrigued with both a bizarre attraction of youthful curiosity and needed company. The sun broke through the gray, white clouds and began shining through the slats to interrupt the banal darkness of the shadows. Infiltrating bit by bit. A flat board of light shone on the side of Righty's face and Ezekiel could see the redness of his stretched cheeks and the toll he had paid living in motion. A gathering of glistening liquid had gathered under the hair of his nose. His right ear disfigured and scarred with burns. Ezekiel wondered how God could do this to a man, despite anything he could have done to deserve it.

"How long you been out here?" Ezekiel asked.

Righty began picking his nose as he answered. "A long time."

Ezekiel watched him a moment and then looked off across the cool river. The sun's rays brilliant and omnipresent now.

"You live under here?" Ezekiel asked, nodding to the train tracks.

Righty gave him a puzzled look, then he looked up to the tracks, and then back at Ezekiel. "I live where I live."

Ezekiel began to grow frustrated with Righty's ambiguous answers. "Well, God knows ya live somewhere, right? Ya have to have a place to rest yer head."

Righty sniffled and said, "God has nothing to do with it."

"What?" Ezekiel asked, near exasperation.

"You speak of God when God is no concern."

Ezekiel spit into the dirt and crossed his arms across his chest. The frustration beginning to build within his veins as the ever-ready furnace of his short-temper stoked.

Righty continued, "God, as you say, is a trailblazer that knows it all. Knows it all up and down." He pointed his finger up then down in an exaggerated motion.

Ezekiel did not want to talk about God nor anything to do with him. "I think God likes to watch us wander," he growled.

Righty coughed and began a prolonged retch as if holding the final note in a song as he leaned forward. He spat out what appeared to be mucus with a tincture of red but Ezekiel couldn't tell for sure.

"You alright?" Ezekiel asked concerned, leaning forward with Righty, trying to see if he really was alright.

"Of course He likes to watch us wander, fool. Everybody is wandering. God wanted it that way. Anyone who wanders is lost and anyone who is lost must be found. Who should find us then?"

Ezekiel looked hard at the disheveled and broken man whose wily words were almost ordained by the wisdom of

Solomon in some outlandish time. A man of woes and trials, pain and loss speaking through years of experience and travel. An understanding only achieved through a life lived hard as stone.

"Are you sayin' we are all lost?"

"God made the road. We have to walk it. But He makes it so the road leads back to Him, no matter which way we choose to take. In the end, we don't have a choice. No choice at all. People just don't see that. Don't see it." He spoke out loud but too himself, shaking his head. "That's why I hate Him."

He stared at Righty intently. "I hate Him too."

Righty made no gesture. His stomach shifted and twisted with hunger or conviction. The truth he had been taught all his life felt bitter yet his guilt troubled his soul at the thought of complete betrayal. Of his father's faith. Of his mother's faith. Of his brother's faith. He needed faith in something and he wanted to believe in the God this strange man spoke of. The God he once thought he knew but now questioned and searched for faulty answers and contradicting ideology. He wanted to hate God. To hate Christianity. To hate religion. To hate those who believed in a God he saw tear his family apart with his allowance of all things wicked at the same time preaching that He loves us. The only love he felt of God's was through the back of a hand. But the words he spoke scared him.

"I got some beans if ya want some," he offered to Righty, who had begun to sort the brown stones from the grey stones with his bare feet. His features intent and focused, silent a time before saying, "God didn't give us eyes in the back of our head."

"What?" he replied but Righty gave no further response.

After a moment, Ezekiel got ready to stand up to retrieve his sack but stopped when he heard Righty's voice.

"Your daddy must have been a preacher. Preacher's children are always runnin' from God for awhile but they find their way back. Sometimes not all in one piece," he said, raising his stump in the air. "It is better to cut it off so we're told. Sever whatever hinders us from doing good. But what is good? I've stolen. I've drank till my heart gurgled its beats yet I am still good. Good is man-made. A word. An idea. If it is made by man then it is going to have problems. It's going fail. Good, or whatever God says is good, is inside you deep. Deep inside." He stopped as if interrupted and saw the two mounds of brown and grey stones. He looked up with his dark brown eyes into Ezekiel's face with a startled gaze and excited voice.

"Which would you choose?"

Ezekiel felt his face contort at Righty's wild question, catching him off guard. "Huh?"

"Choose. Choose. Which one would you choose?" he said urgently, pointing his stained hand toward the two piles. The faint sound of a whistle came from a distance.

"Hell, I don't know. What does it matter?"

"Everything matters! Pick a pile, please. There's no moment like now to choose a side so choose. Quick." The transient man's persistency had made Ezekiel forget he was starving. He examined the two piles and then the face of the grimy, eccentric and felt lost at the back end of an inside joke. He picked the first that came to mind.

"Brown, then. I pick brown."

Righty sat back and his eyes spoke disappointment. His body released its tension and his head hung slightly as he rose to his feet. He gazed solemnly over the water through his tangled hair then turned and began to leave. Ezekiel sat in amazement and confusion, not wanting the company to be leaving so quickly.

"Hey, where ya goin'? Was brown the wrong choice?" He called after him.

Righty stood covered from head to toe in light. Every scar and bruise, wrinkle and hair illuminated and visible. Ezekiel had underestimated what the road had taken from him. Righty turned and met young Ezekiel's eyes.

"There's no room in heaven for those who sit on fences. No room at all. People just don't see that. Don't see it at all..."

He mumbled along as he turned, walking drudgingly up the gravelly embankment, shaking his head in bewilderment. As he crested the small hill and disappeared, the earth began to rumble to life once again, the whistle of the coming train imminent. The roar of the vessel grew louder and louder till all noise would be subdued by its power. Ezekiel sat as the stones, grey and brown alike, chattered to life around him and Ezekiel thought about what Christ had said about rocks talking. With the force of the train overhead, Ezekiel thought of his brother again and the memories returned with the sound, strong. He leaned over and emptied what lay of his stomach onto the rocks, alone again.

Wounds

       I press the button for the first floor and we head down. Clemens is with me but not completely, still stumbling out of his stupor. The ding opens the doors and I notice through the lobby doors a crowd outside. I tell Clemens to sit and he listens for once. I try to appear as inconspicuous as possible as I head out of the lobby with the duffle bag, weaving in between bystanders. As I return from dumping the bottles and trash from the room in the hotel's dumpster, I see our black Cadillac limousine with the tinted windows pull into the covered esplanade outside. Inside, I find Clemens sleeping, slouched on the floral couch. I nudge him and he startles awake. We stand and walk through the hotel doors straight toward the backseat of the Cadillac giving the hotel guests who would recognize Clemens little time to act. The zealots usually find out where we are staying and camp outside, waiting for Clemens to emerge. Some would follow us from city to city like groupies. Others were homeless or insane, fanatical. We called them God Groupies for fun but I admired their passion. Sometimes even envied their dedication. I couldn't let them see him like this. I can't break their faith no matter how askew its premise may be. Clemens always does have a heart for the lost, for some reason. Maybe it's from us being on the road so much. I don't know.

The boyish valet nods and greets us as he opens the car door, trying to increase his tip. I push Clemens in and slap a wad of cash into his youthful hand before he shuts the door. I notice his awestruck smile staring into his hand as the small group of zealots begin to crowd and push around the door, calling for Clemens and waiving Bibles in a frenetic way. The car pulls forward and out into the sunny open air leaving the shadow of the chaos waning in the rear. Bill greets us with a white smile and I tell him to take us to the convention center as quickly as legally possible. He nods and the car accelerates quickly with a fierce growl from the engine.

I attend to Clemens as he fumbles his seatbelt, missing the latch and mumbling something under his breath. I reach over him, buckle the belt with ease and sit back as he stares into his lap like I had just completed the world's largest puzzle in seconds. I ask him if he's alright and he just smiles with his head down, the blood gathering in the veins under the bluish bags of his eyes. I make a note to myself to do something about those bags before tonight's meeting.

"You hungry?" I ask but he doesn't answer so I take it as a no. Over the past few months his appetite for food has been non-existent. All other appetites are voracious.

"We got a call from that news station requesting an interview again. What do you want me to tell them?"

"Tell them God told me not to do it. That always works," he answers, uninterested. I hate it when he gives me that answer. Anything that is difficult, he tells them God won't allow it and he's just obeying the Lord. I've heard other evangelists use it too.

Putting my seatbelt on, I relax and lean my head against the grayish leather headrest and close my eyes. I suck in long breaths and exhale slowly to relax. I do this to clear my head. It works most of the time. I ask Bill if he can turn the air up.

"You think the Lord has plans for us, Ger?"

I open my eyes and look at Clemens, his head leaning against the tinted glass, darkened shapes flashing past in blurred glimpses.

"I sure do, boss," I say. I can smell the soap heavily in the backseat. Refreshing in a way.

"Really?" His damp hair slicked back tight and sheik.

"If not then I'm expecting a warm afterlife."

He smiles a lethargic smile without looking at me like he feels obligated to humor me.

"What about you? You believe the Lord looks after us, don't you?"

He pauses and sits despondent, weighing the gravity of the question. "I don't know. It's different. Just different."

"Different?" I ask.

He shuffles a bit in his seat. The sun lighting the side of his face and forcing him to squint, even through the tint.

"When I was a young boy, I loved to go fishing out at the lake over yonder by the house. You know that lake, right?"

Before I can answer, he resumes.

"I told ya bout it, I'm sure. Well, I would go out there any chance my hand touched a pole to toss the line in the water. We had cats and crappie mainly, but if you got lucky, you may snatch a bass. Sometimes Je...Jeremiah would come but he was never one for sittin' there and just staring at water. Told me it was stupid. Bothered me none so most the time I was by myself. As far back as I can remember, I always wanted Pop to come with me out to the lake. It was something I always thought would really be the stuff, you know? Us relaxing and having a peaceful moment. But no matter how much I ask, he would never oblige me."

He scratches his gray scalp and coughs.

"Anyway, I still had this hankering for fishin' with Pop. I guess in my mind it was a safe place. A new place where things just started over. I would always ask but he was usually too busy. Over and over again. Till one day he come to me and say, 'Boy, why don't we head up yonder to that lake you're always pesterin' me about tomorrow?' Well, I hop scotched like a toad on coals at the prospect of that. Didn't sleep a wink that night. I was a bonified owl. Well, first sign of light, I'm up and out of the bed, puttin' on my clothes, grabbin' my gear and my bait and ready to go. Pop comes in all groggy and such, but up nonetheless, and he grabs his gear and we head out walkin' to the lake. Now, I'm shakin' like a wet cat for excitement, imaginin' all the fun times we're gonna make and when we get there, Pop ain't said but one word to me the whole way. I try to conversate but he just sits there, prayin' to hisself, ignorin' me and the fish. He didn't say nothing. Just stared out across the water, rubbin' his hands together and mumblin' to hisself. We stayed there a couple hours and left with no fish and no words between us."

He stops talking, looking at his lap despondent. I think to speak but he beats me to it.

"You know, when we started, I was filled up but now, it's all drained outta me. Like God poured His spirit into my soul but there was a leak somewhere and now I'm all dried out. It's just different."

He was staring straight into my eyes with those last words. Staring like he expected an answer to a hidden question that I didn't have the answer for. Like I had the consolation he needed and he was just waiting for me to say it. His eyes dropped and he repositioned his chin in the palm of his hand, elbow on the door, and his face bounced off the reflection of the dark window. He stared out as to watch the busy world pass by like fleeting moments of dreams too impossible to stay.

I witness a sadness, a humanity, in him I'd never before seen, expressed only through the eyes and spirit of someone who has gone through an inexplicable life of turbulence and pain come out clean, only to damn himself back to that pain he fled from in the beginning. Like he has looked back on all his achievements and deeds of his life and second-guessed his intentions; his purpose. This scene is just another scattered piece to a puzzle with no image.

My heart cracks at the sight of him. I sense his vulnerability and my soul nudges me to say something. I know my words never come out as eloquent as Clemens but I feel the need, no matter how awkward, to say something. To say something. I don't know what but something. Anything. I part my lips slightly only to hear nothing but air escape. I turn and face my dark window with a dejection of missed opportunity. My mind tells me it is the Holy Spirit prodding me. My mind is always telling me it is the Holy Spirit but my heart is telling me something completely different.

We sit in a regretful silence as we pass through the urban and cluttered streets, everyday people performing everyday tasks in an everyday city. The life outside passing us by without a care in the world and Clemens doesn't even notice or care. I imagine he feels like he's sinking, deeper and deeper into the cold, black abyss, farther and farther away from the God who's trying to grasp his hand, feeling the pressure of the waters fill his lungs and muffling his cries for salvation as his purpose is slowly diluting with the swirl of the waters.

Or maybe it's just me.

He turns his head at me with those conflicted, blue eyes and subtly smiles that gap-filled grin.

"What?" I ask.

"How bout that cigarette?"

1930

"Come on, preacher boy. The Lord won't let you drown. Even if you is a queer."

"Yeah, Clemens, don't be yellow-bellied and swing."

The taunts and jests of the three boys carried up to the branch where he stood in a sturdy live oak, both encouraging and discouraging his attempt with each insulting statement. The hot sun raining down, warming everything and bleaching the three white boys to an almost phantasmic state.

"I ain't no queer and I ain't no preacher, goddamn it," he retorted from on high. The words odd and thick as they came out, as if regurgitating something he wasn't to have eaten but ate of anyway. The rope was frayed and callous in his prepubescent hands and he gripped it tight, feeling the pressure release from his fingers every time he readjusted his hold.

The three boys stood with squinty eyes and heads cocked near the shore of the lake, standing knee high in the shallows. The noisome red-head called through his hands as a make-shift megaphone, "Clemens, even Petey ain't as scared as you. Give it a jump."

Petey gave no mind to his comments and joined in silent support of the red-head. The other said nothing, bashful, removed in stance from the two.

Ezekiel stood in his gray boxers, concealing his paralytic fear of water from the trio, not just for pride's sake but for his own humility. The humid summer air moist and oppressive making the water almost inviting to Ezekiel. Through smooth talking and evasive maneuvers, he had been able to postpone this inevitable meeting at the rope where he knew he would be forced to plunge to his death. Now it was here and it terrified him.

"You keep raggin' me, I'm gonna bust all ya'll faces up so folks won't tell it's ya. I won't lie."

The gang laughed.

The red-head responded, "You ain't doin' nothing. You cain't even swing from that tree without pissin' yourself."

"Hell, no, I ain't afraid."

"Clemens, you're a worse liar than you are a fighter. Jump or I'll push you out that tree." He stood with his arms crossed over his smooth chest. His red, fiery hair curled wildly atop his scalp, his vibrant amber eyes emitted an air of violence and mendacity and arrogance.

"Why don't ya pray, then? We're afire down here," the red-head complained.

Ezekiel's black bangs stuck to his wet fore head just above his lids, the sweat gathering under his arms. He looked as if he had already plunged into the cool water. The shade from the thick leaves of the giant oak tree created an unbearable sauna. Petey and the other boy began splashing toward him in the knee-deep water, throwing sprays in a playful yet irritated manner.

"Let's go, we ain't got all day. We want to swing too, you know," Petey called in his gravelly, thick voice. He held a fat bullfrog in his hand. "Freckles here is gonna pop you like that frog if ya don't."

Freckles rubbed the circular scars across his face subconsciously. He cast a shadowy glance to Petey at the mention of his moniker but remained reticent.

"I'm tired of this, Ezekiel. You better swing and quit. This is getting' ridiculous. I'm gone give you to five otherwise, I'm gone kick the fear outta ya. One..."

The red-head's counting only made Clemens more irritated. The voice grating inside his ears like some demon's natter.

"Two."

"I'm jumpin' John, hold a minute."

He rocked on his soles; his toes curled and futile, grabbing the bark. He took deep breaths, in and out, as the hurricane of anxiety spun violently in his gut. The heat growing like a looming beast among the leaves.

"Three."

Clemens felt something hit his chest. Then another sting popped on his thigh. The sting and throb that followed concentrating on the areas of impact. He saw John and Freckles searching in the water along the shallow shoreline. Petey was now holding the bullfrog, pulling on its rear legs and extending it to an unnatural length.

"Stop throwin' rocks, you fools. Yer gonna hurt me."

Freckles rose and tossed a stone, just missing Clemens face and ricocheting off the sturdy oak with a sharp thud.

"Hey, quit."

"Four," John hollered.

"Alright, alright!" Clemens hastily yelled, rearing back as his feet lifted off the branch and hung limp and defenseless over the sweeping waters. He could feel the blisters forming in his palms and the blood being squeezed out his knuckles. The motion of the weightless swing sent the hurricane high into his throat and he feared he may vomit. He could hear nothing from the trio as his eyes watched the brackish blue water turn into vibrant sky blue. The warm wind pushing against his thin body; suspended in space. His hands released the weathered rope and he fell, back first, as if vicariously watching himself, into the shallow water. He felt a surge of intense pain scatter across the skin of his back like being slapped by the palm of God. Following the pain, he felt the cold water rush over him, flooding his face and funneling into his nose and mouth. He feared he was drowning until realizing that his backside was resting on the rocky floor of the lake's shoreline. He rose up out of the water, spitting and shooting water from his nasal cavity, standing waste deep in the water with the sun beating down upon his red and white skin as water dripped off his extremities. John waded over to Clemens with a victorious smile as his knees pushed ripples across the surface of the lake.

"Did I tell ya or did I tell ya? God wouldn't let you drown. Glad ya grew a pair and finally got outta that tree. Wasn't so bad, was it?"

Clemens aggressively wiped the water from his face, swiping his hand in a downward wipe as he spat water from his lips. He glared at the red-head, the nerves still tingling across his back and the rocks poking underneath his feet.

"I coulda broke my neck. Why didn't ya tell me the water was so shallow?"

"What's got into yer trousers?"

"I coulda died, Jakes," Clemens growled.

"Take it easy, Clemens, you're fine now, ain't ya?"

"That's not the point. Don't ya ever think about what could happen? What if I had dove headfirst?"

Jakes laughed to himself, dismissing Clemens question, "You weren't gonna dive headfirst."

"How do you know?"

"Cause you ain't got the integrity to."

Ezekiel shook his head and waded forward, brushing past Jakes and nearly knocking him over into the water. John Jakes' face flushed to match his hair.

"Where you goin'? Huh? You runnin' again? Huh? Runnin' back to that God of yours? Your God ain't gonna help ya cause you'll always be chicken shit. Just like that drunk daddy of yours. Hidin' behind a God that don't give a damn about you or anything He created."

Ezekiel Clemens felt the rage he had been suppressing come to a boil. He turned around and faced this boy with no limits and saw his father's eyes. His hands closed and, in a fit of impulsivity, swung a right fist into the side of John Jakes' neck with a thud, missing the target he was aiming for. Jakes winced, head cocked to the side of the impact, and he let out a holler as he grabbed his throbbing neck. Clemens cradled his hand, feeling the pain rush to his fingers. Jakes shot a black-eyed glance at Clemens and rushed in, releasing blow after experienced blow upon the newly acquired feather-weight. Clemens fell as John Jakes stood over, swinging blind fists at anything belonging to Ezekiel Clemens, connecting sporadic, creating a typhoon of waves and pain. Clemens felt dream-like, as the water poured over his beaten body. It lasted a few seconds before Freckles and Pete grabbed Jakes' arms and pulled him into the water and under. He struggled as they all emerged from the water. "Let me go! Let me go!" he hollered between gulps of air.

Clemens sat in the cold water, feeling warmth gush from his nose and a throbbing throughout his body. In the water, chest deep, he watched the blood drip quickly from his broken nose into the water, dissipating in the immense liquid of the lake. The noise of the trio wrestling demons mute to his ears. With each drip, he felt the martyr. With each drip, he felt like Paul. Then he realized, battered and broken in the shallows, that he had nothing to die for. A causeless martyr, grasping for a shaky ideal to live for.

He walked home alone under the blue sky, his shirt over his shoulder. The light brown dust kicking up in puffs of smoke as his feet shuffled along homeward. The road was bordered by a parallel fence that opened to a vast field of cotton. The wispy webs stuck to the bare plants, wind giving the field life. He cradled his nose, blood dried across his face and chest, resembling war paint of a defeated warrior.

"He ain't got no right to say that," he mumbled. "No right at all." He walked further on in the humid air, acting scenarios should time be reversed. "I ain't runnin'. I ain't never run from nothing in my life and I sure ain't hidin' behind no God either. I don't need no God to protect me."

His rants were interrupted by the rumblings of an old truck in the distance. He watched a dark speck and a puff of smoke growing as it came. He veered his path toward the edge of the road and continued walking, glancing at the approaching vehicle. He would rather have it just drive past than stop. After a time, the truck came close enough to see the driver and it slowed. He put his head down and continued on until he heard the engine's whine waning until it idled next to him. He stopped and looked up at the visitor.

It was an old pickup truck that had the appearance of being a restoration; the paint almost unintelligible and no side windows. The engine emitted a hissing when idle that irritated the ears and the heavy smell of exhaust came from the rear. The driver resembled his vehicle. He wore long, greasy hair that was an old grey and his face stretched and full of brittle hair.

"What happened to ya, boy?" the man asked in a sleepy drawl.

Ezekiel gazed full into the man's face. His eyes bright and blue as if they were eyes that didn't belong to his body.

"Nothin' happened."

He turned the ignition key off and the engine dwindled to a rest. "Somethin' happened. You look like hell all over." His voice was demanding yet subtle. Clemens eyed him a moment, noticing the scars and wrinkles upon his chest.

"A fight is all."

The man gummed his few teeth in a pondering demeanor. His leathery forearm draped down the ledge of the window revealing his cracked elbow. He wore denim overalls with no shirt, his heavy body visible underneath.

"A fight, huh?"

Clemens nodded. The heat from the day heavy on his shoulders. His nose seemed to surge with each subtle movement.

"What's yer name?"

"What business is it of yours what my name is?"

"Well, then, where you from?"

"Nowhere you need to know."

"Nowhere, huh?" He smiled a gummy smile as if entertained by Ezekiel's defense. He spat into the dust. "Well, what were ya fightin' fer then?"

"Jus' fightin' is all. Ain't nothin'."

He looked at Clemens a moment, then ahead down the desolate dirt road.

"Well, it ain't worth fightin' if you don't know what yer fightin' for."

Clemens shrugged. "What you want, old man?"

The old man's eyes narrowed, peering through heavy slits and fueled by some unknown fire.

"I know your type. You ain't nothin' but a boy that don't know."

Clemens eyes lolled in their sockets and he began walking again.

"Hey, son," the old man called.

"Leave me be, old timer. Why you ridin' me?"

"You need to understand somethin'."

Clemens stopped, looked at him. "What's that?"

He shuffled in his seat, groaning, and settled himself, preparing for a long stay. He looked out across the cotton fields forlorn as if his dreams rested on the borders of the horizon and he knew they were to stay there always, unattainable. Clemens' nose began to ache and he could sense the swelling in the cheekbone under his right eye.

The old man finally turned his time worn face to Clemens' and said, "I knew a young man like you once. A long time ago back before the war begun. A positive and eager young feller. He dreamed of being somethin' greater than anythin' he knew growin' up in these lands and he had faith in his dreams. He knew what he wanted and how to get it. Fixin' to head east over yonder mountains to make his way in the world. To have somethin' to live for. When the war come, all that changed. At first, he was ready to fight. Believin' he was gonna change somethin' in the world. Fight a country that did more bad than good and make life better for those being oppressed. They sent him overseas as part of the 177th Division straight into German territory before he even got his feet wet. For the next few months, he saw and did things he ain't ever told nobody. Things a man ought not do. When he got back when the war ended, he was a shadow of a man. Somethin' was wrong with him like he left hisself there. I asked him how he felt about the war and such, he looked at me with big hollow eyes and said that when he started, he thought he knew what he was fightin' for. But when he got there, he realized there was no cause for what he was doin'. Looked me in the eye and told me he was the devil's now, after what he done. He had killed men that didn't deserve death more than he and he didn't know what for. I asked him about God, he said to me that God doesn't condone the suffering of man but he sure enjoys it. He say that if ya do anything in life it has to be for a reason and if ya have no reason then ya have no life. A few months after I spoke with him, he disappeared. Never saw him again. Some say he took to the road to find his way in life and make a livin'. Others say he was runnin' from his demons. You know what I think? I think he just couldn't fit in anyplace. Ever since he been on the road, travelin' and workin', tryin' to find somethin' he ain't ever gonna find. All the time runnin' somewhere got him nowheres."

He stopped and wiped his forehead of sweat with the back of his hand and gazed in nostalgic wonder upon creation.

"It's burnin' hot," he remarked.

"What was he lookin' for?" Ezekiel asked.

"Huh?" he spoke nasally, putting a hand to his ear.

"I axed what was he lookin' for?"

He paused. "What are we all lookin' for?"

The old man gave a closed lip smile and his eyes looked moist and sad. He turned the key of the ignition and the battered truck coughed and sputtered to life, disrupting the quietude of the scene. He shifted the car into gear. "You get on home now."

Clemens just stood reticent as the strange old man shifted the old vehicle into first gear and putted along the dirt road leaving a growing trail of dust in his wake until it obscured his view and the truck vanished into the horizon. He watched the dust settle before starting his way again, still deciphering the story he just heard.

It wasn't until he saw the light from his home that the fear came. He stopped a good distance from the house in the coming twilight and waited. He listened for any voices. All felt still and calm. He crept over to the cow's trough and washed his face and chest of the dried blood. His nose bulged, swollen like rising bread. Using his shirt, he dried himself and snuck on tip-toe homeward.

The front and only door whined a soft creak as it opened into the living room. There, resting in the ancient rocking chair before the fireplace, his father's profile sat motionless with his head down reading from his black, leather Bible, his hand resting under his chin in deep concentration as the flicker of the flame danced upon his features like hellfire. The old fear rose in him again. He stepped in placing his dirty bare foot on the floorboards and it moaned his presence. His father's head shot up and faced the door sparkling black eyes. When he saw his son, his eyes softened and his back relaxed. "Where you been?" he asked.

Ezekiel froze, unable to speak. The words there but his body wouldn't allow him to speak.

"You want to answer me, boy?" his father said annoyed at his perceived defiance. He rose out of the rocking chair and tossed the Bible onto the table next to him. He advanced with a powerful and looming gait towards Ezekiel in the doorway. Ezekiel's heart began to pound and he bit his lip tight. His father's eyes widened and a foreign look of concern arose in them. Ezekiel saw his white eyes and began to unthaw.

"Dear God," he exclaimed when he saw his son's face. He put his calloused hand under Ezekiel's chin and lifted to get a better look at the damage. His mustache creating an ever-thin emptiness to his lips.

"How did this happen?" he asked after studying the wounds a moment. Ezekiel debated whether to lie or tell the truth.

"I...I...got in a fight."

"A fight? A fight with who?"

"Nobody," he lied.

"Son, who did you fight with?" His voice was tense and foreboding.

"I...c-can't say," he stuttered. He could feel the clog in his throat and the omen of tears beginning in his eyes.

"Can't say. Why?" he vociferated.

"Because you'll be mad at me." His face began to cringe with the tears and before he could even fight it, they began to flow down his cheeks.

His father looked at his boy sobbing. He put his hand onto his shoulder and ushered him gently into the kitchen where they sat at the homemade dining table that his father had crafted himself out of pine. One of the legs was too short and caused the table to rock. He pulled a chair out for Ezekiel to sit in. The room was dimly lit by the afterglow of the fire so he retrieved a candle and lit it.

"You sit here and I'll get somethin' for that eye."

Ezekiel sat and recovered from his emotional break-down. His father grabbed a piece of cold meat from a dark stone cooler near the back of the kitchen and slapped it onto Ezekiel's right eye. The coldness felt painful and relieving all in one intense sensation. He pulled up a chair and sat down facing his son. His dark eyes unusually empathetic and nurturing. They sat this way in silence except for Ezekiel's intermittent sniffles for a few minutes. Finally, he spoke, "Were you with that Jakes boy?"

Ezekiel shot a panicked eye and then, reluctantly, nodded yes.

His father sat back in his chair and rubbed his hand down his face. His countenance morphing.

"How long have you been hangin' with that boy?"

"I don't know," Ezekiel answered lazily, angered and afraid.

He pulled his chair closer, dragging the legs across the floor in a demonstrative manner as the grate echoed in Ezekiel's ears.

"A couple months, is all," Ezekiel uttered quickly, noticing the line he was dangerously close to. His father stopped and looked to his side out the kitchen window.

"Well," he said without averting his gaze," what should we do about this?"

Ezekiel shrugged, defeated.

"What did Christ say about our enemies?" he asked raising his eyebrows.

Ezekiel snorted. "To turn the other cheek."

"Good. Good. Now did you?"

Ezekiel shook his head.

"That's right, you did not. You did not."

He sat back in silence adjusting his suspender straps as the flicker of the candle moved about the kitchen. He looked off into the darkness, pontificating on some thought kept from his son.

Ezekiel sat, slouched, with the cold meat pressed to his face.

"I'm sorry."

His father turned to him, hesitant to speak but an eagerness present until he closed his lips and returned to the darkness.

"Did you win?" he asked.

Ezekiel shook his head. A faint semblance of disappointment lingered on his father's face. "Well, you're takin' over your brother's duties."

"Sir?" Ezekiel asked.

He turned and stared into his son's face, abandoning his thought. He held in his mind the image of his own father's gaze and the trepidation it conjured.

"Can I ask you something?"

He nodded, crossing his arms over his chest.

Ezekiel felt his nerves rattling but he knew that now was the best time to ask. If any time would suffice.

"Did you ever get in a fight when you were a boy?"

His father inhaled deep. "Yes. But I won."

Ezekiel hung his head, the meat wet on his face. The exhaustion setting in on him now.

"Did you get in trouble with granddad?" The question slithered out of his lips like some forbidden snake and Ezekiel almost fled at the realization he had asked. The old bruises awakened from the past.

"What?" his father asked sharply. His eyes narrowed and a great battle seemed to be brewing behind those opaque windows. An old battle fought a lifetime. He looked away from his son in restraint. His teeth clenched tight and his lips thinned behind his full mustache. Ezekiel felt the static of anxiety in his gut.

Suddenly, he grabbed his son's shoulders with a powerful grip and stared hard into his son's eyes. The fingers pressed deep into his young muscles and pain began to fire off like sparks. Ezekiel's tears paralyzed, the meat thudding on the table.

"Why would ya ask that? You ain't got no right to ask me that," he growled through his teeth. His hands trembled as he spoke. Ezekiel froze, waiting for the strike like lightning. His father held him this way, breathing heavy.

"Get to bed," he growled, startling Ezekiel as he released him and stood up. He sauntered to the small kitchen window with his hands on his hips and his back to his blood. Ezekiel froze a moment in his seat, staring ahead liberated of an impending doom. His heart beating fast. He turned his glance to his son and saw him still seated there.

"Get!" he hollered as if commanding a dog.

Ezekiel jumped up and walked briskly to his bedroom without looking back. He passed his parents' bedroom and saw his mother sitting on the edge of the bed. Her ghostly face stared at the floor, statuesque. He paused and watched her before continuing to his room and closing the door behind him. Jeremiah sat on the edge of his cot looking at Ezekiel. He stared back and an interchange of understandings passed between them.

"You alright?" Jeremiah asked.

Ezekiel dropped his eyes and went to his cot to the side of the small bedroom and fell onto his bed in the dark staring at the planks of wood on the ceiling. The bed creaking with his weight. Jeremiah watched him in the darkness.

After a silence, Jeremiah said, "You know, he really does love us."

Ezekiel looked at his older brother. "Sometimes the glass is half empty, Jem. Doesn't matter how you look at it."

"It doesn't have to be," Jeremiah said in the moonlit dark. His voice a strong whisper in the warm night air.

Ezekiel turned to face the wall, putting his back to his brother. The moonlight shining through the tiny square window onto Ezekiel's back. Jeremiah sat and watched his brother's shape in the dark. He knew him like he knew himself and right now, there was nothing to be said. He laid on his wooden bed with its thin mattress and uttered a soft prayer under his breath.

Vipers

The convention center appears through the windshield, nestled between two skyscrapers in the urban circus of city life. It always amazes me every year; the rounded architecture and mirrored glass surrounding the immense building; the marble sculptures of abstract modern art accenting the mosaic exterior. It's always a pleasure to witness and I feel blessed to behold it. Since our first televised meeting so many years ago, I have held this place in reverence and regret. It's difficult to explain.

I ask Bill the time and he says 10:45. We're late. My pet-peeve is punctuality. Clemens causes it and I can't help but resent the hardships he puts me through. His indifference is almost unbearable. Yet I'm still bound by loyalty to him in a profound way that I can't deny. Like when a prisoner spends half his life in prison, only to be free but still bound to penal life.

"Gerry, that is a mighty fine building. One has to wonder if the Lord ever admires what He's done. He knows I sure do." The smoke from his cigarette curls and rises throughout the air of the vehicle as it comes from between his fingers, pointing in the direction of the building.

"Yeah," I retort, discarding his comment in both annoyance and preoccupation. The tobacco musk is invasive and it reminds me of older days. I glare at him but he just stares back, dragging in the smoke deep to exhale again. He has that subtle smirk.

"Bill, go ahead and drive the car around the back. Take that side street along the west side, where that café is, and there's a loading zone in the back. That's where we'll enter in."

"Sure thing, sir," he copies and makes the left turn to go down the street. As the arrow turns green, Bill accelerates shortly, then slams his foot onto the brakes, squealing, causing Clemens and me to lurch forward. Clemens hits his forehead on the back of the front seat and hollers a more surprised than wounded shout.

"Good God Almighty, Bill, what you braking so hard for?" Clemens chides as he puts his hand to his forehead, attempting to rub away the discomfort. "I about got the devil knocked outta me."

"Sorry, sir, that there homeless fella run cross the street and I almost hit him good," Bill says. "It's all I could do to not hit him, sir."

"Don't worry 'bout it. Forget it. It ain't yer fault. The Lord's lookin' after us and him. Praise Jesus." Clemens sits back, rubbing his head, searching out the windows for the man Bill was talking about. Of all the things Clemens does that bother me, it is his gradual display of righteousness, especially whenever we are heading to a meeting or event where others are going to be watching and listening. It stings me like wasps.

I catch sight of the man as he breathes heavily, standing on the corner of the sidewalk, staring at us. I know he can't see in because of the tint but he can see Bill. I nudge Clemens and he looks in his direction. The man is older with light brown skin and a mature, mingled mustache. His eyes are saggy and forlorn like something painful lurks the halls of his skull. I can tell he's obviously poor. His faded jeans are torn white at the knees with a solid, green buttoned shirt that's missing a button in the middle. Life seems to have dragged him through a colander.

"Poor soul. Lord, help that man to find You before it's too late, amen. Praise Jesus. Hallelujah," Clemens prays through his cigarette. I bite my tongue because it is all I can do.

The Cadillac passes the man watching us. I study him as he continues to watch us until he shrinks and disappears from view when we turn the corner to the rear of the building. Something about that man haunts me. Something in his eyes and demeanor. Even as Bill pulls into the loading zone, I still picture him standing on the sunny corner, his eyes still watching us with a vacant pain vanishing into the past. The car drives along the backside of the building and makes a left turn into the loading dock where the large, high metal door lifts up for trucks unloading equipment. Bill puts the car in park as I look for the event coordinator I spoke to on the phone.

"Here," I say to Clemens, holding the bottle of drops toward him. I see the small, door open with three figures standing outside under the overhang. He grabs the bottle without a word and squeezes two drops into each eye effortless. He blinks repeatedly as he asks, "When are the other guys gettin' here?"

"They're at the hotel. Bill will be picking them up and bringing them here in a few hours once everything is settled."

"We gotta have all the fellas here for the prayer meeting, Ger. I just want you to remember that," he reminds me though I need no reminder. He knows this and his assumption of my ignorance is insulting.

I sigh. "You ready?"

He reaches in his coat pocket and produces a bottle of cologne and sprays it all over himself in more than a mist. I can't help but cough as he answers with a yes. I say to Bill, "You wait here and I'll let you know. You know the routine."

Bill turns three quarters of the way around and gives me a look to say that he knows. No sadness or anger, just understanding. It sickens me but this is the way it is, especially with ministers and it just reminds me that men of God are still men.

Bill leaves the car running as Clemens and I hop out into the mid-morning sunlight and walk the length toward the open door where three men are standing awaiting us. I notice Clemens still is holding his cigarette and I whisper to him to get rid of it. He turns his back to the men, takes one last drag, and tosses it on the ground in a small shower of sparks. I hand him his large sunglasses from my coat pocket to help hide the redness that the drops may miss. He slides them on and puts his hand out palm up to me and I place the chewing gum unwrapped into it without a hesitation and he tosses it into his mouth. Almost like second nature. He exhales smoke and I exhale nerves as we reach the group of men standing in the shade. I notice the old one with white hair checking his wristwatch and whispering to the young, clean-cut man standing next to him. The short younger, good ol' boy extends his hand to greet Clemens.

"Glad you could make it, Pastor Clemens. We are honored to have a prophet of God grace this place." His voice has a slight twang but seemed diluted with years of repression and urbanity.

"Much obliged, young man. I'm very glad to be here myself. God is going to do miraculous things tonight, gentlemen, miraculous. I sense the presence of God right here as we speak. Glory to God." He obnoxiously smacks his gum and I see that it visibly irritates the older gentleman.

I try to keep from rolling my eyes at this nonsense but I don't know if I'm successful. The older man's nose rises and falls with disdain as his head is slightly forward.

"That's what we want to hear, sir," the good ol' boy replies.

"How was your stay pastor?" the skinny man with big ears asks.

"Fine. Fine. Thank you," Clemens replies. "The Lord blessed me with a fine sleep and a vision that tonight, the presence of God will come down on these people like fire upon Gomorrah."

It's all so funny and sickening I don't know how to feel. I think of my wife and kids and really, truly miss them right now. I wonder what they are doing now without me.

"Pastor Clemens, I just wanna say what an honor it is to finally meet ya, sir," the good ol' boy exclaims. Clemens loves it when young kids say that type of stuff to him. It feeds him.

"I notice you got a bit of twang in your tongue, son. Where ya from?" Clemens asks.

"Well, pastor, I grew up not far from Jackson."

"Jackson? Ain't it a small world? God is marvelous I must proclaim. What's yer name, son?"

"Jeremiah Cole. I'll be coordinating the service tonight. If you need anything, anything at all, you let me know and I'll get it for ya. We have plenty of volunteers and a local group of the best musicians for worship. Only the best for one of God's own."

I notice his accent loosen and become more prominent the more he talks with Clemens.

"Je-Jeremiah," Clemens stutters. "I had a brother named Jeremiah."

"Really?" Cole exclaims with curious surprise. "What does he think about the great things you're doin' for the Lord?"

Clemens keeps an unenthusiastic smile under his glasses as he pauses. He seems to stare off and I wonder how he will respond to this whole exchange considering. The gap in conversation is reaching a point of awkwardness and, just as I am about to intervene, Clemens disrupts the moment.

"Well, now, you haven't introduced me to these young men, here," he says, changing the subject as if coming out of a daze. His gregariousness reemerging from its trance.

"Oh, forgive me, sir. This is Lyle Jenkins, an associate pastor fresh out of seminary," he gestures toward the lanky kid with the big ears, "and this is Rev. Sonny Masters, pastor in the sponsoring church for tonight's meeting. Sonny preaches every Sunday. Hasn't missed a service in twenty years, I believe. Ain't that right, Sonny?"

As everyone extends hands and exchanges greetings with obligatory smiles, I watch Clemens give a quizzical look to the finely dressed men. Lyle looks like he's in his mid-twenties, still naïve in the ways of the church and Sonny about Clemens' age. However, I can tell just by looking at young Lyle that he is a few ounces short of a pound.

"A fellow leader of God's people. Amen. And what church might you preach at, Sonny?" Clemens asks as he continues shaking Sonny's smooth hand.

"I preach at the Church of Christ the Redeemer on the corner of 7th and T Street, between St. Michael's and the Lutheran church. It's not far from here, probably a few blocks down that way. I'd love to show you someday. It would really lift the church's spirit to have a genuine prophet speak encouragement."

Clemens nods his head, grinning a faux smile with that wide black gap between the two front teeth. His sunglasses make it hard for me to read his eyes and he likes it that way. He likes to always be one step ahead.

"Well," he responds, "maybe one of these days, good Lord willing. You have the gift of tongues in your church, Reverend?"

"We are Pentecostal, Pastor. What you think we are? Baptist?"

A communal chuckle goes around the circle. I can't stand church politics and the arrogance between believers. I know Ezekiel felt this way once. Maybe he still does.

"Well, Sonny, maybe one of these days I'll be there, good Lord willing." Clemens says, wiping a tear off the top of his cheek.

"I understand your busy, Pastor. These big meetings must take a lot of energy and I wouldn't want you to go beyond your capabilities. You still are a man."

Clemens countenance changes as if he took offense to that last statement.

"I can do all things through Christ who strengthens me, Reverend."

"Amen but one must know himself as to not wear down what God has lifted up," Sonny replies. A hint of tension is beginning and I know what this could become.

"Especially with all the divine miracles that are so common in your meetings," Sonny continues. "How many people have you healed? Must be in the thousands." The tone is unmistakable and I just watch.

Clemens has his hands on his hips, revealing the golden wristwatch he got as a present from the evangelical network that started to televise the meetings. On the reverse of the clock face, it says "For the Prophet Ezekiel Clemens". We all can sense the sardonic tone of Sonny's voice and the air is taut. I notice Sonny eyeing the bright gold plating of the strap and the sparkling border of the clock face. I imagine a cocky smirk under those tinted sunglasses of Clemens'.

"Oh, Sonny, I have nothin' to do with it. It's all the healing power of Jesus Christ. I'm just a vessel, plain and simple. I'm like the dough and God is the baker. He make what He will."

He took a step closer to Sonny, brushing his speckled black and white hair from around his temple. The gum smacking. I can tell what he's going to say.

"Besides, I've got a rest at my home over in California comin' up and I'm sure, once I've rested up, I could make it out to yer little church. There's nothin' like the Pacific air to cleanse one's soul, amen? You know, it's hard to find time for one self when you have been handpicked by God Almighty to shepherd his flock." He rubs his hand under his chin looking at me in a fake, pressed way. "I would love to hop on my jet and make it back here and meet your humble congregation. You have an airport, right? Oh, it don't matter much. Hey, I can pick ya up in my Cadillac limousine and ya can show me the town. How's that sound? My treat for dinner of course. If you are still willing and it's what the Lord is callin' me to do...Of course."

Sonny's eyes convey confusion and anger and bewilderment in a manner I've never witnessed before. His face reddens to a comical color, cheeks slightly puffing.

Clemens cracks that pretentious gapped smile again as he gives Sonny a smack on the shoulder with a boisterous "Amen!" and proceeds toward the door to the back of the center, leaving Sonny, Lyle, and Jeremiah reticent and bewildered. As for me, I saw that coming a mile away.

"Glory, hallelujah, praise Jesus! Let the healing begin!" He exclaims as the two doors burst open into the show, echoing his enigmatic voice into the darkness beyond the door frame. As he disappears into the dark, we can hear his slightly flat song about treasures in heaven fading. The three turn and look at me, as if for answers and I just shrug because I have none. Lyle looks back at the door and shakes his head, "The Lord works in mysterious ways, I guess."

Sonny chimes in. "We can only hope so."

The door Clemens burst through swings back and shut and I'm standing outside with Sonny, Jeremiah, and Lyle in a semi-circle. All three of us standing speechless as if something incomprehensible has just happened.

"Well, Lambough, how does it feel?" Sonny asks me with contempt as he continues to stare where Clemens disappeared. I give him a quizzical look. "How does what feel?"

He faces me with a bizarre look of incredulity. "You know. To have to clean up after that?" He says, pointing his thumb back toward the door. His face leaves no trace of humor.

Does he know? I try to play it calm and act dumb, now adding lies to my already bruised conscious. "The only thing I clean are clothes, Pastor. Nothing more."

He chuckles an unbelieving laugh and gives me a skeptical, humored stare like he knows all the ministry's secrets and sins and is testing me like God would test his own. I keep my right hand behind my back because I know the shake it gets when I'm nervous.

"Listen, Gerald, I may not have proof but I have a hunch. I've been a pastor for twenty-five years and God speaks to me as he does to any man. I have the gift of discernment and my spirit is telling me something that I can't deny and I know, God knows, that somethin' is not right with all this. Not right at all." He gives a glare toward our vehicle where Bill is parked.

I follow his eyes and see the irritation behind them. "What are you trying to say, Sonny?" I feel unconvincing. "That Ezekiel Clemens is a fraud? A false prophet who is conning souls into eternity penniless?" I do my best to sound accusatory and perpetuate the absurdity of the statement but I feel inside that I'm completely unconvincing.

"I didn't say that. You did."

I smile and stand speechless. Sonny casts another bitter glance toward the car. His bushy grey eyebrows like canopies above those eyes.

"Is there a problem, pastor?" I ask.

He casts a sideward glance at me and then back to the car as the sides of his jaw tense like he's grinding his teeth.

"He your driver?" he asks with an arrogant nod toward the car.

"He's in our car," I reply. His cheeks flush a bit but not with embarrassment and I wonder if I should change the subject.

"It's just you don't see that much, is all," he says.

I feel myself becoming defensive, ready for a battle I should probably not fight but my emotions sometimes get the best of me. This is one thing I have the temerity to fight for.

"A man is a man, pastor. If God looked through your eyes, you might consider yourself in trouble," I reply with a sharp cut of words that normally don't flow so easily. He rolls his eyes, huffing his cheeks and pulling up the sides of his pants causing his belly to bounce freely.

"There that color for a reason, Lambough."

If I ever felt like cursing, now would be the best time. I feel my hands become clammy in their fists but Sonny speaks up before I begin to fight.

"As long as he stays in the car." His response seems to conclude the subject just as I'm ready to fight. I feel my heart begin to beat slower. Tonight is going to be interesting.

"That boss of yours needs some common sense," he remarks. The more I look at this man and my boss, the more questions I have for God should I ever meet him. How can God attract such representatives?

"Ezekiel is a good man," I say pathetically.

He snickers with an obnoxious laugh. "All I know is what I feel and I feel something wrong about that man." He looks into my eyes and I feel the risings of anxiety in my gut, desperately trying to stay afloat with my lies and deception. For an instant, I feel like I am Ezekiel Clemens. Like he and I are intertwined in our deceit. And in a way, I guess we are. I see Lyle and Jeremiah just standing, listening to this exchange with terse body language. In an attempt to escape the possible trappings of my lies, I bring them into the conversation.

"How do you feel about this, Lyle? You have the same hunch as Sonny?"

Lyle looks at Sonny for guidance. His eyes give a glint of frenzy and panic. "Answer him, Lyle. Make your own choice, son," he tells him.

Lyle stares at the ground with his head cocked to the side, shuffling imaginary dirt on the pavement with the toe of his brown leather boot. He seems to be struggling with what he really feels and what he feels he should say. "I don't know," he mumbles. "I guess he's alright with me."

Sonny rolls his eyes and stares off to the distance with his hands on his hips. Lyle seems disappointed with himself for saying the wrong thing.

I look down to Jeremiah, with my arms crossed and back arched, giving the impression that I want an answer. He looks from me to Sonny and back at me as all eyes anticipate his answer. He looks to his right at nothing and says, "Ya'll can think what you want but my hunch is that Ezekiel Clemens is the God-honest truth. He's a man of God if I ever seen one and this meeting tonight is going to bring thousands to Christ and possibly heal some of 'em too. Now, Sonny can think what he wants but I think he's just jealous that he ain't got the gift of healing. None of us do. God has chosen Clemens to be a leader." He looks me right into my eyes. "He's a prophet of God just like Billy Sunday or William Branham and I'm blessed to be here tonight. Now if you'll excuse me,

I'm going to make sure Reverend Clemens has everything he needs. I'll see you fellas inside."

He abruptly turns and marches into the convention center, swinging the door wide and entering the pitch dark beyond it.

"That kid is gonna make a good preacher one day," Lyle remarks.

"Oh, shut it, Lyle. He's nothin' but a fool," Sonny snaps as timid Lyle drops his head from watching Jeremiah, staring at his boots again. Sonny glares at me with condemning eyes and I glare back though inside I'm shaking. "We all are," he retorts.

He gives Lyle's skinny frame a push as they head in to the darkness of the door and I'm left standing, alone and ponderous. I close my eyes tight but not enough to completely block out the light through my eyelids. No matter what I do I can't hide from the light. In this moment, I send a prayer to God, my only form of constancy.

"Lord, help me."

I want to say more but my lips, just like in the car on the way here, seem paralyzed by an unknown force. Maybe it's God or maybe it's Satan. Or maybe it's just my cowardice.

I give Bill the sign to park the Caddy in the chain-linked parking lot around the corner of the loading zone and he nods as he always does, smiling and understanding, and backs out of sight. I stand outside, in the shade of the convention center, feeling the pressure of my struggle increasing. Is this the life God has planned for me? To be an accomplice to blasphemy? To spend my nights and days far from my family for the benefit of one man? I ask these words to God as I rub my hands across my eyes, hoping He'll answer. After all I've seen, I don't know if God will answer me. "God, what will you have me do?" I listen for a few minutes with nothing but the sounds of the street echoing dimly in the background. Maybe I've been forgotten by God as a penance for my sins. Or maybe I just don't know how to listen. Maybe He's just not there. So many unanswered questions in this life.

I spy a pay phone along the side street we just drove down and feel for enough change in my pocket. I walk into the sun and reach the pay phone. I check the street to the corner, expecting to see the dejected Mexican man standing with those piercing eyes at me, but I see no one. I step into the booth, pick up the grimy receiver and hold it to my ear. My hand sticks to the receiver. Why don't they wash these things? The dial tone is loud and buzzing and I dial the number into the faded panel and listen for the amount I need. I fish out the thirty-five cents and place each coin into the slot, each accompanied by a metallic clang. The phone begins to ring and I scan the inside of the booth and notice the obscenities scribbled and etched into the glass by a dozen lost souls. Among the slander and profanity and sexual invitations, I see the etching of "God is Love" as if it is a lone lighthouse among an angry sea. I close the door to hear better but my nose catches a whiff of urine and I decide to keep the door open.

After three rings I hear a young boy's voice answer.

"Hello?"

"Hey, Willy. This is your dad."

"Hi, dad," he says with nonchalance.

I glance at my watch. "What are you doin' home? Aren't you supposed to be in school?"

"I'm sick." I know he is lying and he's conned his mother into believing it. This is an issue that always arises when I'm out crusading.

"You're not sick."

"Yes, I am." He blows two fake coughs into the phone as if to validate his malady.

"Can you get Mom for me?"

"Ok. When are you coming home?"

I hesitate. "Soon, buddy. Soon."

"Ok. I miss you but I know God wants you there."

I hesitate again. Taken back by the profound voice and understanding of my child.

"Yeah. I know He does too. Can you get your mother for me?"

"Ok. Mom?!" he screams into the phone and I can hear the ringing in my ears as Ruth comes to the phone.

"Hello?" her beautiful voice asks and I realize how much I've missed her.

"Hey, Ruthie."

"Hey," she says excitedly. "I didn't expect you to be calling this early."

"I had to call you." One sentence is all it takes. She always has a way of bringing the problems of mine to light.

"You alright?" she implores.

"I just miss you and the kids is all." I pause. "Sometimes I wonder if I've been doing what I'm supposed to. If it's worth all this time away."

"You're doing what God wants you to do," she reassures.

"Am I?" My voice is uncertain and I know she can feel it.

"What's wrong, Gerry? What's bothering you?"

I don't know how to answer. Again, I'm lost for words. I want to spill these poisons of mine into the phone but something stops me and I don't know why. My heart desires confession but my shame is too great.

"I'm just tired. I had a long night and my head hurts. Anyway, how are the girls?"

"They're good. They miss you."

"I miss them too. I noticed Willy was home again."

She pauses. "Yeah, that silly kid is sick again. Can you believe it?"

"No, he's not and you know it."

"Oh, I know but he's my little guy. I can't say no." She hints a laugh as she resolves this. "It's nice to have a man around the house."

A silence fills the booth and I realize that she regrets ever saying that but it still cuts me deep.

"I'm sorry..." she pleads.

I cut her off. "Don't be."

"How's Ezekiel doing?" She's trying to change the subject.

I hesitate. "He's fine. Doing what he does."

"That's good."

"Well, I better get inside and make sure everything is in order and ready for tonight. We're expecting ten thousand to attend tonight."

"Really?" She sounds surprised but in a fake way. "That's wonderful."

"Yep." My voice sounds disinterested in my own profession and I can't imagine her caring any more.

"I gotta go, Ruth. I'll call you later on."

"Alright, dear. You call me anytime, understand?"

"Yep."

"I love you."

"Love you."

I hang up the phone and sigh in a moment in time where anxiety and shame are suspended and I have been given a grain of peace. The words "God is Love" stand out to me once again. I wonder. I turn and head out the booth and return to the convention center. From a side view, I think I see the Mexican man staring at me from the corner this time but again, I see the corner vacant except for the passing cars. I wonder what it is about that man that haunts me. Maybe I identify with his sadness.

I see Bill standing by the car and wave to him and he returns the gesture with a tilt of his cap. I walk across the loading area and enter the darkness and prepare for another meeting for the Glory of the Lord. If not the Lord, then something.

1926

The old phonograph revolved and scratched the old timey hymn throughout the small home. She stood at the kitchen sink, washing dishes in a tin bucket filled with lather. She hummed the record's melody to herself, smiling as if the words carried her back to happier times where she felt she really shall not be moved. She watched her children playing outside the foggy kitchen window; their high, muffled voices echoing through the vacant yard. Abigail tried to keep up with her older brothers in a game of tag. She waveringly ran, nearly losing balance repeatedly, until she finally lost her battle and tumbled into the dirt. The roaming chickens scuttled about as she fell. Her maternal sense perked till Abby's brown, dusty smile and innocent laughter arose from the ground. She grinned then winced at the cut across her swollen upper lip. She closed her eyes in pain, bringing a soapy hand to her mouth and felt the slightest warmth of blood swell from the opened wound. She continued her washing, hoping to scrub away the dirt and the filth. She scrubbed faster and faster; her eyes poured fear, hurt, and anger as she sang.

She looked to the calendar above the sink and followed the crossed days until it landed on Saturday. She listened to the song, savoring the jovial melody and the laughter behind it.

She felt guilt for wanting to leave earlier. A guilt instilled through years of masculine teachings and interpretations of the Word that condemned the legal separation of husband and wife, regardless of the circumstances. A condemnation ordained by God Almighty and enforced socially by every God-fearing man, woman, and child. She had often wondered what it was that drove man to destroy what he loves. Watching them play outside, she knew what she must do to protect her children. She mouthed the words of the hymn as she wiped her puffy eyes, sniffing.

She continued to scrub the dishes while she watched Jeremiah help Abby to her feet. Ezekiel was irritated about something and she could faintly hear his sharp voice across the yard, even above the phonograph. His gait and tone so similar to her husband she felt the fear seize her then subside. The song ended and another began.

She heard the voices fade then the wooden gate of the property's fence creaked open behind the music, the rigid and fragile greetings from her children, and then the voice. The stern voice she could feel inside her. Her heart sank deep within her chest. She looked out the window. The lank figure unsteadily looming forward. He had come home early and his step was staggered. Her mind began to spin. She quickly wiped her eyes with the hem of her dress and ran to the old phonograph, switching off the music; the hopeful lyrics vanishing. A sharp, high crack came from the kitchen and the remnants of one of the white plates lay fragmented on the soapy floor. Her lathered hands went to her mouth. She trembled at the long, wailing creak of the screen door coming from the front of the house.

The sturdy boots trumped closer and closer on the wooden floorboards, bringing with them terrible possibilities. The steps seemed loud and deliberate, reverberating the silence and thickening the air. She stood waiting, dripping. The man whom she loved and hated appeared around the worn and splintered doorframe. His dark blue eyes slightly visible underneath the brim of his straw hat, giving an inquisitive stare. He tossed the black Bible onto the kitchen table, startling her as it plopped, leaning with his shoulder on the doorframe, arms crossed. She noticed his missing ring finger but looked away. An anticipatory silence lingered in the air, thickening the potential. She brought her hands down to her sides, avoiding his gaze as best she could.

"Did you finish yer sermon, dear?" she asked.

He didn't answer. His mouth moved in a chewing motion causing his mustache to rise and fall in a pompous fashion, a slight smirk moving with his lips. He fixed his gaze over at the broken dish on the floor and nodded in its direction. "D'you break that dish, Clem?"

She nodded. Her heart breaking just like the instigating dish.

He cracked a smile, dropping his head and chuckling to himself. "Clem, I love ya but you do some of the dumbest things sometimes. I mean, you can't wash a single dish without breaking it? Is that it?"

He was staring at her again, the smile fading away with his patience. "You wanna answer me?"

"N-n-no," she stuttered out, the fear in her voice rattling with every consonant. Her eyes were drilling holes into the floorboards.

The children stood outside the door, listening with cautious ears to the tension they could feel in the yard. Jeremiah held his sister in his arms, whispering assurances to her innocent ears. Ezekiel stood alone with white knuckles. The scalp under his black hair warm and fiery.

"Now you gonna lie to me, Clementine. Lie like the sinner you are. The Good Book warns us about liars and deceivers. Proverbs heeds us to be wary of those who lie. Should I be wary of you, darling? Should I be worried that you are lying to me, not only about the dish but about playing music when I'm out of this house?"

She glanced up quickly in a wide-eyed look of surprise.

His voice shattered the tranquility that had once dwelled there like a gunshot through nature. She closed her eyes tightly and uttered a hushed prayer to God.

"You think I'm an ignorant man. You think I can't hear that cursed music coming through the walls outside? Christ, woman. What else you doin' behind my back?"

She kept her face downward, lips incapable of speech and limbs filled with lead. He pointed a flaccid finger at her, waving it like some improper tool of instruction.

"I know what yer doin'. Yer foolin' around. Yer spreadin' those legs like some whore of Babylon!"

Shivering again, her face cracked and contorted in fear and despair, opening the cut he had given her wider and wider. She began to do what she vowed she would never do in front of him.

"Don't you do that. Shut that off right now," he demanded.

He paced back and forth, pulling his hand down his face, across his mustache and off his chin. The boots clacking a vengeful dance like a bull preparing to charge.

"You quit that right now, woman."

She had begun to sob in loud sucks of air. Her defenses crumbling before him. She hoped the children wouldn't see her like this. He huffed air out of his nostrils as his dark eyes narrowed.

"I said quit!" He growled through his teeth taking a step toward her, grabbing her cheeks between his thumb and fingers, squeezing, pushing her against the nearest wall. He could feel the shape of her teeth through the flesh. The sour musk in his breath putrid, inches from her nose. The whites of his eyes cracked with leaking red wires, so terrified, she had ceased to shake. They stood for an eternity; frozen in an execrable painting. His wild eyes fearsome. His hot breath heavily poured in and out of his nostrils, malodorous and impious.

"Please," she whimpered, softly, mumbled through his fingers. "Please, Regal..."

He dropped his head, the eyes softening but refusing to submit. He slapped the palm of his hand hard and angrily against the wall behind her head, rattling the iron cross that hung there. He cinched his eyes tight, restraining his conscience. Raising his face to Clementine, he examined her puffy eyes and his craft upon her. The cuts and red patches of skin, bruises beckoning peace.

"You lied to me, Clem. You lied..." His voice began to crack as he choked back tears, damming the reservoir of inadequacies and inhibitions.

"I didn't lie to you, darling," she softly replied.

For a moment, she could see the pain his drowning eyes held. His grip on her cheeks loosened, the blood flowing once again past his fingers and in her veins. Slow, methodical, she raised her hand and stroked his rough cheek, an intimate moment rife with potential. But something in his stolid dam cracked and the reservoir burst through his mind, body and soul and flowed through his palms. He saw the cross above her blonde hair.

"Don't touch me. Hold your tongue," he commanded.

"You're not that man, Regal. You're not him..." she said but she knew that her brief haven was about to crumble.

Jeremiah and Abigail huddled together in the dirt of the front yard, singing the once hopeful words that had so briefly filled their home. Her high voice and his feudally tried to dilute the sickening violence behind those walls. Jeremiah put his hands across her precious ears, cradling her head. Ezekiel stood grinding his teeth, tears running, dropping into the dirt, creating dark brown patches around his bare feet.

"Shut up! Just shut up!" he yelled at his siblings; their surprised and puffy eyes staring blankly at him.

"Don't sing to God! Don't do that! God has nothing to do with it."

Jeremiah replied, "Don't blame God for your anger, Ezekiel. God has a plan."

"I hate His plan! I hate all this!" Ezekiel screamed.

Jeremiah ignored him as the sibling's song resurrected louder this time with more conviction. With more hope.

He listened to their faithful song, the cries of terror from his mother and the beastly rants and slaps of his drunken father. He cursed the God, this so-called God of Love, who fueled the violence behind his father's dark eyes. A violence that had come to be known as family.

He burst through the front door and saw his father straddling his mother on the floor. She lay on her back with her hands outstretched toward his clenched fists in futile protest. Her nose imbued, leaking down the side of her cheek. His father possessed by some unknown force. He had not heard Ezekiel approaching and was surprised when he felt a slight pain on the side of his right cheek. His head jerked to the side. He turned and saw his son, cradling his fist in his other hand. Ezekiel never thought his knuckles would throb so much. He glanced up and saw his father looking at him with perplexity. Regal alternated his glance from Ezekiel to Clementine before standing erect with his black and blue fists smeared in blood. Clementine rolled onto her side and spit red as she placed her hands on her face, shaking.

Ezekiel stared down at his mother in shock. Her face swollen and red and unrecognizable. Everything moved in slow motion. He saw her helpless and beaten, hopeless. Strong tears slid down his cheeks. He saw the iron cross next to her trembling body. Its shape an island among the blood. The rage had left and despair had replaced it. Witnessing such horrors gripped him, trapped him in a scene where all innocence had abandoned this place.

Clementine saw her son before her and reached out her hand to him as her mouth screamed for him to run. Her voice and the world came back to life around him with full force as he felt his father's powerful grip around his arm, pulling him. Ezekiel's legs dragged as he fought and kicked and spat at his father, his mother's cries receding in the house. His head swirled. He cursed his father and hit his leg futilely, desperately with his free hand. Regal walked without a word until he reached the door and flung his son as one would fling a dead animal out into the dust. Discarding something cumbersome and irrelevant from his sight. He looked once upon his disheveled flesh and blood in the dirt and saw his other children huddled together, eyes blazed with the intensity of a wildfire. Ezekiel, panting and distraught, knew he could never be free of his father's grasp.

Regal turned his head and spat into the dirt, his chest rising and falling, adrenaline and alcohol surging through his veins. The cloudless, beautiful day stood above and around him. His black shadowy frame menacing and ominous. He gave one last silent warning and grabbed the handle of the front door and slammed it. The top hinge creaked and then splintered into pieces, forcing the screen door to tilt on its only anchor and hang helplessly before the children, leaving a sliver to a scene they knew more than they should and cared even less to witness.

The Thief

The door I and many have entered through opens to an industrial hallway of fluorescent lights that stretch down the gray concrete walls lined with various doors. The ceiling is snaked with piping and electrical wiring and every ten feet a fluorescent bulb orbits the path. I walk toward the end of the musky hall looking at the blank doors until I come to the door that has a nameplate that reads, "Pastor Ezekiel Clemens" in gold lettering. I turn the door handle and enter without knocking. It's a typical dressing room for any major celebrity. Bright, round bulbs surround the three paneled vanity mirror. To the left is a black, leather couch and a mini-fridge. An impressive replica of Van Gogh's "Starry Night" hangs above the couch and, fitting to tonight's celebrity, a classical portrait of Jesus Christ. I imagine Jesus differently, not so white and handsome. The eyes of the painting stand out to me as if watching and pleading with me for something. I look at the coffee table and see it is inlaid with delicate jewels and, presumably, fake gold.

I walk over to the fridge and open the door. Just as I expect to see. The finest black caviar imported from the Caspian Sea; Ruinart champagne chilled; a wheel of moose cheese; Italian white truffles grown in the most rural portions of Tuscany. Pure opulence. Exclusive. What sickens me most is the fact that I know Clemens despises all these foods.

He loves waffles and chicken, fried catfish and grits. That is what he eats when he does eat. But he requires them to be present at every meeting to his specifications. He only knew about these items from a magazine he saw at the station director's home. The only item he would consider to eat would be the Godiva chocolates. And of course, the Ruinart.

I close the door and stand in the room a moment, reveling in the silence. The bulbs around the vanity mirror are bright and illuminating. I walk over and sit down in the chair, staring into the three paneled mirror. Dear Lord, how I've aged. I look like a smoker. My eye lids are saggy. My hair has retreated down the middle, leaving a tarmac of skin and all that's left is one long strip along the sides and back. Has this all been time's handiwork? Forty-eight years worn but visibly it looks much more. All I can do is stare because regret is self-abasing.

I grow tired of myself. I sink into the leather couch and close my eyes. As I begin to enjoy my solitude, I hear loud steps advancing down the hall, louder and louder, with a faint whistling of what sounds like "Blue Moon of Kentucky" until the door bursts open and clangs against the wall.

"Gerry, it looks great in there. Absolutely great. You should really go in there and check."

I open my eyes reluctantly. His dark, baggy eyes scan the place, making sure it measures up to his qualifications. He nods his head in agreement with himself and walks over to the mini fridge and peeks inside. After some agreeable grunts, he grabs the Champagne bottle and the Godiva chocolates and takes them over to his comfy chair before the three paneled mirrors and has a seat, whistling his tune. He checks himself out in each mirror and adjusts his collar, smoothes his hair, and bares his expensive teeth, making a sucking noise to dislodge anything in there. I wonder how he can change gears like this. I wish I had his ability to shut off my convictions at will. To not feel the confusion and shame as I play the part of a leader.

"Not too bad for my age," he says to the air, admiring himself. "A few grays ain't hurt nobody, right Ger? At least I ain't got your problem."

I watch him in the reflection as he dawdles over himself; completely enamored by his own image. In times like these, I can't help but wonder what went wrong. I wonder how a man who experienced what he experienced supernaturally could freefall to such an unconscionable state of pride. I look in his blue, bloodshot eyes as they reflect off the mirrors and I see no hint of the man I used to know. Neither does he, I imagine. He runs his hand across his scalp, slicking his hair. After he finishes, he reaches for the champagne bottle and surveys the room for something.

"Hey, where's the..." he begins.

"Clemens," I interject.

"What?" He still looks and peruses for the cork screw with determination.

"Not now. Please." My voice sounds cowardly in my ears.

"Lord, Ger, it's just a lil' sip is all. Ain't no need to..."

"It's too early," I say.

"Christ turned water into wine. I don't think he cares if..."

"I know, Ezekiel, can you shut up for once?" My voice sounds angry and terse in my ears. He freezes and looks at me with wide eyes; the champagne bottle dripping condensation from his hand. Our eyes meet and he recognizes my seriousness.

"Alright," he says and sits down in his comfortable chair facing me. His countenance subversive and quiet but I can tell he's annoyed by his licking lips. I rub my eyes and exhale a deep breath.

"I've been thinking about things," I say.

"Things? What things?" he asks obnoxiously with imploring eyes. As I look at my boss and mentor, what I was going to say escapes me and I am, again, speechless. I can't help but feel he needs me. The silence grows and I scramble through my mind for something to say that sounds even mildly important as what I made it out to be. His face is full of concern and impatience at once and I see his foot beginning to tap.

"You want a raise, Ger? I can give ya a raise. The Lord has blessed this ministry immensely and I have no qualms with givin' ya somethin' to pad yer pockets with, ya understand? How much ya want? Name it."

"No, no, no, I don't want a raise. Please. I don't want anything from you."

"Are ya sure?"

I nod persistently and he shrugs the deal away. I'm kicking myself repeatedly for my stupidity. My body feels drained, empty, and I want to cash it in but the day has just begun. Before I can even make a decision, Clemens voice revs up and he starts searching for the cork screw again only this time he's being sneaky about it. I pretend to not notice.

"Anyway, the musicians seem like alright fellas. One of 'em says he played with...uhh...Hank Williams. Played guitar or something like that. Good enough for me anyway. Even if he can't play a lick, they won't know the difference out there anyway. Oh, the television crew wants to know where to set up so can ya be sure to tell them where and such? Get my good side, alright?" He stops searching a moment and looks at me on the couch as if struck by a profound thought. "Ya done well, Ger. I can't thank ya enough for all ya do for this ministry over the years. God is keepin' you in mind, I know it. Treasures in heaven. Treasures in heaven."

A wave of bittersweet fills my mouth and I choke back the sting of bile in my esophagus. It's as if my spirit has been poisoned enough and now is fighting to regain its morality. Like I'm dragging on a cigarette from Lucifer. I rest my head back and stare at the ceiling, listening to Clemens searching for the cork screw so he can drown his conscious for another day.

"Have you thought about calling Abigail?" I ask.

I hear his movements stop for a momentary pause and then resume. He doesn't answer.

"She's your only sister," I say and realize that statement never made sense to me. Whether she's the only one or one of many doesn't discredit her importance.

"She's my sister, is all," he replies blankly, emotionless. I know he's afraid of what she might have to say to him after all these years.

"She deserves some answers."

"Maybe later."

"Why'd you want me to find out where she was then?"

He continues searching and searching, faster and faster with more perseverance. Right now, I just can't take it.

"I'm gonna go and make sure the aesthetics are ready," I say and rise from the couch. "I'll be back."

"Yeah," he responds absently, still opening and shutting drawers and prowling for anything.

"Hey, Ger," I hear Clemens call as I stand in the open doorway with my hand on the handle. I turn to face him and he stands tall looking at me. For a moment, I sense he wants to tell me something important. That maybe he wants to open up about his past and his present and possibly, his future. For a brief moment, I get the feeling he wants to purge himself and begin again. To wipe the slate clean.

"Can ya toss me a smoke?"

I feel myself exhale, shoulders dropping. I rifle through my jacket pockets by rote until I come up with a stray in my interior pocket. I pull it out, stare at it, and then at Clemens, and toss it to him. He catches it and looks at me with a gap-filled grin.

"I can always count on ya, Ger. Yesterday, today, and forever." He mumbles as the cigarette dangles between his thin lips. Lips that are a barrier to his most dangerous weapon. I guess all lips have poison, it just depends if it is used or not. He pulls a matchbook from his pants pocket and strikes it, lighting the end. It flickers into embers and he drags, hard and slow, sucking in the toxicity that he will spew later before an unsuspecting audience that will devour his every word like manna. I can't deny his ability to speak because I was his first victim. I continue to watch in a disgusted trance as the smoke filters out of his nose and mouth like a serpent and I wonder how God could love a creation like man. What is it about mankind that God finds so appealing and worthy of unconditional love? A being that's sole purpose is to praise but instead presents the one who granted life to it with disappointment and betrayal and evil. How can He love a being that destroys all that it loves? My thoughts are not your thoughts is the only explanation. I guess I'll never know for sure. I turn without saying anything and head down the cold hallway toward the "sanctuary" to make sure the stage is set for another night of televised hypocrisy. As I take each step, I can't help but get the feeling that something is looming. Like the walls are closing in on me and I'm helpless to stop it.

A young man passes me in the hallway and I catch a glimpse of his eyes in the dim glow of the lights. They seem to shine at me but I know that isn't true and I nod a gesture and he nods back, paying no mind. The breeze of his passing is cold and my heart begins to pound. My skin surges with bumps. Did I pass under a vent? It's nothing I suppose. I reach the end of the hallway and walk into the auditorium of the convention center. The bustle of voices and movement hit me first. Stage hands, technicians, set-up crew. The immense room dwarfs the scurrying inhabitants of it and makes anything we are doing seem insignificant and petty. A thought occurs to me that maybe God views all of this in the same way. All these meetings and gatherings to bring those closer to Him only further distance us from our goals. Maybe God is disgusted by what goes on. This must be me talking now.

The auditorium is shaped like a big-empty rectangular warehouse with a giant terraced stage on one end. The foldable seats are being set up by many volunteers in infinite rows and they are only half finished. Looking at their job makes me appreciate mine. Maybe not. By tonight, there will be thousands of these seats filled with people full of eagerness and faith and, presumably, many more will be standing in the back. It's all just a big show for Jesus. Jesus, Jesus, Jesus. The light grey stage stands about eight feet off the ground with its only access points coming from backstage and a small staircase on the left-hand side. This is where the believers will come to be "healed". The podium with the giant gold cross on the front is centered on the stage and a bright spotlight bathes it in illumination but keeps flickering. Clemens always demands the brightest spotlight be on him during the service.

Examining the set-up, I notice the short figure of Jeremiah Cole on the front of the stage, directing the musicians wildly with his hands. I hear the faint yells at the back of the building and they grow as I approach. The worship leader is pointing his finger in Cole's pursed face as the argument begins to make more sense.

"...not playing "To God be the Glory" or "Swing Low Sweet Chariot" or any other tune I had to hear my grandfather sing at church. Those tunes are old and the people want newer..."

"I don't care what the people want. Pastor Clemens plays old time hymns and I ain't gonna fight with some local, churc..."

"...I've been playin' music longer than you've been alive so don't start actin' like you're the..."

"...don't want that hippy, heathen Love Song music poisoning our meet..."

"What seems to be the problem here?" I ask, feeling the need to intervene before holy blows are exchanged.

"Mr. Lambough," Jeremiah Cole starts excitedly, jutting his thumb toward the man holding the guitar, "this musician here doesn't want to play any old time hymns that Pastor Clemens wants to be played at his meetings and frankly, he's going against the Lord by havin' drums in here as well." He stands with his hands on his hips breathing heavy and bothered. Expecting agreement. I look at the young musician. Young by my standards but he's probably in his mid-thirties. His hair bordering on what some would consider "sinful" in length and his jeans taper down to a bell.

"What's your name, son?" I ask.

He takes my hand. "Timothy, sir. I just want to say tha..."

I interrupt him calmly, "Hold on a second, Tim. Let's take some deep breaths and come to a good resolve over this whole issue. Alright?" He nods and I look at Cole and, reluctantly, he nods as well.

"Now, listen. Just by looking at you I can tell that you have a good heart. Your passion for your art obviously displays that. And, Cole, I admire your desire to stay true to traditional values as well. The church is founded on tradition."

He shrugs, slightly flattered but still annoyed. Short people are always like that: easily bothered and difficult.

"Fighting over something as trivial as this is completely arbitrary. Do either of you think God cares whether we play new songs or old songs? As long as He is glorified, time shouldn't matter. Are we agreed?"

They all nod and shuffle about like children being chastised.

"Now, as far as the drums go. Did not the psalmist rejoice and praise God through the clashing and resounding of cymbals and the beating of drums? Didn't David also say to 'let everything that has breath praise the Lord'? If the Bible states it, then do it."

They glance at me and at each other. "Alright," Tim concedes. Cole looks at Tim then me and finally says, "Ok."

"Great. Jeremiah, can I have a word?"

I usher him away from the band toward the other side of the stage and say in a soft tone, "Listen, you have to pick your battles in these instances and that battle wasn't the right one. Focusing your attention on whether you play 'Amazing Grace' or 'Jesus Is Just Alright' is what creates other denominations, understand?"

"But that..." he blurts out.

"Regardless, other things are more important than music. Things change and we have to adapt to it or we'll be an outdated ministry with a dying congregation."

He looks around the auditorium, sighing big puffs of air in and out and I can see the beads of sweat around his forehead. It isn't a secret this is his first meeting.

"Is this your first meeting?" I ask.

He nods his head up and down. "I never thought it would be this hard, sir. And the fact that it's Ezekiel Clemens makes me feel like...like I want to lose my guts."

Placing my hands on his broad shoulders, I look into his eyes. "You relax now, alright. The meeting doesn't start till this evening. We've got plenty of time. He has a way of working these things out." My words strike me in my own dilemma. As if God is speaking through me to me. Jeremiah Cole, the young, optimistic event coordinator, accepts what I say and begins to calm down. His shoulders relax and he opens up. "The sound man is late. We got all the spotlights working except for the one over Pastor Clemens. That one keeps shortin' out on us and we can't figure it out. Security is shorthanded and demanding more money than we originally agreed on and I ain't got any more money to give 'em. And the florist won't be able to deliver the flowers for the podium till three and we have a local nursery bringin' in twelve-foot palm trees that weigh more than the Cadillac you drove up in and we got no way of getting them through the door with the amount of people we has. The television crew for the network that is televising the whole thing says they can't be here till later this afternoon to set-up and..." He sighs a long, exasperated sigh. "Addin' on the fiasco with the band just sent me over the edge is all. I ain't cut out for this sorta thing, Mr. Lambough, I thought I was but I just can't..." He trails off, dropping his face to the floor overcome.

I stand looking at this young kid, eager and wanting perfection of everything. I see a hint of myself. The eagerness and optimism I once felt so long ago now a distant, dull feeling that has been enshrouded in dimness for what seems eternity. Is spreading the gospel supposed to be this way? So taxing? Sadly, Paul's plight is not my own. My plight rests in my heart and behind the door that reads Pastor Ezekiel Clemens.

"Son, these things have a way of working themselves out, understand?" I advise.

He nods. I put my hand on his shoulder again. I don't know why I keep doing that. It seems so Christian. "We can plan all we want but it won't make any difference if God has otherwise." He smiles sheepishly and laughs a little as I smile back.

"What time is it?" I ask and he looks at his watch and says, "11:30. Why?"

I span the busy auditorium and then declare, "I'm hungry. Let's get some lunch."

"Alright. Is Pastor Clemens coming?" he says eagerly.

I hope not. I hope I didn't say that out loud. "Let's go find out. Come on." We go from the stage through the back door and take the long way around to Ezekiel's dressing room. The back hallways are almost like a labyrinth. Thick piping and tubes and cases of electrical wire run the ceiling and the cold, grey brick of the walls is lit in fluorescence that makes the eyes strain. When the sound of the setting up fades, Jeremiah's voice speaks up.

"Hey, Mr. Lambough, I want to apologize for the way Sonny was earlier. He ain't got no right to say such things. Especially as a member of the church."

I admire the kid's conscience. "It's fine. Really." I can't help but think of how the kid from Mississippi is coming to the aid of my driver.

"I believe we are all equal in the eyes of the Lord," he admits. A nod will do so that's all I give him. We continue to walk through the dark halls.

"How long have you been with Pastor Clemens?" he asks.

"A long time."

"Was he always the way he is now?"

I hesitate, going into that mode I go into when certain questions are asked about Clemens' life. I've been lying for such a long time that I switch over automatically like my mind is computing excuses and falsities that are appropriate for the individual asking. I don't know what the truth is if there is any.

"You know, a prophet of God an' all?" he clarifies.

I decide to change the subject.

"So, you're from Mississippi?"

He smiles. "Jackson, yessir. Grew up in a Pentecostal church with about fifty members in a rundown building. No electricity or heating of any kind. That was a big congregation where I come from. In fact, I believe it wasn't far from where Pastor Clem-"

"You have any family?"

"Yessir, my mom and pops still live in Jackson and go to the same church I cut my teeth on. No siblings though. Well, I had a sister but she died at birth. We was twins but it never affected me much cause I didn't know her or nothin', you know." The conversation pauses as we pass through a large door that opens to yet another hallway. Various doors that led to the custodial rooms lined the walls. We pass workers sporadically carrying boxes, cords, tape.

"What made you leave Jackson?" I ask.

He thinks a moment and then says, "I just had an itchin' to go. God wasn't callin' me to do anythin' in Jackson. He had bigger and better plans for me. If I had stayed where I was, I probably would've ended up doin' nothin'. Actually, it was a sermon I heard on the radio that Pastor Clemens gave that really inspired me to do great things for God. He spoke of how he was runnin' from God and he met a man who's hand grew back. I couldn't believe it and I knew. I knew."

"You really think that much of Ezekiel Clemens?" I ask with a tone I felt came across as rude, pretentious, but doesn't hinder Cole's excitement on the subject.

"Sir, I think he's the greatest minister I've ever heard. He inspires me to do so much for God that I get goose bumps all over just thinkin' about it. Tonight, this night, is like a dream come true for me, I swears it."

My heart breaks in two ways at this statement. One, because this poor, naïve child of God is so unaware of his hero's transgressions and the other reason because he truly believes, without any doubt, that this man of God named Ezekiel Clemens is an honest-to-God prophet. This same man who cradled the toilet purging himself of his consecutive night of debauchery and sin just hours ago is the man God has appointed to lead the world to Him. I knew he could inspire but, after all my years of aiding him in this circus of spirituality, I had never seen evidence such as this.

Evidence of a young man who will dedicate his life to God and ministry because of the words that one man, not a god or angel or ideal, but a man, would say into a microphone before thousands of broken people around the globe. In a way, I envy him.

"Is it true Pastor Clemens has a brother named Jeremiah?" He asks.

"Had," I answer absently as we walk.

"Pardon?"

"Had," I repeat louder, more pronounced. "He had a brother named Jeremiah."

"Had? What happened to him?" he asks. His brow showing an honest sympathy. The dank smell of old water fills the hallway.

"Can't say. He doesn't talk about it much. Drowned, maybe. I know he was the one that found him though."

"Really? Lord, poor man. Must be hard to lose a brother," he remarks. A tinge of sorrow in his voice.

"Maybe. I never had any so I wouldn't know," I inform. My tone sounds insensitive and I hope Cole doesn't think I don't care. But would that be the worst thing?

"Does he have a wife?" he asks.

"No."

"Do you know why?"

I've wondered this myself, since most fellow ministers of his time have families and wives. I asked him once but he never gave me a straight answer. Too much honesty for that sort of relationship.

"He told me he wants to follow the example the Apostle Paul set. Paul said that to be a true disciple, it is best to be a bachelor to wholly devote yourself to the spreading of the Gospel. Something like that."

He shakes his head in disbelief at Clemens dedication. Truly marveling at the measure of faith in one man. "He sure is a man of faith," he says with admiration. I realize now that Jeremiah is in awe of the idea, the myth, of Ezekiel Clemens. The true man is hidden in our blind spots. The man is just a figurehead.

We stop before the door that leads into the hallway where Clemens' dressing room is. Before we go through, I turn and face young Jeremiah Cole and look into his eyes that are so full of hope and say, "I'm going to give you some advice and you can take it or leave it but I want you to know something."

"Ok," he says. The fluorescent light shining directly over him. I pull my pants up from slipping and then say, "The one main difference between God and man is that God never changes. He is the same as He was when He first breathed life into Adam but man? Man will always change. That is why you must always look to God if you want to make it through this life. Faith in man will only lead to disappointment and hurt and pain and loss but faith in God will sustain you. It will feed you. If there is one piece of advice I can give, it's this. Are you listening?"

He nods.

"Man is God's greatest mistake."

His face gives a confused look but he nods as if he understands. I feel it sounds too pessimistic and grim. What am I saying? My words didn't come out like I wanted them to. Sometimes my mouth is too slow for my mind. When I turn and open the door, I'm thinking to myself that that speech was intended for me more than Cole but I think we both are lost.

We pass the threshold and I hear the door of Clemens' dressing room open. A blonde, pale skinned man wearing khakis, sandals, and a white dress shirt steps out. I recognize that this is the same man I passed in the hallway when I left the dressing room.

My first thought is that Clemens may be dabbling in sins I don't even know about. The man looks at me and I see those same lit eyes I swore were illusions and am paralyzed inside by them like my legs have fused to the floor. My stomach shudders at his presence. I stop as does Cole and we just stare, unknowing and witnesses. Clemens' door shuts behind the man and we stand in an unarmed, silent standoff. He looks at us with those transcendent portals that must lead to another world. I sense something beyond understanding and fear it deep within my spirit, a reverent terror with no name. My body feels cold all over and I want to break down and collapse, weak and powerless. The man, about thirty feet away and sparsely lit, turns his back and walks, silently, in the opposite direction for the exit. Inside my chest, my heart is pounding and pounding. A bright glimpse of sunlight flashes at us and causes Cole and I to flinch and turn as the mysterious man opens the door. When we look back, the door is shut with a loud clack and he vanishes. I look at Cole and he

has a panicked look in his eyes as if begging for an explanation. I don't have the slightest clue.

Our bodies reawaken as if from a deep sleep, no words
between us, and we walk briskly down to Clemens' door. I
turn the handle and walk inside, half-expecting to see a dead
body or the devil himself. I hear something and look next to
the mini fridge in the dark and see Clemens, lit by the fluorescence of the hallway's lights shining into the room, cradled in a fetal position, pale and ghostly and mumbling, terrified as if something dead and gone had just visited him
from the grave. I yell at Cole to run after the man and see if
he can catch him. Cole stands their bewildered and I yell at
him louder and more forcefully and he shakes to life and
runs to the exit. I flip the switch and the light floods the dark
dressing room. Clemens shrieks and my heart wants to escape my chest cavity. I go to Clemens' side as he lies in the
corner, grasping the bottle opener he had been so desperate
to find in his white, clamped fists. I pick him up under his
arms to lay him down on the leather couch but my touch
sends him screaming.

"It's me. It's me. Calm down. Calm down," I say trying to
soothe him. Once he relaxes his thrashing, I hoist his heavy
body onto the couch.

"Ezekiel, what happened? Who was that man that was in
here? Ezekiel?" I prod. His eyes are darting here and there,
distracted, across the room, elsewhere and he keeps clawing
at the couch as if trying to escape something unseen. I don't
know what to think or feel at this moment. The chills and
cold still atop my skin.

"H-He knew. He knew," he mumbles through his lips. "Dear God, he knew! He must have been sent. He's come for me." I lay my hands on him to stop him from a publicity nightmare. His eyes are wide and alert like his survival is dependent on it. His skin feels cold and his normally reddish face is colorless. In my mind, I'm trying to understand what just happened. Is he dying?

The door opens and Cole enters the room.

"Did you see him?" I yell.

Cole shakes his head. Cole sees Clemens on the couch acting possessed and irrational.

"What happened to him?" Cole asks. I can see the intensity in his posture. I feel Clemens pulse and his heart is flowing like rapids through his veins. I hope his heavy heart can take the test.

"I don't know. I don't know. He could have taken something or that man may have given him something as well. I just don't know." I try to think but shame comes over me at the thought of his death. The shame of relief. Ezekiel begins to mumble to himself, transfixed in some other bewildered state.

"Is he gonna die?" Cole asks.

"I don't know. I've never seen him like this." Am I capable of performing an exorcism?

Cole begins to come back to reality. "I'll call a doctor."

"No! No!" I yell grabbing Cole's wrist as he turns toward the phone on the vanity. My instincts surprise me. He looks at my hand and then at me, almost offended that I would so blatantly stop him without cause. I think of the best excuse I can.

"We have to have faith that God can heal him." Ezekiel's words coming out of my mouth. A product of my environment. My tone is so convincing it scares me.

Jeremiah Cole, the young and naïve follower, nods his head agreeing and I can tell that he feels shame for not having faith. I turn my attention back to Clemens who is lying motionless now. His eyes stare up toward the ceiling and he continues to mumble incoherence. I listen close to try to decipher any information he might give me.

"Jesus...how could he...God sent him. God sent him to me...Jesus, help me. Oh, Lord Jesus, save me. What have I done...what is done in darkness will be brought to light...what is done in darkness will be brought to light..."

This is me, on my knees, perplexed and helpless, cradling Ezekiel Clemens in my arms as his mouth vibrates insanity. Who was that man? A sensation of supernatural fear grows within me. A fear of complete loss of control and mystery that cannot be harnessed or attained. Is he dealing with forces beyond the spiritual divide? I can't help but think these thoughts. I realize Cole is still in the room and turn around to see him pacing, rubbing his forehead back and forth. I call for him to come over and ask him to get a bucket of ice. He stands and I instruct him to not tell anyone about this. Not even Sonny and Lyle. He agrees and darts out of the room, leaving me and Clemens alone.

He's shivering so I take my suit jacket off and place it over his torso. He hugs it close and seems to be relaxing from this ordeal. Sweat saturates his shirt and his face is regaining its redness. The mumbling stops and he looks at me as if just now recognizing that I am here with him.

"Gerald," he says. His eyes moist with tears.

"I'm here, boss," I assure him. I assure myself. God, give me assurance. He closes his eyes and breathes deeply through his nose. "W-What's going to happen to me?"

"What?" I ask, hoping he could have answered that question for himself.

He looks at me with slanted eyebrows. "I gotta sit up..."

"Who was that man in here, Clemens?"

He shakes his head and tries to sit up.

"Clemens, listen." I scream, slamming him back down onto the couch's cushions. My sudden rage surprising us both. He looks at me wide eyed and subdued with my arms pinning him down. His strength no match for mine. "If you're dealing in something had anything to do with this, I'm walking out right now. You understand? I can't be a victim of this anymore. This sickness unless you are straight with me. Who was that man?"

"I don't know who he was!" he screams back. His breath heavy. "I don't know."

I raise my eyes to the wall and see Jesus' face staring back at me and I want to slap the perfection off of it. What is He putting me through this for?

"You're lying to me, Clemens. You've been lying your whole life."

"I swear on God Almighty, I don't know who that man was, Ger."

"Was he selling to you?" My hands still rest on his chest, holding him down but I refuse to let him up till he speaks truth.

"No, Ger, no." He seems hurt at my question. His voice seeming to try and reassure me in a soothing way. I can feel his bones in my grip.

"Don't lie to me..."

"I ain't lying, damn it! It's the truth!" he barks at me, shaking with the weight of passion. Now I know he's telling me the truth. I relax my arms a bit.

"Well, what did he want?" I ask.

He averts his eyes from mine and I can tell he's hiding something. He says nothing.

"Ezekiel, what did he want?" I say the words sharp. Emphasizing my frustration while emphasizing my words. He doesn't answer but only looks away.

"Does this have to do with your father?" I ask. The nerves in my gut tremble as I ask. I can feel my muscles cramping in my fingers. His eyes show a mixed emotion of anger and surprise. "I need to sit up..." he says again. I can tell he's irritated.

"Does it, Clemens?" I ask again. My voice is strained and loud now, louder than I've ever heard it. I can feel my usual level of patience waning. Cole will be back any minute and time is running out.

"Ger, let me go," he says, trying to grab my hand. When I feel his fingers on my skin, I know that our partnership has been building to this moment of conflict. Everything piling up like snow on a roof. It can only take so much before the roof gives way.

"Clemens, tell me now! You stupid, ignorant man! You're just like your father was! Speak to me!" The words come out, messy and harsh, and they hang in the air a moment like poisonous snowflakes. I never knew his father but the words came out, impulsive in the moment. His eyes fill with rage and he struggles and writhes to be free of my grip. "You shut the hell up! I am not my father! What would you know about fathers? Huh?" He was almost growling now. I struggle to keep him subdued but his lean body is full of surprising fight. When I said what I said, I expected a verbal retaliation attacking who I was. That is just how Ezekiel Clemens is. I look to the door, almost expecting Cole to burst through and see us engaged in this juvenile sprawl. By God's graces, his young optimism won't have to see this.

"You're nothin' without me, Lambough. Nothin' but an ordinary man doin' ordinary things. Nothin' but a husband an' father with no purpose in life. Nothin' but a bastard that no one will remember," his animosity was spiteful. I can't deny that his words hurt but I have to be empathetic as best I can.

"You are your father, Clemens." I repeat to him and he gives one last violent surge of rage at me but my position holds strong. The weight of age benefitting me for once. He begins to settle and struggle less. We both are breathing intensely from the escalation. My mouth feels dry and sticky and, for some reason, I realize I haven't eaten anything all day. The door swings open and in comes Jeremiah Cole with a bucket of ice. He's breathing heavily as if he's been running laps around the building.

"I got it, Mr. Lambough," he says between catching breaths. "Who woulda thought...it be so hard to get ice...without a good explanation?" He smiles as he places the bucket on the floor next to me. Then hunches over on his knees, breathing like an engine.

"Did you tell anybody," I say rather rudely. Cole doesn't seem to notice my shortness.

"No, sir...I barely had time to."

I sit back and release Clemens. He rises on his elbows breathing deep breaths. I wish I could get him alone again.

"How is he?" Cole asks concerned.

I look at Cole. "Best as can be expected."

"Oh, praise the Lord. You alright, Pastor?" he says loudly as if speaking to a geriatric. He leans over me and stares at Clemens' face. My heart is still pounding from arguing with Clemens and I feel no closure to the issue. So close to something real, to another piece of the puzzle. Maybe redemption.

"Son, the devil was trying to test me," Clemens speaks to Cole, the red back in his face. "Ya see, Satan wants to bring down those who do right in the eyes of the Lord. Thank the Lord Jesus I overcame his attack."

I can't take this. I stand up and grab Cole by the crook of his arm and lead him out of the room and into the hallway. The door shuts and I pace a small path in front of it.

"Cole, listen here," I say pointing my fingers. "You are going to have to be my right-hand man tonight, alright?"

Cole looks excited and nervous all at once. "But, sir, I have to take care of everything goin' on out here and..."

"Forget that. I need you to help me with Pastor Clemens, alright. This is much more important."

"Alright."

"Alright," I repeat and continue to pace. My mind keeps going back to Clemens. Why won't he tell me what that man wanted? Who he was? What else is he hiding from me? I need to focus. Focus. I return my attention to Cole.

"I need you to watch over him right now while I do some other business, understand? Stay here and don't let him leave this dressing room until I come back and tell you to, alright?"

"Alright," he says meekly.

"Good. Go in there and I'll be back soon." I place my hand on his back and usher him back into the room.

As his body hits the door, he hurriedly asks, "What are you gonna do?"

I push him through and as the door shuts, I tell him that I'll be back. The door clicks and I compose myself and my thoughts a moment in the fluorescent lighting. Lord, what is going on today? I sense a shadow on the day. An important shadow that with it brings only darkness and I am terrified. I need some fresh air so I head toward the door that led me into this mess, the door that hopefully might lead me out of it.

1928

The boys sat outside Bidley's General Store, which at night transformed to a bar for the few who would use it. Each sat nursing a cola they purchased with the money made working for the cattle rancher, Mr. Mayhew. The ancient rancher had offered them two dollars each for a week's worth of hard labor, digging, feeding, and scooping. "I won't hire ladies," he warned. He had a long, leathery face abused by the sun with a frowning mouth hidden behind his brittle white beard. His only friend Regal Clemens which, no doubt, led to the boys obtaining the job in the first place. It was a long week but they had shoveled enough dirt and manure to earn a treat rarely received and deserved entirely. They placed their ten cents on the counter and even Bidley couldn't hide his smile at the two's success.

"Thanks," Jeremiah said politely. Ezekiel nodded his gratitude. Bidley looked down at them from behind the bar and smiled a pitiful smile. His face round and jolly with eye lids that were beginning to sag, revealing the red lining of his eyes. Teeth set in his mouth as if at random.

"How's yer daddy's sermon comin' along?" he asked, polishing a glass with a dark, stained rag. Jeremiah took a quick sip. "He's doin' the Lord's work, he is," he hiccupped.

He smiled as they raised their glasses to him leaving. "You boys tell yer daddy ol' Bidley's greeting," he said as they disappeared into the day.

Jeremiah sat on a flat, wooden bench, slouched with his knee up and foot on the seat that lined the row of buildings on main street. He wore a red, checkered shirt defiled with sweat and dirt. Jeans designed to match. Light brown hair hung just above his eyes as he dipped the glass bottle back and enjoyed the sting of the bubbles on his throat. He belched and looked over at his younger brother. Ezekiel lay with head back and chin up, looking like a child drunk who had staggered about before falling onto the same bench to sleep off his drink. His smooth cheeks and black hair were as grimy as his habiliments. He clasped the sweating glass in both hands as they sat in the shade of the awning, escaping the humid air and absorbing the wastefulness of the summer.

They sat watching the town's daily clamor and busyness as they drank. Rarely witnessing new events, people, or anything that broke the banality. Time did not govern their stay and they relished the freedom of it. Jeremiah took a swig of the cola and commented, "Now I know why nobody want to work for that crazy fool."

Ezekiel lethargically rolled his head toward Jeremiah. "My arms are so tired I can't even lift 'em." They sat silently enjoying the presence of each other. A subtle happiness that can pass by without acknowledgment if the mind isn't looking for it.

Jeremiah watched the limited array of people walking and shopping and conversing in the streets as Ezekiel bordered on the verge of sleep. Most people he saw attended his father's church and he would waive periodically when noticed, dutifully. His father had found the job for them. Jeremiah had believed it was because Mr. Mayhew had owed Regal Clemens a favor, whatever it may be, that they even got the job since there were plenty of colored boys who would have worked the same job for half the money.

"You done good, Ezekiel," Jeremiah said. No answer from the other side of the bench. Jeremiah kicked and Ezekiel shot with a start.

"What? What?" he stammered, looking down at his pants darkening.

"Hey! Now ya gotta give me some. It's only fair."

Jeremiah laughed. "I don't gotta give you nothin'."

"Come on, now. It's only fair," he reasoned.

"Ain't gonna happen."

Ezekiel sulked, "Whad'ya want anyway?"

"Nothin'. Forget it."

Ezekiel wiped at his legs without remedy, stretched his arms and back as he yawned and then took a sip of his cola.

"It's all sticky now," he observed with a hint of annoyance in his tone.

"You complain too much," Jeremiah chided, "you ought ta be happy with what ya got."

"I'm happy," he scowled. "Ain't I happy?"

Jeremiah ignored him, gazing cross the street toward the shop that read 'BANK' in big bold letters across the doorway. Inside, he could see the tellers, dressed in fine suits with ties cordially aiding the customers with their money. He liked the thought of making money, of being someone who had it and what came with it, but he knew there lay more to life than what was made in the world. A young girl with long brown hair lingered outside the bank fussing and pouting as her mother's finger dangled in front of her. He recalled the look Bidley had given Ezekiel and him, a look of sympathy and sadness that held knowledge that warranted such a look neither seemed to comprehend.

"Zeke, you ever think about what you wanna be when you get older?"

Ezekiel looked at his brother out the corner of his eye, suspicious. "Sometimes. Why?"

"Jus' curious. I do it a lot. Where I'll be years from now and what I'll be doin'. Wonderin' how God's gonna put me there and what he gonna use me fer," Jeremiah scratched his scalp and took a drink, hiccupping after. "Life is full a mysteries, ain't it? Like this here pop. How they get the bubbles in there, anyway?"

Ezekiel looked straight ahead, staring at nothing in particular and waiving his brother's comment. His mind wandering in its own future, pondering what fate awaited him, where he would end up.

"Whatever I be, it won't be here," Ezekiel said.

The warm air was heavy yet comforting, laying like a blanket upon them, nestled in its warmth as the cola and shade added just enough chill to make it perfect.

"I like sittin' here," Ezekiel said.

Jeremiah nodded. "Me too."

"Too bad we ain't got some real drink," Ezekiel remarked. Jeremiah looked at his brother, his face grave.

"That ain't nothin' but poison. You're only ten and don't you ever start, ya hear. Promise me that."

"I was jus jokin'."

"Promise it."

Ezekiel paused. "Y-Yeah. I won't."

Jeremiah leaned, took a sip of his pop, and looked down the street. In the distance, he could see two figures, one fat and one skinny, approaching, wearing white dresses and one chattering gaily to the other. Jeremiah sat erect.

"Shoot, look who's comin'," Jeremiah warned. Ezekiel leaned forward and looked down the path and rolled his eyes back into his head as if he were trying to view his brain.

"No breaks in this town, I swears it," he said crashing his head back against the bench. "Can we run for it?" The boys looked at each other, searching for a way of escape. The fat figure waved.

"Well, hello, Jeremiah. What are you doin' out here? Havin' a lil' treat?" the fat lady asked and answered all at once. Her voice melodious though not a melody desired; shrilly and nasal to pierce the ear drum like a blade. Her dress grew less white as she approached and the remnant of old and new stains looked as land on a map Jeremiah could see the stitching between the seams, facing their ultimate test.

"Yep. Jus' sittin' here havin' a pop, ma'am," he answered with a fake smile, staring up at her swollen face, suppressing a snicker at the woman's squeaky voice. He could see in her eyes she was creating some type of falsity right now as they spoke.

"That's so nice. Is it tasty? It sure looks tasty. I know it is tasty. My Lord, why are your clothes so filthy?" Her eyes fell over to the scowling face of Ezekiel, arms crossed, staring straight ahead, brow pointed and visibly irritated. "Oh, I didn't know little Ezekiel was here with you right now. How are you, sweetie? Good? Good."

Ezekiel answered without looking at her, "Fine."

The skinny, homely girl stood silent. She was younger than the fat woman yet always attached to this domineering personality. The big brown eyes of the young, skinny girl downcast and embarrassed, swaying just behind the girth of the large woman, casting furtive glances at the two. The fat one grabbed her arm and pushed her forward.

"Jeremiah, this is Emma. She's gonna start goin to your daddy's church soon. I've been workin' on her for some time and I finally broke her down to be saved. Ain't that just the tops?" Emma smiled avoiding Jeremiah's gaze. He smiled as all boys of fourteen do when they talk to someone of the opposite sex.

"How do ya do?" he asked.

She replied soft, "Fine, thank you."

"You wanna kiss her, don't ya?" Ezekiel commented under his breath. Jeremiah punched him in the shoulder. He grabbed his upper arm in surprise and shot a stare his way. The fat one and Emma didn't catch his words or the cause of the sudden violence.

"How's your mother, Jeremiah? I don't see her as much anymore. Is she doin' good? I'm sure she is."

"She's fine. Just fine, Miss Wordman," he answered.

"I would call her to ask her how she is doin' but ya'll don't have a telephone. When is your daddy gonna keep up with the times? God don't got nothin' against electricity, you know. Why preachers all over the world got telephones."

"He is who he is, ma'am."

"The Lord knows it. He surely do. Well, your sister must be getting so big. She's what? Six years old now."

"Four years old. Same as she was at church on Sunday."

"My how the time does pass," she remarked ignoring his statement. "When my Charles was four, he was the most funniest lil thing you ever seen. He would say the most silly things an all I could do was just laugh and laugh. I hear your sister likes to play with you boys. She's quite a tom-girl, she is. Hope she don't turn out funny, ya know." She laughed a close-lipped and her face resembled a balloon about to burst. She fanned herself with her gloved hand, the gelatin surrounding her arms wiggled with each wave.

There was no worse fate for a teenage boy on a summer day than to be verbally imprisoned by a parental acquaintance. Ezekiel simply stared away looking perturbed. Both boys knew this would happen when no means of escape appeared and their spirits were crushed because of the horrible luck that had befallen them. However, there was one form of escape.

"That's quite funny, ma'am, but I'm afraid we're gonna have to get home now. Our Pa 's expectin' us," Jeremiah informed. Ezekiel shot a glance.

"Oh, ain't that a shame. We was havin' such a good conversation. Well, say howdy to your parents for me. Lord knows how we jus' love your folks."

"I sure will do it, Miss Wordman," Jeremiah said standing. Ezekiel followed and they stepped past the two ladies into the bright sun. Ezekiel kept his silence as they passed. Miss Woodman eyed them as they left and then leaned close to Emma's ear and whispered loud enough for the boys to hear, "That Clementine must be losin' her head to let those boys outta the house like that." She made a tisk sound and continued her stroll down the walkway. Emma obediently followed, stealing one last glimpse.

When they were out of hearing range of Miss Woodman and Emma, Ezekiel punched Jeremiah back in his arm.

"Ow!" he hollered. "What?"

"You know what? Why ya gotta say that? Now we gotta go home."

A loud pick-up truck rumbled past carrying furniture, kicking up a storm of dust. The boys waved their hands through the cloud.

"It ain't right to lie. Jus' cause you don't wanna go home don't mean I have to contradict my beliefs."

"It ain't fair. It jus' ain't fair."

"Oh, quit your whinin'. Pop probably won't be home anyway."

"Why ya gotta be so righteous, anyway?"

"I jus tryin to be a good person is all."

"I jus don't wanna be home," Ezekiel mumbled. They walked through town silent, holding their empty cola bottles. The store windows caught their mute reflections, mirroring the itchy air between them. They walked till they reached past the borders of the small town and then followed the long dirt road that led home. The march felt eternal. Both walked slow and similar gaits as if they cared not to reach their destination.

They passed an old, blue house with broken windows and a sagging porch. The old paint sporadically scraped and torn by nature and time. A slight breeze strolled through the air. The tall leaves of grass swayed along the fences and the cotton field rustled to life. The dust they kicked up flew about frenetic and dissolved into the sky. Ezekiel walked with his hands in his pockets.

"It's pretty hot," Ezekiel remarked. His statement hanging in the air as if waiting for its match.

Jeremiah gave a quick glance his way. "Sure could go for a swim."

Ezekiel turned to Jeremiah as they walked. He returned the look. Their eyes exchanged the same thought and Ezekiel smiled for the first time that day. They picked up speed as they walked down the dusty road and as they came to the fork, they looked at each other.

Jeremiah contemplated the straight path ahead that lead home and then turned to his right down the path lined with ironwoods and sinuous brush that led to the lake. An old dog limped across the dirt road as he looked thoughtfully in its direction. Ezekiel watched his older brother without aversion, anticipating his decision; the sweat christening his scalp as he watched. Jeremiah looked full into Ezekiel's face with a serious countenance, his fists on his hips and said, "I never said when we had to be home, did I?"

Ezekiel smiled a wide gap-filled grin. Soon, the boys were running full speed toward down the road, the hot sunlight overhead, yelling and whooping with joyful defiance as clouds of dust filled their wake. The old dog scuttling down the path cowered into the dry brush as they ran past.

They swam the rest of the afternoon until they were exhausted. Ezekiel waded in the shallow end, overcome by fear to attempt the rope swing that had been affixed to the thick live oak next to the shore. They lay supine on the damp embankment under the shade of the trees. The sun falling in the west as they dried their half-naked bodies, glowing orange fire-like. Their dirty clothes piled together in heaps. A black crow cawed in the silence above them then flew.

Jeremiah hummed an old hymn. Ezekiel knew the melody tired of its constancy of his brother's lips. "I just love the way it sound is all. Makes me think of heaven," Ezekiel remembered hearing his brother say one time talking with some other boys. Soon, his hum became words and he sang of never meeting this side of heaven.

"Why ya sing that song?" Ezekiel asked, interrupting.

Jeremiah sat up on his elbows. "What ya askin' for?"

"Jus curious is all," he replied, the crook of his arm resting over his eyes. Jeremiah stared at him a moment, sorting through his mind. "I likes it is all. I don't know how ya couldn't."

"Why?"

"Huh?"

"Why?"

Jeremiah hesitated. "It's hard to explain. It gives me some hope, I guess. Hope in the future."

Ezekiel lay silent, staring into the bundles of leaves that clung to the branches. Their skin was tender and moist. "I think I believe in God. I just don't know if I want to."

"Why you sayin' stuff like that for?" Jeremiah asked irritated though he knew the root of his doubt. "Ma and Pop raised us to believe, not doubt."

"I don't know what I'm sayin'," he confessed. His demeanor metamorphosing to a darker shade of person like the idea of sub ordinance proved too strong.

Jeremiah debated whether to ask and decided he needed to. "Is this cuz of Pop? Is that it?"

Ezekiel's lips pursed tight and he repositioned his legs.

"Why don't God wanna help us is all I really am askin'?" he blurted out. His voice cracked and he tried to mask it. "They is all these awful things happening to people every day and if God was up there, if He really cared about us down here, then why don't He just stop it all?"

Jeremiah waited to respond till he knew exactly what to say. He prayed a silent prayer to give him the words that would console his brother's soul. When he felt ready, he said, "Look, Pop is Pop and God is God. You can't be mad at God for what Pop does and vice versa. Pop chooses to drink cuz he wants to and God done have nothin' to stop him because He's got other plans in store. Member when Paul said to rejoice in our trials? Maybe he was on to somethin'."

Ezekiel sat up. His shoulders and arms red and warm with sunburn. "But He can stop it, can't He?"

"Yeah, I guess if He want."

"Then why the hell don't He? Why don't He jus kill Pop then?"

Jeremiah sat up straight and slapped Ezekiel across the face with a loud pang, swiftly. Ezekiel shuddered and grabbed his stinging cheek, eyes full of shock and terror that melted to anger at his brother's action. A sudden remorse fell quickly on him though he tried not to show it.

"Don't say that. Don't ever say that. No matter what he does, he's still your Pop and nothin' is gonna change that."

Ezekiel fought back the tears that were desperately trying to break free. He hunkered down inside and sat brooding.

Jeremiah sulked, watching the horizon and setting sun. Ezekiel simmering between sadness and anger. A slender snake swam atop the water near their embankment, fluidly writhing its body in a hypnotic motion as it paralleled the shoreline.

"Sorry," Jeremiah said after a moment.

Ezekiel sat with his arms crossed looking in the opposite direction. "Ain't nothin'," he said.

They gathered their clothes and walked barefoot along the dirt path for two miles until they saw the smoke from the chimney of their home. They stood atop the small hill, hesitant. The youthful afternoon just a fleeting moment and now they were forced back into an adult world where their presence should be forbidden. The sky's color faded dark and the home and horizon were becoming blank silhouettes in the waning light.

Ezekiel looked at Jeremiah. "I hope your right about God," he said.

Jeremiah smiled a discomforting smile in return. He placed his arm around his younger brother's neck, standing joined in familial comfort, brothers again before the storm.

"Me too."

Wilderness

God, what is happening? Is this a test or am I wandering in the Valley of Decision? I think back to what Judas must have felt when he kissed Jesus in Gethsemane as I walk down the corridor, heading somewhere but I don't really know where. Just away. Jesus' eyes are what would convict me of my betrayal more than anything I am sure but the knowledge of what I had done would be terrible as well. Terrible beyond description. I know Judas felt it. How could he not? Today, I feel I am a modern-day version. My pockets heavy with thirty pieces of betrayal. Except I don't even realize how attached I am until after the fact. By doing nothing, I've allowed everything. The full effects of my conspiracy are being made evident in my mind as we draw closer to this massive gathering of faithful sheep and I, the wolf's apprentice, am aiding in their demise by hiding the truth. Christ said the truth will set us free yet I've fought it most of my life. Something so simple and liberating but still so terrifying it holds my tongue.

I don't realize it but I am outside in the sunlight, exiting the same door that the mysterious visitor vanished through not more than fifteen minutes ago. Just as I expect, he's nowhere in sight. The air is warm now and welcoming and I stand bathed in light and exhale deep, deep breaths of release. It still does nothing for my anxiety. I hope Cole is keeping an eye on Clemens. Should I have left him alone? The street has increased in activity since we arrived earlier. The pay phone has a heavy woman in a flat dress wedged into it and she seems upset about something. Her swollen arm waving like a conversational conductor orchestrating an argument. Near the chain-linked fence surrounding the parking area, I see the black Cadillac sitting in the shade of the convention center's massive shadow with Bill sitting inside. I tap down the steps towards Bill to ask if he saw anything. To maybe get some more information on this mess and another voice that will help my mind clear. Hopefully, Bill can bring reality back to me. He looks like he's laughing at something on the radio and, as I get closer, I see that his face is down and he's looking at something in his lap. He doesn't notice me come up and startles a bit, fumbling the book shut and stutters, "Y-Y-Yes, sir. What can I do ya for?" I can see the black face and big ears on the cover. I lean my elbows on the sill of the open window and look down at the comic and then at Bill and he just smiles sheepishly.

"I never outgrown it, I guess," he admits with a smile. His coarse curly hair now white. Bill's face reminds me of one of the faces belonging to a rancher in those old westerns I watched when I was a kid. Stretched and gruff. Exuding a harshness and ferocity that made you hesitate without thinking. In contrast to his features, Bill is as simple and gentle as a breeze.

"Never mind that, Bill. Have you been sitting out here the entire time?"

"Haven't budged an inch, sir. I've been sittin' here readin' the whole time. I guess reading. I look at it more for the pictures than anythin' else. Never could read well. You know...considerin'."

I look around to see if maybe he's watching us. Getting some heightened ecstasy at the confusion he's brought us. I only see a couple with a baby stroller and the fat woman in the phone booth.

"Did you happen to see a blonde-haired guy in a white shirt and khakis come through the door? About this high?"

"No, sir. I just saw that young, short fella come through not too long ago you was with lookin' kinda scared. Seemed like he was searchin' for somebody but he didn't find who he was lookin for. Other than him, I haven't seen a soul."

I massage my eyes, hoping to pressure the stress out. Little gray-white circles pop in varying intensities as my fingertips slide across. Pressure the pressure until it cancels itself out. It never works but I do it anyway. Just like I've always done.

"You alright, Mr. Lambough?" I hear Bill ask me. When he says my name, I know he's truly concerned. That's what I have grown to love about Bill. It's not the years he's been chauffeuring me and Clemens around and that he has never, in all these years together, asked for a raise he deserves. It's his empathy. His joy. His constancy. These are simple things I've complicated in my life, by choice or circumstance. Ironically, Christian charity has encrusted my heart with bitterness. I wave my hand. "Oh, I'm alright. Don't worry about anything. I was just hoping to speak with him. It's not important."

Bill looks at me incredulously and opens his mouth to speak, then stops, dropping his eyes back to his comic.

"What is it, Bill?" I ask.

"Uhh...it's nothing," he replies. "Nothin' important."

"You can say whatever you want to say to me, Bill. I'm your friend"

He examines my gaze with almost admiration and then says, "Gerald, I've been drivin' for you and Mr. Clemens for a long time now and I always wanted to ask ya something about it."

"Yes." I feel my gut begin to dance.

"I just drive and don't ax much questions. I'm thankful I has a job. I am very much. Never had any problems with any of ya'll but...I know somethin' not right with pastor."

"What makes you think that?" I've failed at my job. I must have. Or am I that disconnected from everyone?

"A man can just tell by lookin' in another man's eyes."

My head is swimming, grasping at excuses.

"I ain't gonna say nothing bout it to no one. Just wanted to hear it from you." His eyes are genial and warm, displaying a sincerity that touches my heart.

I pat his shoulder. "He's being tested, Bill, just as Job was."

Bill nods saying that he'll be praying for the pastor. I thank him and pat the sill with my hand as I walk away with full trust. Bill is better than all of us I would venture to say. Man needs to be simple and how we complicate the simplicity is beyond comprehension. God laid it out easy and plain in those seven days. Creation must have been at peace and tranquil until he blew breath into a dust bowl and formed what I would call a mess. Couldn't even follow one uncomplicated rule. I imagine the fruit tasting bitter and sour and Adam and Eve realizing the severity of the first evil they partook in. I feel bitter thinking on man and I realize I would have eaten too. I am no different, one of the mistakes. I wonder if Jesus feels like it was all a waste of time, a thankless martyr with a grudge. I wonder because I put myself but how could I possibly understand?

"Bill," I say as I stop and turn. He looks to me. "You're a good man."

He smiles before I turn around and, for a brief moment, I feel a true sense of connection with someone. I'm standing in the driving lane of the parking area, surrounded by the living world. I see the door that leads back inside and then ahead toward the street and I resign with myself that I deserve a break. Toward the street I go where the fat woman is talking on the phone. I'm not sure where I'm going. I decide to walk around the block to clear my head, maybe my heart. If God wants to talk, I'm willing to listen. I cross the street successfully and follow the stained and tattooed sidewalk. Without realizing it, I'm avoiding stepping on the cracks for fear of bad luck. Then I realize there is no luck. Only a mysterious plan that seems like luck. I pass a deli that sits at the corner of the side street and where we almost collided with the young Mexican man. I scan the area briefly but can't see him among the many pedestrians so I keep walking. The shadow of the building is cool and a touch crisp. Is that man walking behind me? I periodically look over my shoulder, expecting to see blonde hair and piercing eyes but they are never there. Could a man like that scare Clemens without knowing something? My only guess is he gave him something to take that made him lose it like that. That doesn't explain my fear. Why did I have fear? Cole felt it too, right? He did because I saw him freeze as I did.

A small liquor store, windows opaque with cigarette and liquor ads, is set quietly into the brick building. Through the signs and grime, I see the cashier handing a brown, wrinkled bag to a man who takes it and walks toward the door. He opens it, jingling the bells. He sees me and stops. By his clothes and smell, I can tell he lives on the street which contrasts highly with my nice suit and shoes. He scans me from the toes up, moves past me and then leaves down the street. I watch him, limping on his left foot, and it occurs to me how out of touch I am with not only myself, but with the people I've dedicated my life to helping. Christ would have spoken to that man. Would have helped him in some way. But me? I am an empty suit. Nothing but fibers interwoven to look the part of someone who cares. He turns the corner, tipping the bag to his lips and disappears. Something of him reminds me of Ezekiel in some way. A little of myself as well. Clemens always had a heart for the folk of the street. In the early days of our ministry, we would rarely keep the gift offerings we received. Just enough to pay for bus fare and food. Maybe lodgings. Anything else was given away. Clemens always wanted to give the money to the homeless, the wandering.

That was an old time though. I wonder if Ezekiel Clemens hadn't become Ezekiel Clemens, he would probably be that wandering man.

Putting my hands in my pockets, I stroll along, head down, watching the cracks again. Avoiding the cracks just like I always do. I pass other stores and places of business. A shoe repair place, an antique furniture store, a bookstore that smells like old paper and binding as I walk past the propped open door. Young and old people pass me on the street. Some avoid eye contact, others glance just as they pass, some stare without regard. Each face slightly different than the next yet terribly the same. All afflicted by life. It truly is a nice day. I think of the children at Sunday School, clapping and singing innocently that this is the day that the Lord has made. If only they could keep that joy, that unbridled faith when the rapid decline of adulthood sets in. Maybe, just maybe, they would know true love. Not the love that man has created but a love like a rock. A love like faith, not of reason.

Near the corner at the end of the block of the brick building is a record store and I feel an impulse to step inside. I haven't been in a record shop since I was a kid, before it all happened. Maybe I can connect again. Shelves of records and the menagerie of posters rekindle a nostalgia in me that I both despise and welcome. I don't think about the past much. At least, not my past because that is what it is: the past.

I'm overwhelmed at the collection of music. Genres I've never even heard of are inhabited with names and faces all too foreign to me. I feel so old. So useless. What happened to the olden days? The record player in the front is playing some bizarre music that sounds erratic and distorted. It doesn't even sound like music. It smells in here and I wonder if I'm smoking drugs as I inhale the fragrant air. When I came to these stores, there were only a few styles. I really liked the blues. I think it was because I identified with the heartache they spoke. The musical catharsis that the gravelly voices sung was always something that made me feel not alone. The nostalgia wears off quick because everything is changing so fast. This music is killing me. The sad part is I never even noticed the change coming. I turn to walk, spying the bluegrass section. I shudder. Quickly, I leave the store to continue my walk as I turn down the sidewalk on the other side of the building down an alley.

Bottles and trash are scattered all over this damp street, hidden away between two giant structures. I place my hands in my pockets to fight the chill. The gauntlet is isolated and eerie as if the bustling life respects some unwritten law to leave this concrete and brick tunnel to the creatures that dwell in its crevices. The people of the streets know this law and it parallels so much of humanity. No one wants to confront the unwanted.

The alley and record store, and maybe other factors, make me think of life. My life. A life I have pushed back into my brain to forget and move on from. Horrors free of pain but still ghosts in my mind I can never forget nor move on completely from. It is who I am and what makes me me. Since I found the Lord, it makes more sense. More sense than without him, I guess. But it doesn't erase anything. The thick air reminds me of when it first happened. The cabin air. Vivid and surreal at once like your brain is wanting to remember but forget at the same time in some mental b-battle. I can still hear his voice. His h-hands on my arm-ms. The smell of h-h-his breath, him changing m-m-me, banjoes a-and f-f-f-fiddles b-banjoes and f-f-fiddles Father, h-help me-e-e. Though I w-walk through t-the valley of the shadow of d–d-death I-I will fear n-no evil for thou art with me. God, it's coming back. I exhale deep. In and out. Remember your salvation. There was a time when I was blind, but now I see. I know I am saved from it. I know it. But it still comes back unexpectedly like a dark and grey flash. Never free of the memory but the pain. However, now there is no fear. Just a memory of my life I've been redeemed from. There is more to be redeemed though. The anger, the hurt, the indecision. The communion of the devil and the beverage he mixes all poured down my throat as I sit not knowing I was drunk. A past, my past, that is fragmented, disjointed, yet always there and sometimes not there at all. Why do I always feel like prey?

The grayness of the street is heavy with a frigid humidity. It feels like eyes are watching me from the cracks in the brick, the concrete. Yellow eyes prying, devouring faith. I look behind me but I am alone. Alone and afraid of the fact that there is something God wants to talk to me about and frankly, I don't want to listen. I think of my beautiful wife and the day we met and it warms me. I miss her on these long tours. Going from city to city, meeting hundreds of people at once with a hundred names, fighting to keep the ministry afloat from all the darts and arrows thrown our way. It's on tours like these that I wish she was with me. My rock. My fortress. My constancy. I miss the touch of her hand and the sound of her voice. Not the metallic voice traveling wires but the live, fresh voice that rejuvenates my heart. A voice that reminds me life is not as dark as man makes it to be. There is hope within our opposite and God put only the best parts in her. Took the good rib. I hear something digging through a mound of papers, bottles, and food and see a small figure scurry away, its tail scurrying behind it. She always had a way about her. A confident and gentle slight movement that made me feel safe and secure. An aura, I guess. She never held my mistakes against me nor any secret resentment for what I was before she knew me. She never focused on it as I used to. I think down inside, she is glad to have me the way I am. Not for any self-serving purpose but just as an unconditional love should be. Just as God's love should be. God's love is, I'm sure. Seventy times seven. I hope.

Small puddles line the outer edges of the alley, close to the buildings and sit stagnant. Next to a large dumpster, I see the shape of a man huddled, wrapped in blankets and newspaper from head to toe sleeping. Up ahead, the end is near. Life continuing its perceived importance and unnecessary bustle. I'm glad it's coming because I've had enough of the cold and gray path I'm on.

I feel warmth as I step back onto the street and life follows. I check my watch and realize I've been gone too long. Picking up my pace, I walk in the direction of the convention center. The shops and restaurants pass me and I glance sideways, hoping to just catch a glimpse of what the store is all about and who is partaking. Curiosity, no matter how small, is still a powerful thing. As I pass a bar, I snatch a quick peek and think I see blonde hair and vibrant eyes. My heart jumps and I stop to look through the open door but see nothing but a drunk with black hair and a bushy mustache hovering over a mug. A sad spectacle. I see him there, hunched and alone, and wonder who he is, why he's there. I decide to go in despite my conviction.

The bar has a musky, thick smell. The lights low and the jukebox going with some odd song talking about being born in the wild. I feel watched and my gut is flitting. The man at the bar doesn't notice me, just looking into his dark mug of beer for something. I think to myself if I should have a drink. God knows I deserve one after all I put up with. Clemens was right. Christ made water into wine so it must not be that bad. Is one drink really a sin?

I step up to the bar and clumsily slide onto the stool. The bartender is washing some glasses by the sink and doesn't bother to look up at me. The place feels morose. The wall behind the bar is lined from end to end with hundreds of drinks. So much that I can't begin to choose. Vodkas, wines, beers, whiskey, rum. So many variations on a drink with one purpose. The bartender notices me and lumbers over at his leisure, sleeveless and tattooed.

"What'll it be?" he asks in a gritty voice as the smoldering stub of a cigar pokes out from his lips. The smell is strong and it makes me slightly nauseous, more so than Clemens. I peruse the mass of bottles and containers behind me like I'm reading a foreign language. It's different being in here. I've only seen bars from the pictures and I haven't seen many of those. When I got saved, I never went in one because of the church. So many choices. My stomach feels flustered and nervous. Like I'm rebelling against my father. What would one drink do? Am I a sinner for one drink? If Clemens, a preacher, can condone a sip of alcohol, why can't I?

The bartender shifts his weight impatiently, thick arms bulging, and I say the first thing that comes to my head.

"Water, please."

He rolls his eyes, fills a dingy glass with iceless water and slides it to me with just the right amount of force so that it lands directly in my hand. I look down at my hand, grasping the glass and say thank you without any response from him. Out the corner of my eye, I notice the drunk glancing at me from under his straggly hair. Since his mustache is so bushy, I can't tell whether he's smiling or scowling. I raise the glass in a mock cheer and sarcastically remark, "Just a little thirsty." Just a little thirsty? I take a swig quickly to escape briefly from this foreign land. It's uncomfortable but not evil and I think the church gets those two mixed up a lot.

"You ever been in a bar before?" I hear the drunk ask. I place my glass on the counter. I'm regretting not ordering a real drink. I must look like an idiot.

"It's that bad, huh?"

I think he smiles because the sides of his mustache elevate slightly as he takes a sip of his beer. The remnants of it dripping from the hairs of his face. The smell of alcohol reminds me of Clemens and a desire to have a proper drink is almost audible in my ear. He swallows then looks at me, up and down, as if examining my appearance. When he's done evaluating me, he asks, "You a damn preacher, ain't you?"

I burst with a laugh and he looks at me like I'm crazy.

"You a church man at least," he affirms, rather serious.

I nod. "Every day of my life. If that's what you want to call it."

He nods gravely and takes a drink again, then stares off toward the vast bottles on the wall behind the bar with an almost reverent expression.

"I was a church man once."

"Really?" I ask. Figures.

He nods. His greasy hair dangling in strands. His face red like Clemens but with deeper creases and lines. A battlefield of a face.

"I was born on a pew. Which ain't no exaggeration neither. My mama pushed me out right there in the church. Pop! Hell, the preacher the one who delivered me in more way than one." He let free a horrendous, gurgling belch.

"Is that right?" I took a sip of water to avoid the smell and then asked, "Why'd you stop going?"

He brushed his face with his fingers, itching the ruffling facial hair before he continued. "Got tired of it, I suppose."

"Tired of what?"

He replies in an obnoxious voice, "The whole damn thing." He shoots back a shot of liquor and continues, "You a church man, tell me somethin'. Am I goin' to hell cause I don't go to church?"

I feel my face flushing and I look at my harmless drink before me with malice. I say, "I don't know. It depends, I guess."

"Depends? Depends on what?"

I shrug, "On what you believe I would assume."

He nods his head in a bobbing motion, cup cradled in hand. He returns from his thoughts and says, "So I ain't goin' to hell?"

"Sure." I take a drink. The bartender has not stopped giving me a nasty look since I came in and I wonder if I should just leave.

"Why is there so many different churches anyway? Don't they all believe the same thing? Jesus and God?" he asks. His impulse is obviously affected by what he is drinking.

"Well, everyone wants to believe the way they want to," I try to reason. To try to explain why my belief is so fragmented.

"It's ridiculous is what it is. You either believe in God or you don't. I don't understand all these denominations. They all is dumb if you ask me."

"Why is that?"

"Because if you all believe that there is a God and that there is a Jesus, then what the hell you need all these other churches for? Huh? Just two streets over from here, you'll run into four or five churches with different names for the same thing. Baptist, Lutheran, Mormon. God Almighty, it never ends. In ten years, they'll be more churches and then more churches that all believes in God, Jesus, Mary, Buddha, and even the president. It's crazy. In my brain, they is the Bible and everyone should just go by that because all these churches is givin' me a headache. You got a bunch of batshit crazies starting churches cause they wanna sing different songs or go to church on Saturday or wear those queer robes. Who picked those out? It don't make any difference what day you go to church. Right? Right?" He prods me with his finger and returns to his beer.

I take bigger sips of my water, imagining it is a real drink. Imagining it is taking me away. He shakes his head, all worked up, and takes a quick swig, then continues loudly, "It won't surprise me if they create a church for everybody that want one. The Church of Joe. The Church of Lionel. Hell, church man, I could have my own church. Meet right here in this bar. Our sanctuary. 'Our Father who art in Heaven, pour us another shot.' And if you think God can't meet me in this place then you don't know God at all. You know? Maybe we'll have communion with real wine and peanuts. Get drunk in the name of Jesus. Hallelujah! Hehehehe."

My mind began to think of ways to get out of this when I was interrupted by the drunk again.

"Don't you see, church man? Religion, the church. It's all part of man's plan to take over for God and make a few bucks in the meantime. Soon, we won't even need God in church. What's the point if we just change faith until it goes our own way? No evil, no sin. Everybody is just OK. Hunky dory. No heaven, no hell. Peace, man. You watch, church man. Unless they want to stop fightin' like cowboys and injuns, it's all going to hell. Going to hell in a hand basket as my mama used to say. Down, down, down..."

His words mumbled off and his face becomes serious. He burps wafts beer and peanuts across my face. That settles it, it's time. I stand to leave and he reaches his hand out and grabs my arm. Either steadying himself or wanting to impart some more of his theology on me. I look down at him and he up at me until his face narrows, looking at me and slurring, "Give to God what is God's and gi..."

He stumbles hurriedly off his stool, disappearing around the corner under the bathroom sign, hand between his legs. I don't know what to say or do. The bartender is looking at me as he continues to wash the glasses. I ask him how much for the drink. He looks at me without a hint of cordiality and says, "It's a glass of water."

I nod and head out into the street. The fresh air has never been so fresh. I return to the convention center. Now I know why I never go in bars or talk with people much. I reach the corner and see the convention center in full view. Glad to be back. Sort of. The telephone booth is still filled with the fat woman and she covers her face in her hand as she continues to talk on the phone. Soon, I pass the booth and feel compelled to speak with her. To ask her what is troubling her or if I can help. I tell myself that if I see her again, I will talk with her. I promise this to myself and God. Just like I always do.

I am at the door to the convention center now and I do one last scan of the area. No one. Nothing. I take a deep breath and enter. As the door whines open, I can only hope Jeremiah Cole has subdued the enigmatic dragon. Yet in my heart I know nothing can stop Clemens but God or death. I think of the drunk and wonder if I'm crazy for considering what he has to say. Maybe God has left this place or man has evicted him. Maybe He was never here.

1940

Ezekiel and Gerald sat at the yellow counter of the diner early the next morning, each with six dollars in their pockets. The previous night had been a successful service, attracting around one hundred visitors in a fairground building

The robust waitress came over to the two, holding a pot of dark coffee. "You boys look beat." Her red hair curled upward, layers of makeup accentuated the wrinkles in her skin. Her white apron now a collage of spatters, drips and smears against her pastel blue blouse.

Ezekiel cradled his cup of coffee in palm and smiled. "It shows that much, huh?"

"Not too bad, but enough," she replied, refilling their mugs.

Gerald sat sipping the hot cup, face down and shoulders forward.

"Well, when doin' the Lord's work..." Ezekiel informed as he emptied the container of sugar into his cup.

"Is that so?" Her eyes conveyed a faux surprise as she rearranged the cutlery in the napkins like a blanket.

"God's honest and blessed truth. We had a service last night over at the fairgrounds had 'bout one hundred folks. The Holy Ghost was movin' like a hurricane, praise Jesus. We were blessed enough to stay with the Millers last night.

Gracious God-fearing people with compassion and love more than I've seen in my years."

"Yes, they are generous people. What denomination you comin' from?" she asked.

Ezekiel smiled as he thought a moment. "Let's just say we belong to God's church."

She laughed through her lips, waving a playful hand at Ezekiel. He shifted and smiled sheepishly, keeping set eyes atop her blouse.

"You look like a Holy Roller to me."

Ezekiel snorted into his coffee as he drank. Slim streams dripped down off his chin as he wiped his face, smiling.

"Guilty as charged," he confessed with his hands raised. She giggled, leaning on the counter. Ezekiel began examining her curves before snapping out of his gaze.

"Ummm. Well, now, we're hittin' the road again when we are finished up here with this here pleasant talk and coffee to continue and spread God's blessed word across this great country. In fact, we been across the great nation from California to South Carolina, from the end of Texas on up to Montana preachin' the gospel of our Lord and Savior Jesus Christ to any an' all who'll listen. Includin' yerself," he said, tipping his mug.

She laughed, her biceps framing her chest. "So, we have a couple of good ol' preacher boys, here?" she observed. "And what is ya'll's names?"

Ezekiel straightened and adjusted his shirt sleeves. "I am Ezekiel Clemens. A sinner who ran from God and was lost but now is found, by His grace. And this here handsome man is Gerald, my friend and advisor. We both came from the depths of despair to be raised up by the saving power of Christ Jesus and, in return, we dedicated our lives to spreadin' the good news."

She folded her arms and looked with a disbelieving curiosity at the two. "You're the one who gives the sermons, I would venture to guess."

Ezekiel leaned back a bit. "That's what the Lord has blessed me with."

"I see," she eyed his left hand and asked, "Is there a woman behind this man of God?"

Ezekiel's face flushed, "To be a true messenger of the Lord, a man must focus all his attention on the spreading of the gospel of Jesus Christ. To be able to do what God truly intend for us to do, then one must keep himself free of attachments, so to speak. Think about these men for a second: the Apostle Paul, Stephen the Martyr, John the Baptist. All these men called by God had no wives. No women. It would be too difficult with all these...distractions." He smiled, picking up his mug to sip. "I'm a bachelor for the Bible, darlin'."

She bit her bottom lip, sneaking glances at the youthful man with his jet black hair and thin, scrappy frame. She brought her attention to Gerald, who had thus far been reticent.

"What's your take on all this, sweetie?" she asked him.

Gerald looked shyly at the gregarious waitress. He shifted on the cushioned barstool, his weight on his elbows as he sat.

"I...uh...I...don't know. I..." he stammered out before trailing off. Ezekiel looked at Gerald and placed a hand on his shoulder. Gerald relaxed, his hands shaking subtly. Gerald took a quick sip of his coffee to keep his mouth occupied, wincing as he burnt his mouth. The waitress looked on with confused eyes like a frightened child.

Ezekiel burst in, "He's had a long night and he gets nervous sometimes when he talks with new people. He's but a boy, just eighteen this year."

The waitress shifted her eyes over to Ezekiel, back to Gerald, and then again to Ezekiel. "I meant no harm by it. I apologize."

"Ain't a problem at all. Not at all," he replied with an uneasy smile. The friendly exchange became uncomfortable and stale.

"Ya'll need anythin', just let me know."

She left and busied herself with something in the kitchen. Ezekiel could see her whisper something to the cook and he looked in their direction.

Left alone, they sat silent. When finished, they paid the waitress the cost of the coffee. Ezekiel tipped his broad hat to her in thanks and cordiality. She was short, no longer her effulgent self. They picked up their middle sized suitcases that held some clothes, Bibles, and whatever else they acquired over the course of their meanderings, went out the glass door into the day. The morning sun bright, reflecting off the wet roads as they walked down the sidewalk. Farmers and construction workers about, gathering feed and supplies for the day's work. Most the shops still bore dark windows.

The odd couple walked in silence till they reached the bus stop, using money from the offering to purchase a ticket to take them north where they hoped to find a church willing to hold a meeting. They sat on the wooden bench. No one around. The morning air tense. Across the road, sporadic passer-byes spoke greetings to each other. Ezekiel's voice broke the air, "Ya thinkin' about him again, ain't ya?"

Gerald stared at his lap, reticent and solemn. Ezekiel blew a ball of air through his cheeks and rubbed his face with his hands.

"Eight years. That's how long I've known ya, Ger. Eight years me and you have been up and down and across this country doin' what we wanted and now what we feel God has told us to do. Facin' all kinds of persecution and hardship all for the Gospel of Jesus Christ. Even got held up together at knife point in Wichita, remember? But that is nothing compared to what's goin' on inside. Now I know you had a hard life. Harder than any most people had to face. But there's a point where the pain needs to be faced, Ger. A point where ya gotta give it up and not hold onto it any longer. All the shame, fear, guilt, anger; all of it wants to be released unto the Heavenly Father."

Scraping his shoes across the surface of the concrete, Gerald froze in himself.

"Now, listen, Ger. I want to help you be rid of this pain. Cast it away into the sea of forgetfulness. Christ said that the truth will set you free. So please, Ger, confide in me. Tell me, tell God your story to be rid of this filth."

Gerald shook his head. "I can't. I c-c-can't."

Ezekiel put his hand on his shoulder. In a gentle voice, he said, "I know he hurt ya. I know he did things to ya that will always be there but unless ya open it up, it's just gonna get worse."

Gerald shook his head, gripping the edge of the bench.

"You can do it. Together, we can do it. Open up to me. Let me heal you. Quit hidin' it inside and let the darkness of the past be redeemed by the light, in Jesus Name."

Gerald cinched his eyes, hoping that by making the confrontation disappear, it would do just that. He opened his eyes and looked down the road, watching for the bus. Ezekiel held his hat in his hand, rubbing his fingertips around the brim. He popped his hat onto his hand, stood, and walked off down the sidewalk a few steps.

The bus appeared, rumbling, and stopped hissing like some wounded beast before them. The silver doors opened and they gave the driver their stubs. The old man nodded coldly and took them in his hand without much regard. The bus was full of passengers, both male and female, young and old. They found a seat near the middle and placed their belongings in the hold above them. Gerald took the window seat. He sat on the stiff cushion and looked out the window, huddled and hugging it like it was a gate to a freedom that he would never enter but still found comfort in knowing it was there. Ezekiel sat and unbuttoned his suit jacket, blowing out an obnoxious sigh.

He swiveled his head. Across the aisle, a mother and her son. Behind them, an elderly man with a burgundy bow-tie sat alone by the window. Some couples and children comprised the remaining passengers. The lone man, divided from the others by three rows, disappeared into the seats as if he held no existence. Ezekiel stared as the bus rolled forward, headed north, leaving the buildings of the town within five minutes and entering a landscape of flatland pervaded of corn stalks, wheat, and eternal horizons. The bus bounced along. The wheels a dull murmur in the silence.

Shortly, Ezekiel scanned the occupants again. His decision to test the mother and son directly across the aisle soothed his energy. After several failed attempts, he succeeded, grasping eye contact with the mother. She gave him a cautious look and he nodded, smiling. She nodded in return then focused her gaze forward.

"It's a mighty nice day," he said matter-of-fact. She held fast to her rigidity. The young boy peeked his fat, freckled face around his mother's body then sat back. The boy whispered something and she shushed him. He conceded his failure. Gerald was statuesque in his position, motionless, lost outside the glass.

Ezekiel took another scan of the bus, heels clicking against the metal floorboards. He revisited the old man near the window, alone. He viewed his surroundings then stood, steadying himself on the seat backs on his way to the back. The man turned his brown eyes and tensed as Ezekiel approached him, looking toward the front of the bus and then back. The old man clenched his fists once limp atop the seat. Ezekiel stopped at the seat and the man spoke in a low and gravelly voice preceding Ezekiel's own.

"I got a right to sit here jus' the same as you."

The voice froze him. His face sagged from his cheekbones and dark skin, scaled like leather, bore a life weathered. Atop his head, short, white curls of hair fuzzed around with a slight bulge in his gut that jutted just above his waistline.

"I know ya do, brother," Ezekiel obliged.

The man squinted, eyebrows slanted. He stared at Ezekiel with a weary caveat.

"What ya want of me?" he asked.

Ezekiel smiled. "Just some friendly conversation, is all."

The man's red eyes watched as if trying to penetrate some confidence this stranger sought. He sniffed, rubbed his chin, gently, then returned to the window. The bus bounced them both as a mother bounces her infant. Ezekiel kept his eyes about him, gathering his thoughts, wondering if this attempt at cordiality would be fruitful.

"Where ya headed?" Ezekiel asked.

The man turned his gaze from the window, his lips curling slightly. "I'm goin' where I'm goin'. That's all ya need to know."

"I understand, yer anger, brother, but it...."

"I ain't yo brotha, understand?" he bit back.

"Christ said that we are all brothers. Every man is the same in God's eyes despite our color, creed or character."

He looked Clemens up and down with his brown eyes, resting on the golden cross dangling just beneath his shirt.

"You a preacher?"

"You could say that," he said smiling wide.

The old man huffed like one would to a joke.

"Well, preacher, God's eyes ain't got no credence in this world," he said. "This here's a man's world. A white man's world." He turned his head to the window, facing his hazy reflection.

"God's eyes are all that matters, despite what man says," Ezekiel retorted.

The man adjusted the opening of his grey, checkered suit jacket. The ends of his sleeves frayed and his long fingers protruded from them like branches.

"God, huh?" he exclaimed. "What is God? You seem like the type o' guy that wanna talk regardless so, tell me. What is God?" He crossed his arms and slouched back. His tongue brushing his teeth behind his lips.

Ezekiel smiled. "What is God? God is the creator of the heavens and earth. The beginning and the end. The provid..."

"No, no, no. I don't want yo standard response yo give to church goin' fools. I don't want what ya learned in Sunday school. Tell me, what is God?" he interrupted in his woeful baritone.

"Sir, I don't know what ya mean?"

He chuckled through his teeth. "Sir?" As if he seemed entertained by the notion of such respect. After he regained his composure from laughing, he said, "I'm askin' simply what is God? Is God some idea that s'pose to help me? Is God somethin' I'm s'pose to respect? What is He? Cause frankly, I ain't got no cause to be servin' no God that ain't servin' me."

"Well, we ain't suppose to expect nothin' from God. He expects it from us."

"That's a bum-shot deal. Straight up suckered into nothin'. Then why the hell yo wanna serve him fo'?"

Ezekiel sat down in the red seat in front of the old man, placed his arms across the top, and rested his chin on his hands.

"My brother once said that ya gotta have somethin' to believe in. Somethin' or someone to serve," Ezekiel replied.

The old man rested his saggy head on his knuckles as he leaned against the window. Humoring this inquisitive visitor. "That's funny comin' from you," he retorted.

"What makes ya say that?"

The old man pondered a moment as if debating whether to continue. Recollecting. Gathering. His sad face gazing forlorn into the landscape, lips and skin cracked like roads on maps. The only moisture visible lay in his eyes.

"I've had my share of woes. And my share of God. The man who used to whip me and my ma once told me, 'Between earth and hell, that's where God put the souls o' niggers.' Is that God? When I was a boy, I thought he was right and I figgered I was at that place already. Trapped in a world where I belonged with the souls o' my people in a place forsaken by God hisself. You speaks of servin' somebody and I don't think you even knowed what that means. What that truly means. Serve? I've been servin' everbody every damn day of my life. Never a chance to serve myself. Never a chance to help myself. My family. That's if I hadda family. Only family I knew of was my mama. Never knew my daddy. We did alright survivin' for the most part. If yo consider that life worth livin' for. Since I can r'member I work the fields.

All fo a place ta live and food ta eat. It wasn't much but it was somethin'."

He paused, rubbed his brow, and continued.

"The man who owned me and my ma was a mean sonuvabitch. Mean and angry and hated colored folk like yo God hates sin. He lost two, three workers a year jus' from him beatin' 'em to death. None escaped. The law didn't care so I figgered it was the natural order o' things fo' folks like me. One night, when I was jus' about ten, my mama decide she gonna run fo' it cause she couldn't take it no more. Says to me, 'I won't let him touch me no more, God help me.' So, after he and everone else gone to sleep, we snuck out an' ran without lookin' back. Fo' two days we run an' camped in them woods. They was close too. We could hear the dogs barkin' an' sometimes torches would even light our faces but theys never seen us. Didn't know where we was goin' but my mama had faith. She says to me, 'God will keep us safe, chile.' At night, she'd sing an old song to me about God watchin' over me."

He bit his lip and grimaced.

"We made it two days befo' the hounds catch us," he muttered, shaking his head in bitter recollection. "When they took us back to the farm, Mr. Jessup, that was his name. Couldn't ever fo'get it. He took us to the barn an' tied my mama up by the arms like a thief. Like a criminal. He start whoopin' on mama real bad with a whip. No matter how much she scream he still keep hittin' an' hittin' an' hittin'. He says to me, 'You watch now, you lil' black bastard. This is what happens to niggers when they step outta line." And I watched it. I watched till my eyes bled with her body. And ya know what my thought was at that moment? I thought where is this God my mama's been prayin' to? Why don't he come down and save her? Stop all this. So I prayed out to God myself and ya know what I heard?"

Ezekiel waited. The drone of the bus rolling behind them.

"Nothin'. Nothin' but my mama sobbin' and screamin' as all the blood ran into the dirt an' Mr. Jessup, the devil hisself, stood grinnin' like he done taught a dog a lesson. No God came to help me. No God came to save me."

He looked out the window. The sun illuminating his ancient face of struggles and sorrow. His pain melted away.

"Next mornin' she was dead. Didn't even call a doctor 'cause no doctor would come out to help a colored woman. Especially in the middle of the night. She died where he left her an' I stayed there by her side till she passed. I was there while God watched. What was her crime, preacher? What was her crime? What did my mama do to deserve death upon her? Since then, I often wondered 'bout where God was. I can only think that he's jus' like Mr. Jessup. How could such mercy come from a God who does nothin' when ya ask him? What's the point in servin' him if he ain't servin' you? After that I always thought of God as a white man cause only a white devil could do what he done to us. Smilin' as I went on to suffer the next sixty eight years from field to field, farm to farm with nothin' but a hunchback to show. To be spat at, cursed, beat on, put down every day of my life like I was nothin' but an animal. I seen friends hung from trees cause

162

they refuse to sit where I sit now. I seen white men acquitted of murderin' Negroes an' Negroes accused of murderin' the victims of white men. Coloreds killin' coloreds with no eyes turned to him. No justice taken. It's a sick world I live in. Serve, you say?" He asked again, with sick offense. "I've been servin' my whole life fo' nothin'. And I'm so sick of life and people tellin' me to believe. 'Jus' believe' they say to me. I say no, goddamn it. I hate life. The only person I'll serve is myself. You can tell yo God that if he care to listen."

The words stopped and he returned his gaze to the window. The air sucking in and out of his nostrils. The bus lulled on, trotting forward. The man noticed Ezekiel's lingering presence and asked, "Yo know what the worst part of it is?" He smiled for the first time but joy was not its origin. "I'm free jus' like you."

Without words to say, unknowing how to feel or respond, Ezekiel sat. The old man turned to the banal landscape with no intention to continue. Nothing to be said. They sat awkward till the old man raised his face, eyes glistened, and said, "Get on outta here and think about yo God. I'll hear none of it."

At the command, Ezekiel stood and turned back to his seat. He saw the pale faces of the occupants watching him, receiving his return with shaking heads, lips turned downward. He shuffled to his seat and slouched, heavy and morose as if the man's burden were his to bear. He thought on what the old man had said. He could hear the anger and spite in his words. He could hear the hate and bitterness in his voice. He never wants to be that man.

Gerald hung asleep fixed to the same position. Dreaming of his escape into his world where good is all that is needed. A gray moral realm where nothing is complex. Ezekiel watched him sleep until he shifted into his own realm and dreamt he was bleeding gray blood. There was nothing he could do to stop it.

Conflict

My eyes adjust to the dimness as I stand in the shadows again. My head feels full of water. The recent events seem surreal like distant memories. As if they happened years ago and I'm trying to catch up. I see a figure with his back to the door, leaning against it looking exhausted. My heart skips for a moment, the wave of nostalgia cresting for an instant until I realize it is Cole. I meet him outside the dressing room door and notice right away something is askew. His hair is disrupted from its perfection and his blazer has been removed. As I approach, he lifts his distraught face up to mine.

"Is he in there?" I ask.

Cole nods lazily. He seems overwhelmed and dejected so I place a firm hand on his shoulder. "What happened?"

He surprises me with a loud laugh, awkward and flat. Almost a cackle. A grin spreads across his cheeks like I've just said the funniest thing he's heard all day. Is he losing his head?

"Alright?" he repeats. "I sure ain't alright. I'm as sick as rain, right now." He looks away."I was never meant to be here."

His voice is crackling with hurt or betrayal. And I know it is all my fault. In my moment of self-deprecation, I had abandoned young Jeremiah Cole with a profoundly disturbed man. Not just any man but the man that has defined the course of his life. Can't even imagine what Clemens must have said to him to account for his current state. I lean my head in, almost touching our crowns together. I catch a sour whiff of alcohol from Cole. Why would he smell like alcohol? Is this some bizarre Mississippi ritual I'm missing where Christians get drunk before church?

"Son, what happened? What did he say?" I ask.

The once vibrant man I met earlier today who followed God to this moment in time is not with me in the hallway but rather the remains of what he had been. An empty shell whose spiritual and purposeful meat has been shoveled onto the floor in disregard like unwanted dirt. All from one man's lips. One man's hurt. He bit his bottom lip. His eyes swollen and red as he begins to speak.

"After you left, I stayed in the room with Pastor Clemens like ya told me to. At first he jus' sat there thinkin' and tappin' his foot really fast. I asked him if he wanted anythin'. Ya know. Just if I could get him somethin' to make him feel better. I was still nervous all over because of what just happened. I didn't mean nothin' by it, I swear, Mr. Lambough, honest..." He began to plead his innocence and I assure him that everything is alright. He jitters a nod and wipes his nose.

"Go on, then what happened?" I prod.

He sniffs and continues, "So...So he looks at me with a real mean look in his eyes. So I ask him if he's ok, ya know? And he gets mad and begins to yell at me. Loud. He says to me, 'Ya think God sent ya here. Well, He ain't sent you nowhere. You left Mississippi fo the same reason I did. Ya ain't nothing but poor white trash from nowhere. Ya got your God and your faith and nothing else and look where it got ya. Here to corridnate a meeting for the great evangelist Ezekiel Clemens. That don't mean nothin'.' He stopped for a second and I was hopin he had no more to say but I was wrong. Then he grabbed and pulled his hair like he was gonna burst and I felt truly afraid, Mr. Lambough. I thought he was gonna attack me but he just shot up off the couch and began hollerin' and swearin' and pacin'. I didn't know what to say or do. I just sat still while he was actin' crazy, sayin to me, 'You're runnin'! You're runnin'! and then he picked up the champagne bottle and he done threw it at the mirror. It was so loud my ears popped and I ducked down and all the glass and mirror and drink went everywhere. I was shakin' like a hare's whiskers." He holds his hand out to me to demonstrate. "I look up after a bit and I see Pastor is sittin on the floor, holdin part of the bottle and cryin'. All I can do is watch. I ain't ever seen a man act this way before. Ever. I imagined the worst was over so I says, 'Pastor?' and he looks up at me with the tears runnin' down his face and he says for me to get the you-know-what on outta here. So I got outta there as fast as I could and stood by the door here and waited for you."

He pauses, shaking his head in disbelief. I can't help but do the same. "I can't go back in there, Mr. Lambough. I can't do it."

His voice begins to break. The twang that was so subtle now thick in his words, "I only wanted to do what God told me. Is th-that the right thing?"

I feel responsible for all this. Though Clemens is his own man, I take sole ownership over all of this. Wasn't I the one to fix it all? It's my silence, my selfishness, my fear, my passivity that has caused this and I can't ignore this feeling of disgust and shame. All this time I have been placing the blame on others. Shifting like a gear to everyone but myself.

I grab him in my arms, holding him like a father holds his son and I apologize. I rub my hand over his back and feel him hiccupping his hurt into my chest. My eyes remain dry and blocked as I accept the fruits of my labors. What have I done? As I embrace this youthful believer, I feel the impression that I am not the issue here. I know this impression and I've felt it long ago. I am not the issue here. Lord, what is?

Inside, it is all swirling around. I feel anger, sorrow. God has given Satan the free reign of his unworthy Job to test and punish in hopes of blasphemy. But I am not Job. Nor is Clemens. We are prodigals making our own path only to falter. Following our human instinct to control just as man has fought to do to God since the Adam was formed from dust and wind. Control what cannot be. Through church and legalism, Bibles and sermons, we are a race destined to torment our maker through our own twisted sense of what God is and what he stands for. I am not Job because I have already failed too many times.

Jeremiah, naïve, wounded Jeremiah. I embrace this silent fellowship as he weeps into my chest. The bitter warmth of our bodies exchanging the human plight of emotions. It feels good to be a father just as it feels to receive one. In this moment, I realize my own neglect to this gift. Phone calls an invisible embrace that is all I have given them these past few years. My wisdom and comfort are just words like I am some audible phantom that they know loves them but not enough. How God seems sometimes. I can count on my hand the times I have prayed with them before they sleep or the moments of laughter I have shared. I can't say what my son got on his last math test or what my daughter's favorite toy may be. I know I am a father but there is so far to go. I am miles away from everyone and I am the one who put me there. Lord, they're growing up and growing apart and I'm watching them wane. What of a husband? I am just as much a failure to her as I am to my children. I can see her alone, the bed barely filled with her small frame. Cold and dreaming alone as I work. Christ, is this my calling? Am I doing what you have asked of me or am I satisfying my own needs in this? I hear nothing, feel nothing. and ponder whether that's all that has been up there. Why does God make things so difficult?

I push Cole in front of me. He looks at me embarrassed for letting himself go like this. I pat his cheek and give him a stern but loving look.

"You are right where you're supposed to be," I say firmly. I can feel my gaze on him and know he feels my sincerity. He nods, wiping his face with his hands, sniffling. I straighten my blazer with a pull and sweep. "Now, stay out here and I'll deal with that. Alright?"

"Yes, sir."

"You sure you're alright?" I ask. Procrastinating.

"Yes, sir," he says, "I'll live." He smiles like a child would after being scolded. He stands to the side and I turn the handle. The lights still shine from the vanity and display the chaos that occurred while I was away. The nostalgic odor of alcohol hits my senses quick and I see the fragments of mirror and glass sprinkled in various sizes all around where the rest of the mirror stands. Dark blotches trail away on the light-colored carpet and I can only assume it is blood. I follow the trail with my eyes and see him, sitting with his knees to his gaunt face. His right hand hanging limply, covered and dripping.

He resembles how I saw him this morning, hung over and discontent. Yet now, after all the tension and anger, my soul is dragging the weight of chains. My friend, for that is what he is, is hurting. He's been hurting for years and I have been ignorant. Ignorant to many things in my life. He is the wounded and the wounder at once.

I squat by him. He raises his face to me, eyes dim, clouded, conveying an ache. His ache. An ache decades in the making. The worn face, aged by pleasures and pain. He drops his gaze again and begins to sob. Sobs out years of his life, moaning low. My throat chokes and, for once, the words I am supposed to say are no words at all. I come close and wrap my thick arms around him. He grabs my arms and squeezes mightily with that one wounded hand and I feel all the cars of the past piling up in a colossal crash yet my eyes remain dry. The smell of cigarettes and champagne and cologne permeate my senses and I don't care. Right now it is the sweetest smell.

We sit for what seems forever. Ezekiel, through hiccups, apologizes over and over. Thick and growling words directed

at me or anything. God, me, anyone. Involuntarily, I apologize for my own reasons. Such an unspoken community between us. This must be a true repentance. The moment
passes as if time did not exist. I release Clemens and sit on
the floor next to him. The carpet wet and soaking through
my pants and I notice a red handprint on my sleeve.

"I'll get something for your hand," I inform him as I
stand. Head back against the wall, he stares at the ceiling,
relaxed. I find a hand towel, a nice one at that, and squat to
wrap his hand. The bleeding stopped but I feel it necessary
to do it. I don't know why.

We sit in silence. Exhausted from our catharsis.

"Is the kid alright?" he asks concerned.

"Yeah, he'll be alright," I reply.

We sit in silence again, a comfortable silence for once. I
spy the clock on the wall and I realize that it is almost two
o'clock. In all the commotion, I forgot lunch.

"You hungry?" I ask.

He smiles that gap-toothed grin, "Does a drunk drink?"

1932

Waiting, Ezekiel sat at the kitchen table made from his father's hand. The sun yet to complete its ascent from darkness. His brother and sister remained asleep, the air of the house chilly and his thin coat and open-toed shoes futile against the bite. Yet he continued to wait at his father's request to "rise before the sun." Ezekiel knew to do what he was told without question. It was unusual for him to be up this early alone and even more so that the house lay still and quiet. He sat in the dark, in the silence, and listened to the absence of life. The absence of chaos. Through the window, he watched the grey morning sky birthing its first glimpses of light. He did not welcome its coming for with the light came illumination. With it came awakening.

The sound of soft footfall came from behind and he turned quickly. She glided toward him in her night clothes, a blanket about her shoulders. Her soft smile calming.

"Hi, mama," he whispered.

"What are you doin' up so early?" she asked, pulling the chair from the table.

"Pop wanted me up early."

"Oh," she remarked. "Did he say why?"

"No. I didn't ask anyway."

She adjusted the blankets about her shoulders and glanced into the morning sky. Her supple face held a repressed sadness. She turned her eyes back to her son, reached her hands across the table and took his into hers.

"I'm proud of you, Ezekiel."

Ezekiel scrunched his face. "What is there to be proud of?"

"You're my son and I'm proud of you. You have a gift though you may not know it now. But I see it in you."

Ezekiel looked at his mother's hands upon his and felt filled for a brief moment. He reveled in the affection that came so seldom to this home. He felt warm for the first time that morning.

"He's proud of you, too."

Ezekiel looked into her eyes but said nothing.

"He may not be a good father, but he loves you as much as I do. You have to give him a chance," the words came from her lips as if trying to convince herself more than he. Ezekiel squeezed her hands.

"Jus' cause we have the same blood means nothin' to me," he said.

"Don't say that, son. Everyone needs a second chance."

He let go of her hands and sat back in the chair, scratching the legs over the wooden floor in the silence. Her eyes widened and moistened as she looked to the sky again. She adjusted the blanket again and stood, leaning to kiss.

"I love you," she said as she turned, walking softly back to her room, disappearing as silently as she came.

He sat watching the sky, apathetically scratching at a red rise below his right nostril. The gradual metamorphosis to pubescence a cumbersome road. His physical battle in conflict with his family's. The creak of the rusty, battered screen and groaning floorboards at his father's weight startled him. He turned in his chair and his father walked in enough to be seen. In the faint morning light, his figure ghost-like, surreal. His body caught flashes of grey light as he approached until he stood next to Ezekiel, looking down with dark eyes. In his hand, he held his black, Bible and with the other, he rubbed the thick hair on his upper lip over again, pondering some thought important.

He sat still yet trying to watch him periodically without being noticed. Even at fifteen, he still felt anxious around him. His body conditioned to. After a moment, his father looked at him. Ezekiel acted as if he did not notice and continued to watch the sky through the small window.

"Let's walk," Regal Clemens ordered. Without hesitation, Ezekiel stood and pushed his chair under the table. By the time he had released the chair, Regal was a fleeting glimpse out the door.

They owned a vast amount of land inherited from his grandfather with no limit to where one may walk. The horizontal land was a mute grey, the air just as frigid but worse due to the light breeze that brought with it frigidity. Ezekiel tried to tuck his head in like a carapace much to his dismay. The wind stinging his slender frame. Nose and ears the primary recipients. The soft breeze made a roar in his ears. His father, with similar frame, untouched by the icy wind. The walk much like the air. They walked until the house stood waist high in the distance.

Regal cleared his throat. "How old are ya?"

"Fifteen."

Regal cleared his throat louder this time. "So I suppose ya think you're a man now." The words flat, bitter.

Ezekiel kept walking, hating every step further and further away from the house. "I guess so."

Regal sucked some spit through his teeth, hissing. "Yeah, I suppose I thought that too when I was yer age."

The urge to run struck him, no sprinting, into the open plain. Eyes forward with all this behind. He'd rather camp in this cold, grey landscape than be forced to converse with this, his most personal enemy. Regal thumbed the pages of the Bible, pages layering and falling upon one another, piling in whispy thuds.

"My daddy," he continued, "My daddy was a mean man. Never liked me much. I can't say I liked him much neither. He didn't like the price he had to pay for me comin' into this world."

Ezekiel glanced at his father just ahead of him, enough to reveal his face. His nose and cheeks red from the cold and eyes moist. Ezekiel wondered if it was the wind or not. He had never heard his father talk of his grandfather. To hear the words from his father brought a powerful, sensation. Each carried with it a sullen and wounded tone. The words now, though removed, seemed a difficult confession. If not a confession, then an excuse.

"In this life, ya can't let the past control ya," he muttered, clutching the Bible to his chest.

They trod on in silence again before Regal spoke again. The sky shedding its grey tonality, transitioning into a yellow-orange. The sea of grass bowed to the wind before them. On this frozen day, he felt perplexed at this shadow of a man who tried so heavily to be what was difficult for him to be.

"I ain't a perfect man. I just ain't cut out to be a man," he whispered. "No man at all."

Father and son walked on in bitter silence. Of all the days, he wondered why today his father attempted this tragic change. He spat at his father's tracks he followed.

They walked, Ezekiel digging his teeth into his bottom lip, clenching. Regal said nothing more. Ezekiel, his black hair waving in the breeze, no longer cold but numb. Nor did he care to hear his father's words or care to ask. This complex man that had given him his eyes, his hair, his slanted nose and his wrath was nothing to him in his mind.

Across the plain, the sun rose into a cloudy sky. The breeze dwindled to a rustle, prompting a murder of crows to pass overhead, cawing obnoxious, interrupting the unnatural silence. Ezekiel watched them flapping and imagined taking up on those black wings. Regal never paid mind to their presence.

They walked this lonesome road until Regal stopped, gazing off into the horizon. The house far behind them now and before lay a lifeless plain. He titled his round cap onto crown, hands on hips, as if waiting. Ezekiel jossled his leg, arms crossed in disinterest.

Regal let out a heavy sigh and turned his face toward his son. Ezekiel looked up at the sagging eyes and terse lips, his stomach dancing inside. With quick movements one would make to be finished with some unwanted obligation, Regal handed his Bible toward his son. Ezekiel looked at the Bible and then his father. Regal gave the Bible an insistent shake. Ezekiel took hold of the Bible and saw the hand with the missing finger. He stared what seemed like a long time at it, the opportunity afforded. Ezekiel held the Bible in his hands, examining his gift speechless. He raised his face to speak but Regal had turned and faced forward. Ezekiel blinked persistent eyes, fighting. Regal swayed, looking back to the house. Ezekiel opened his mouth to speak but the impatience took over and, as Regal walked away, he said, "Happy birthday, son."

The wind came fast in the wake of his father's lank figure and he watched, feeling the wetness cooled on his cheeks. The land blurring with the exit of his father.

Knock

We stand, refreshed, and head out the dressing room door. There's an aura between us like a purification. A new birth. Cole is standing there and I can see his body tense slightly as we approach. Clemens walks directly to him, embraces him, and says, "Forgive me, brother." Cole's face is comical in its shock. I can't help but laugh a little.

I tell Cole that we're going to lunch and, without him really wanting to, he comes along. Speechless and probably obligated but it doesn't really matter. We exit out the backside of the convention center into the sun. Bill is still parked in his steadfast spot but, from my view, his head is back, chin up and mouth open. I don't blame him. At his age, I'm surprised he still finds satisfaction out of this line of work or the energy. Or tolerance for the people he works with, including me.

Outside, a large truck carrying palm trees backs up, making loud beeps with each inch. A short, fat man is directing the driver back with wild hands, then redirecting him forward, back and forth. Soon they start arguing like spouses, stopping, and then proceed to finish the task at hand. Cole and I look at each other and he lets out a deep sigh.

"Everything's fine," I assure him. The words strike me as the mantra for my life. Everything's fine, everything's fine. We stroll past the truck and around the corner. I tell them

of a diner just ahead and we all agree to eat there out of con-
venience.

"Get a taste of the local color, huh, Cole?" Clemens says
smacking him square on the back like they are old friends.
Cole gives an uneasy chuckle but I can tell he would rather
be somewhere else. I spy the phone booth empty and it
dawns on me I need to call the other ministry members.

"You fellas go on ahead. I have to make a call real quick,"
I inform them. Clemens nods, smiling, while Cole's eyes
widen as if to ask where I'm going. In an instant, Clemens
has his arm around Cole and is escorting him as they go on.
It's funny how a young kid like Jeremiah Cole can be enamored with this idea of a man so much and when that idea is
shattered, fear sets in quick like glue. Love turns into hate
too fast. Life is just funny that way.

I head over to the phone booth and, after looking at the
size of it, can't imagine how that woman even managed to fit.
I pick up the receiver, reach into my pocket for the number,
and then dial. It takes me a second to realize the receiver has
something sticky on it and, frankly, I don't care to know what
it is. After I get through the operator and the concierge, I
manage to get a hold of somebody.

"Hello?" a shaky, gruff voice asks.

"George, this is Gerald."

"Who?"

"Gerald. This is Gerald." He's ancient so the sound of
my voice must be reaffirmed. Back in the war, he lost half
his hearing to a grenade and hasn't found it yet.

"Oh, Gerald. I couldn't hear you there. Lost half my hearing to a grenade back in the war and haven't found it yet. What can I do for you?"

"A favor?"

"You got it, sonny."

It always makes me laugh to hear old folks use those generic terms of endearment that they apply to anyone remotely younger than they are. Monikers like "darling" or "sweetie" or "bud". I wonder if I'll use those someday? Calling waitresses "honey" or something.

"Can you get all the members together and have them here by five?"

"What?"

"Five, George. Five."

"Five?"

"Yes, George, five o'clock. Get them here by five o' clock. Alright?"

"Have I ever let you down?" He always says this because it's true. Probably always has been. "Remember that one place we went to back in fifty five and I had to get down to the church by six and I...or maybe it was fifty three. Was it? I coulda swore it was fifty fi..."

"Great, George. Great. Now make sure you get everyone here by five. No later. Five o'clock. The service starts at six thirty and we have to have prayer before that, understand?"

"I got it, sonny."

"I'll send Bill there early to wait for you so you can be here at five o'clock."

"Bill?" he asks confused. I always have to do this.

"Bill is the driver, remember? You've been traveling with him for the past two years."

"Oh, the colored fella. Right, right. I knew that."

"You know what to do?" This part is important because it shows that his short term memory is still working. Like how you ask a two year old to repeat what you just told them. Like I said, life is funny.

"I gotta get the guys together and meet Bill and be there by five."

"You've never let me down."

"Don't expect me to start, sonny."

"I don't, George."

He laughs a vibrato laugh before signing off. "See you, Gary."

I hang up the phone and smile. I might try calling again later just for my own assurance. The air feels lighter, hopeful. Something the air has been empty of for so long I can't remember what this feeling ever felt like. I exit the phone booth and its eclectic phrases etched on its inside and walk around the corner. Clemens and Cole are standing outside the diner. Clemens chatting as Cole responds by shaking his head like he's listening. I feel selfish again for leaving him. I quicken my step so I can help the poor kid out. I catch up and hear Clemens lecturing on the joys of ministering. "...see the joy in their eyes when ya say a prayer over them is the most satisfying moment in workin' for the Lord."

Whether he is sincere or not is hard to tell. Anything new will last temporarily. Based on what just happened, I want to believe that something has changed but I've seen glimpses like this before. No one just changes. Yet, in me, I have hope. A hope for the future.

As Cole and Clemens get close to the entrance, a beggar, in fact the same beggar I passed earlier, is standing outside the diner. Even from my distance, I can smell him. Ezekiel stops, walks up to the man and places a wad of cash in his hand. The man smiles and nods, his smeared and stained skin making his red eyes all the more visible. I hear Clemens say something about getting drunk on the blood of Jesus instead. I interrupt, startling the drunk, and take us in to the diner to get us seated before some episode occurs.

There's no one there to greet us so we grab a seat. We file into a half-circle booth with each one occupying his section of it. Me on the left, Clemens in the middle and Cole on the right. The seat is faded maroon leather and the cushion has long ago been smothered by the years of abuse. Whatever cushioning is left is visible through the short tears. The corner where we are seated gives us a panoramic view of the diner. The walls are covered in maroon and pink wallpaper. Since we missed the noon rush, our only fellow diners are a middle aged couple obviously disinterested in each other's thoughts and an old woman sitting alone with coffee and a book. The music played overhead is an old country tune with an annoying guitar part.

The waitress comes over with three glasses of water and hands the menus to us nonchalantly. I notice her nails are painted a bright red but, by the looks of it, she didn't put much care into it. Maybe she felt obligated by her boss or something. Her face is tight and angry with too much make up, especially around the eyes. Almost like a purposeful exaggeration. She isn't too old but as I examine her, there's a despair about her face. Something that makes me want to hug her and tell her everything is going to be alright.

Clemens seems energized and talkative, a throwback to an earlier day. Ready to take on the world one soul at a time. Ignited by Holy Fire and wanting to spread the flame. Cole is slouched in the booth, obviously sick with discomfort and hoping to sink into oblivion.

"What'll it be?" she asks in a monotone. It sounds lifeless and agitated to me. Clemens stares at her, smiling wide, and I can tell that he is going to say something. Not necessarily because he wants to but because he has to. It's who he is or what he's made himself to be. The saver of souls, healer of hearts. Just not his own.

"What would you have on this menu, young lady?" he inevitably asks.

She looks down at him and purses her lips. "What does it matter to you?"

"Just curious as to what a pretty lady like you would have to eat?" he asks in his most southern of tongues. I can't tell if he's flirting or converting just yet.

"Are you gonna order or what?"

"I'm gonna order but first I have just one question for you?" he asks, loud and friendly but with seriousness.

She sighs and rolls her eyes, "What?"

"Do you know the road to happiness?" He joins his hands together in front of him and places them on the menu, staring with those dark eyes straight into her tortured face.

She darts her eyes back and forth from me to Cole then back to me skeptically. I just shrug my shoulders and take a sip of ice water. She's the one who's gotta answer the question, not me. Knowing that no help is on the way, she humors him. Clemens has this thing for waitresses. He always feels lead to engage them into salvation. Like all of them are receptors for the Glory of God. I guess he's been running so long that he just knows how to talk with them. Speak their language. But even for Clemens, I don't think this one is going to crack. Not everyone is ready to hear his speeches.

She squints. "Excuse me?"

"The road to happiness. Do ya know how to find it?"

She shifts her weight onto her heels, folding her arms, the notepad dangling from her fingertips and the pencil jutting from her hair. "Do I look like I know where the road to happiness is, buddy?"

Clemens smiles and I know that smile. Revving up for the race. Ready for the challenge. Nothing tickles him more than displaying his feigned wisdom on others. The most bitter and stubborn people with a vehement hatred of all things Christian are the prize that Clemens views as gold. It's the only thing I've seen him genuinely enjoy doing.

"Miss, I can tell by your eyes that life has not been the life you've wanted. Maybe even deserved. I can tell in yer voice that it saddens, maybe even angers you, that life has been short with ya. I can see it written over yer face, darling, that there is people in yer life that have hurt you, let you down, and abandoned you. But there's a road to happiness that is

paved with golden streets. Golden like your heart underneath that stony shell."

He's quite hypnotic right now. The sincere tone, graceful
hand gestures are the work of an experienced speaker. The
same qualities a con man may possess. I check the waitress's
face and, amazing enough, a softening expression surfaces.

"Ya see, miss...uh, what's your name, darling?" he asks.

She startles. "Ma-Maggie."

"Maggie. A beautiful name. There is one way to that road
and I know the man who can take you there. He's only a few
words away and I can help ya call his name. Do ya know his
name, Maggie?"

She glances toward the floor and then back to Clemens.

"God?" It's hard to tell if she's being sarcastic or sincere.

"Close. Jesus. See, I knew ya was a beautiful girl but I
didn't know ya was so smart too," he flatters. Right now, I
know he's sincere. Something within his eyes shows it.

Some red shows through her powdered cheeks and she
smiles a barely visible grin. A smile that looks as if she forgot
how to use those muscles long ago. I wish this would hurry
up so we can order.

"Maggie, Jesus Christ is the travel guide, so to speak, of
this road. He is the only one that knows the way. He is the
navigator of life that will lead us to the Father and the way to
follow him is to ask. Just ask him for guidance on the road
and He will lead you to happiness. Do you want to ask Jesus
Christ to be yer guide?"

They stare at each other. Her face wants to say yes with
all its being but her mind does what it has been trained to do.

To fight and distrust. She's such a sympathetic figure. Walled and barricaded behind layers of abuses to difficult to understand. I don't know her past but I see the effects of it. Just like I see the effects of Clemens' past in all he is. My effects. I am amazed at how what we were makes us what we will be.

The table is at a stand-still. Clemens seems confidant in what she will say. Cole is still slouched and withdrawn like he's hiding. He keeps his face down at his menu as if it holds the answers for all the great questions life has kept hidden since God first breathed life into the dust and created his most beloved and infamous creation. As for me, I am just watching the show.

Maggie bites her bottom lip, fighting and surrendering, back and forth inside like a wave against rock. I've been around people long enough to know the movements of the eyes, the lift of the tuck of the lips, the tilt of the head. They all convey that same inner struggle that happens at sometime in each person when a decision, an important decision, is to be made. An eternal decision. Clemens doesn't take his eyes from her face. Maggie's old defenses kick in and she snaps at Clemens.

"Don't look at me that way. I don't need your superstition to get me through life. What'll it be? You?" She says this looking at me, focusing all her attention on not looking at Clemens.

It takes me a moment to snap out of it. "Uh...uh...a pastrami, please. No mayo."

She scribbles down on the pad. I see the thin page rip but she keeps writing anyway.

"You?" She snaps at Cole, who has slouched and sunk so low the only part of him visible is his head.

"The same," he whispers.

"What? Speak louder. I ain't a rabbit," she shrieks at him.

Cole stutters out, quite louder, "I-I'll have the same!"

Again, she scribbles down hard. Her knuckles are white with pressure. Without looking up, she asks Clemens, "What d'you want?"

Clemens takes a moment to answer but she still won't raise her eyes. In a soft tone, he says, "I only want what God has planned for ya."

At this, she cringes and turns away. I watch her leave and raise a hand to her face before she turns around the corner into the kitchen. I want to do something but what is there to do. Should I run after her? Obviously, Clemens had struck a chord within her. I had to have faith that God would work. That's what life came down to anyway. So what am I to do? Clemens sat back with his head against the cushioned backrest. His eyes moist and ponderous.

"Did you want to do that or was it God this time?" I ask him.

He closes his eyes with his face titled heavenward and he says, "It's always God, Ger."

"You're the preacher, not me," I say, rather sardonic. I don't mean for it to come out this way but sometimes my thoughts overcome my words. But today, my tone is the least of my problems. God knows, I just want a normal meal. Is that too much to ask?

"I hope she don't spit in our food is what I hope," Cole says, rather unexpectedly. These were the first words we had heard him speak in the last half hour. Me and Clemens share a glance and start chuckling. Not necessarily out of humor but out of exhaustion. Soon the chuckle becomes contagious and Cole starts laughing as well. A brief and bad communal joke that was well needed.

A short silence settled on us. Cole took a sip of his water and Clemens seemed deep in thought. Quiet for once. I can tell that he is on all our minds but no one wants to point it out. No one mentions it but it is there. As if he is sitting on the table in front of us like some cultish guru, just waiting for someone to ask. Well, I guess it is up to me.

"Clemens?" I ask.

"Yeah, Ger," he says, fiddling with the cheap utensils.

In my mind, I know what I want to say but, when action is needed, it is much harder to release those thoughts. Instead, I release a part of my caged thoughts.

"Who was he?"

Clemens shoots a bitter glance up at me without raising his head.

"Yeah, pastor, I can't seem to get my head around all this. Who was that man who came to see you?" Cole's meager voice is reassuring to me. It gives me strength to seek the truth. For once, I have back-up.

Clemens glances at us, sighs a deep sigh and says, "I don't know."

Simple and lacking accountability. Clemens's method to success all these years. I stupidly expected a genuine answer when I should have known what I would get. Some things change. Some.

"Ya don't know?" Cole retorts. "Ya have to know. Why did he scare ya so bad? He's just a man." Cole slowly rose from his hiding place. Returning to the optimistic young man he was. "Did he threaten ya or somethin'?"

"'I don't know' means 'I don't know.' I never seen that man before in my life," Clemens says, cutting his bandaged hand into his palm like he was demonstrating karate.

"Ezekiel, don't play this game. Tell us the truth. Please," I plead to him.

"Tell the truth? I'm a prophet of the Holy Ghost. I speak truth everyday and I'm tellin' ya the truth before God and the sweet baby Jesus, I do not know who that man was."

I look at Cole and say, "This is like talking to a Mormon."

Cole shakes his head in agreement. Clemens has a bewildered expression like he has been answering all our questions truthfully. He sits erect, holding his hands hovering in the air as he darts his head back and forth between us.

"What is this? I won't be bullied by you two. I'm tellin' ya, with God as my witness, that I don't know who that man was. What more can I say? If ya can't trust an evangelist, who can ya trust?"

"Clemens," I say to him, putting my elbows on the table, pointing my finger toward him, "First, the title does not make the man, the man makes the title, understand? And second, you haven't answered Cole's question why that man scared the spirit out of you. It's a simple and straight question that needs an answer. Simple and straight."

Clemens releases the tension in his shoulders and leans forward on his elbows. He hangs his head for a long moment and then looks up with his hand in that same karate-chop motion and waves it to make his point.

"Sometimes a man gets scared is all! And I got scared! End of story."

"You kept sayins, 'He knew! He knew!'," Cole said, "What did he know?"

"Look, Cole..." Clemens says raising his arm to do that karate chop motion with his hand but inadvertently hits his glass of ice water, spilling across the table. "Ahh, Jem, ya made me..." He freezes when he says this, whatever it is, and his eyes seem to glaze over as if in a trance, alive but in a different place altogether. Cole and I look at each other sharing the same confusion. Cole examines Clemens' face a moment, waving his hand in front of his eyes to no avail.

"Clemens?" I say and, suddenly, he comes out of it. He asks me what he was talking about and then it comes back to him but his stubborn determination seems to have been left in whatever world he just came from.

"He just knew I was anxious. Just anxio..." Clemens trails off to a whisper, obviously distracted.

As if rehearsed for her cue, Maggie comes back carrying three pastrami sandwiches. Even in her agitated state, she still is graceful with the dishes. Her face pursed and prepared this time. She places my plate in front of me with a clank. Then Cole's. Then tosses Clemens' at him. She stands back with her hands on her hips and asks in a snappy tone, "Anything else?"

I look around the table at everyone. Cole, who must have been starving, is already taking a mouthful out of his sandwich, and Clemens doesn't seem to notice anyone else is around let alone the food. I know he called his brother 'Jem' but I don't understand. He rarely talks about his brother and when he does he is like he is now. Distracted and distant. Almost surreal. She looks at Clemens, probably expecting a second chance at conversion, but seems surprised that he says nothing. She looks at me with a scowl and says, "What's with him?"

I shrug like I always do and reply, "He's just anxious." Cole, feeling better, chokes a bit on his sandwich. Whether in response to my pathetic pun or his voracity I'll never know. She rolls her eyes and slams the check on the table and leaves.

Cole is nearly halfway through his pastrami before I even taste mine. Somehow my appetite, despite its intensity, has waned into just a subtle nausea. I pick up the sandwich and examine it a moment. For what, I don't really know and then take a large bite. It tastes bland and chalky in my mouth except for the mayonnaise. Maybe it's just my state of mind influencing my meal. Food from my home is the only food I've been able to actually enjoy. It's nothing special. The food on the road has no substance or flavor. Nothing to make it unique and fulfilling. There's no definitive explanation for it. There's no explanation for anything in life. Even

God skimps on explanations so I guess they aren't as important as we make them out to be.

The song changes overhead finally as I struggle through a quarter of my sandwich and can't eat anymore. Clemens has nibbled some of the lunch but, mostly, he has been silent the entire time. Cole is seated back, finishing the last of his ice water and returning to the headstrong kid I met earlier today.

"That was probably the best sandwich I ever tasted," Cole remarks, visibly uplifted by the experience. He pats his belly with his hand and I imagine his daddy doing the same thing in another time.

"Boss, you ready to go?" I ask. He nods to my question without really hearing it. I place the money plus a little extra on the table. I think about Maggie and take out a pen, write on a napkin and slide it underneath the money. We file out of the booth and head toward the door. Cole is content and full. Clemens is still suffering and me, the link between this ministry and the world, I'm hanging on by a thread.

I open the door and, as they pass, I spy Maggie going to our table to bus it. She picks up the money, then the napkin. She reads the note a moment and creases form as her face contorts. She puts her hand to her mouth with those chaotic red nails and turns her sad face toward me. I smile because I know she is doing the best she can to say thank you in a thankless world. I see the sparkle of tears that have long been suppressed begin to flow and, in her eyes, I see the gratitude and grace she always possessed but never let free. A victim in a man's world. I head out the door as we walk toward the convention center where more people are slowly trickling in and forming lines outside. A good three hours before the doors even open. I spy some tents and sleeping bags mingled among the people lined up.

After we come around the corner, away from the crowd, Clemens, despondent, asks for a cigarette and I give it to him. He lights up, takes a long drag of smoke and walks ahead of us. His skeletal frame hunched and frail before us, walking alone.

Cole looks at me and asks, "What was that all about?"

I look at him as the afternoon sun comes to warms us as we head down the side street to the rear of the massive structure. I smile and say, "Something she needed to hear."

"And that was?"

I take in a deep breath before I answer and survey my surroundings. "She needed to know she was worth something. That's all."

He pats my broad shoulder and says, "You're a good man, Gerald."

I smile back, touched by the words. In my ears, I hear the kind words of Jeremiah Cole mingle with the condemnations and threats of the street preacher exhorting repentance from the gathering group of people here for the big show and I think to myself, I am not what he says I am.

1932

The townsfolk rumored his brother had found him, floating face down, bloated and grey. Others accused the brother of malicious intent and had done the deed himself. These were rumors of course. How he had died or the circumstances surrounding remained a mystery. The custom of the small town was to not perform autopsies for the sake of the family partially because there were none willing to perform the task. But the coroner's absence was due to the request of the pastor.

The funeral was held in the church governed by his father on a cloudless Saturday a week later, the air perfectly temperate. The building that had witnessed the passings of centuries pushed to capacity with all who knew the departed, all come to pay respects, clothed in the darkest of black and the deepest of sadness to make sense of so unexpected a death. The small community still recuperating from the shock of the reality that life could be snatched from one barely lived. Every member attended including the petty Miss Wordman and Emma, the ancient Mr. White, who had begun to doze before the eulogy, and even Jeremiah's temporary employer Mr. Mayhew, who could not even suppress his loss at this time despite his foul disposition.

With her remaining children beside her, Clementine wept into her gloved hands, moaning a soft, lugubrious mourn. Abigail sat close to her mother, cradled by her warmth. Her eyes puffy and red from the furious bits of sorrow. Young boys watched her furtively, marveling at her delicate features. Regal sat rigid, his face a hollow, colorless, icy complexion. He shed not one tear nor gesture of comfort to his family. Anyone visiting would not know his son had just passed if they were to meet him.

The surviving son sat vacant, wearing the habiliments of death. Detached from the reality of his brother's absence. The thin lacerations marring his cheeks and hands had clotted and were now scabs. His eyes mere orbs imbedded in his skull. His heavy heart beat because nature required, machine-like, solidified inside himself.

Friends and acquaintances offer condolences downcast. Common words "so young" and "what a shame" upon their lips. Regal and Clementine accepted these words of solace though they did not ease the death. Regal would nod solemn and respond on how the will of God was and, "though we may not understand, God has swept his child into his arms to hold him aloft in the heavens." Clementine would concur through gasps of air between retch-like sobs. Abigail, hardly acknowledging the futile words of others but still upheld a respectful and subtle response. Ezekiel, despondent, spoke not a word. No one faulted or judged him considering the circumstance.

The heavy woman played a plodding version of "In the Sweet By and By". Each C a rest by circumstance. The front held a meek remembrance of Jeremiah. A small painting he used to show interest in that hung in the home, a flawless portrait of Jesus Christ, golden shadow coming from behind and the crown of thorns placed gently atop his scalp. Some field flowers scattered around the splintery, box-style coffin donated by the church.

The piano played on. Abigail turned to the statue of Ezekiel. She scooted closer and placed soft hands around his arm and nestled in. He stared at the coffin vacant, unaware of the hands around him. She said, "Do you miss him?"

Ezekiel looked to his lap and then at his sister, his remaining sibling. She began to weep again and Ezekiel held her. He wanted to cry with her but his eyes were as hollow stones.

The song ended and, when everyone had resumed their seats, Regal walked to the front, to the light-colored coffin. He examined it, running his hand across its surface slowly. The atmosphere heavy as he stood. Clementine howled into the still air and buried her face in her hands. Regal glanced over his shoulder and turned to give his son's eulogy.

"I want to thank you for coming out today to mourn the passing of Jeremiah Clemens. My son. Jeremiah was a good child. He had a strong belief in God and always took care of his younger brother and sister. We will surely miss him and the light he brought into our lives. We know he is in a better place now. With the Holy Father." He paused a moment, his eyes glazed with thought. "The one true father. Now, I'd like to open this time up for remembrance."

He resumed his seat. Clementine grasped his arm and continued her emotional drainage. Regal sat rigidly; neither comforting nor mourning.

A breath could be heard in the silence that followed. Finally, Mr. Mayhew, hunchbacked, came to the front. He arrived and scanned across the faces then to the coffin. He spoke with a gravelly, bitter tone, "Jeremiah was a good worker. Never complained and got there on time. If he were still here, I'd hire him again."

Mr. Mayhew returned to his seat, sitting down noisily. The attendees looked at each other, no one knowing how to respond to such a bizarre homage. Steadily, members filed frontward. Some would speak at length of comical stories and others would elegantly describe touching moments of Jeremiah's charity and faith. Some elders came forward and spoke of his respect and kindness to those older than he and of various small tasks he did to help them in their lives. There was a veracious cheer in the air. The short life extinguished praised for such that it gave hope to those who had little. If a life so short could be lived so well, none were exempt from hope.

The endless line of speakers had subsided. Ezekiel stood unexpectedly and approached the coffin. He ran his palm across the top of the cheap coffin, paying no mind to the splinters impaling and imbedding in his skin. A deafening silence pervaded the church, anticipation of what Jeremiah's best friend and brother would say about his loss. What he would say about how painful it was, a sadism in those at funerals who wish to see the internal pain visualized by such a tremendous loss. A desire to watch the complete breakdown of emotions.

He pressed his cheek to the coffin and whispered under his breath. Then, he turned and faced the audience. The face, the eyes, the lips all held fast, unable to tear or mourn. Then, in his young voice, he said flatly, "There's nothing I can say to make it any better. He's dead. Ain't nothin' gonna change that."

The faces looking back made him walk easily straight down the open aisle, past all the sagging and pitiful faces, out the door into the sunlight. A rustle of hushed voices began to permeate throughout the building. The heavy piano player, in an effort to reinstate order, shuffled over to the piano and began playing again. Everyone watched as the door shut with a loud snapping clap sucking out the light. Everyone except Regal Clemens, who had buried his hands in his face.

The door shut behind him. Ezekiel looked into the flat and empty landscape. The redundant horizon broken up by small structures and looming oaks. He held his hand to his eyes to shield the sun, looked around once more, and exploded into a run. No destination intended. He ran headstrong as his insides bashed and clashed and huddled together. Anger hugging sadness and sorrow cutting rage. All emotions tangled in a battle.

When his body could run no longer, he found himself at the lake. He could still envision the pale bluish, grey body floating face down. He unleashed a guttural scream that beheld the tumult within him. He fell to his knees, punching the damp soil, grabbing and clawing with his fingers then pummeling the dirt into his face. Cursing God, his father, the devil, death. Anything.

He stopped, heaving, sitting on his knees and broken, sweat slickening his skin. The loss hit him and he cried without inhibition. Without regard for anyone. A cry that seemed to suck life's energy from him and pour out onto the dirt and mud before creation his purpose. He collapsed and lay prostrate, patched and smeared with dark matter.

He laid in the oak's shade as a soft breeze dried the damp on his face. Exhausted, he could have fallen asleep had it not been for a faint golden sparkle in the shallows. He lifted his head and saw it again as the waters slightly rippled. He forced himself up, first to sitting, then to his knees then feet. He could still see the glint and waded to his knees. The cool water soaking through his pants and into his skin.

Partially buried in the slime and muck lay a cross neckpiece with a chain. Ezekiel eyed it with amazement yet the pang of loss stung him once again. Instantly, he was standing with his brother, holding the necklace before him. Jem held it proudly, dangling it from his fingers saying, "Look what I got."

"Where'd ya get it?"

"I found it."

"Where?"

"On the way home. I think God wanted me to have it."

"Naw, it's just luck."

"Ya think what ya want."

"Is that real gold?"

"Could be."

Jeremiah placed the chain over his head. The cross illuminated from his white chest and Ezekiel marveled envious to have as his own.

"I sure wish I found one," Ezekiel remarked.

"Maybe someday I'll give it to ya," Jem hinted. Ezekiel figured that Jem just might.

He was back in the lake, in the place of death, standing knee deep in muck, holding the cross of his brother. Ezekiel gripped it tight and closed his eyes as the nauseous feeling that had plagued him since returned and he vomited into the water, spreading it across the surface with a plopping noise.

"Ahh, Jem," Ezekiel sloppily said as his mourning poured forth from his lips, "I'm sorry."

In the stillness of the lake, in the ethereal presence of the unexplainable, he heard, or thought he heard, the faintest whisper on the wind. On the leaves. He shrugged it off, wiping his rank lips of bile. Again, the words sounded. It affirmed what he felt compelled to do since that day and now, he knew what had to be done. As if possessed, he mouthed the word.

A violent rustling began in the thicket beyond the old oak. A rattling violence that seemed metaphysical in its voracity. Ezekiel watched in the direction. It grew loud and, in a flash, a doe bounded wildly down the shoreline, graceful even in its uninhibited fear. Ezekiel watched the animal with awe, the tragic event unfolding again before him in all its morbid and grotesque detail. He forced himself to watch the animal through the hurt it produced. He toiled inside himself until

the last glimpse of God's creature vanished into the horizon,
far away from its fear and further from its pain.

Acts

It's now close to three thirty in the afternoon as we walk silently into the loading area behind the convention center. Clemens is beginning to rejoin us, breaking from whatever bizarre spell came over him in the diner. When we passed the entrance of the convention center, we could see a crowd forming out front, comprised of men and women of all ages and even children. Parents and family probably hoping to have an exhibition of the Holy Spirit for their children to see. Some impactful form of existence and its power over us that would either convict or terrify their children onto the straight and narrow path. Seeing children at these meetings over the years reaffirms this idea because, never once, have I seen a child thoroughly enthralled with the word given. However, the authentic look in their eyes when these "miracles" happen is proof enough in the parent's desired effect. I scan the crowd, hoping to catch a glimpse of the mysterious man who has disrupted the day but it is near impossible to tell if he is in there or not. The crowd is just too thick. The faint fervor of the lone preacher on the corner is just a hint of noise now.

It is getting closer. Around two hours before the service begins is when I usually feel the most anxious. Clemens has always told me that anxiety is a form of unbelief in the power of God and that I still had some unresolved sin that was causing my nervousness. I used to believe this nonsense years ago, after he took me in and we started on the road. Now I know that it isn't true and, frankly, I laugh when I hear him say things like that. Anything anyone says is rarely completely true.

I hold the door open as the two enter. I check on Bill visually and notice that he is still asleep, slouched down further. I chuckle a bit and enter into the dim hallway. I wish the world were not so partial to the exterior of a man.

We get to the door that reads "Ezekiel Clemens" and I usher the celebrity into the room and tell him to have a seat. Shutting the door, I face Cole and say, "Now, listen, you've got to help me make sure everything is running smooth as butter out there, alright?"

He sighs a deep breath and says, "Alright."

"You can do this. Being nervous is perfectly normal and, if you can handle being in the same room as Clemens, then you can handle whatever comes your way. If God has deemed it to be than it will be, regardless of the outcome. Now, I'll go..."

"Gerald," he says cutting me off, "Do ya mind if I say somethin' that's been on my mind?"

"Sure, go ahead." I feel that rumble of conviction inside my gut. Somehow, I know what is coming. He shuffles his feet a bit as he stares downward. His hesitation is evident enough.

"Whatever you're gonna say, Cole, just say it. Let's not act like strangers here."

He looks me directly in the eye with a seriousness that strikes me still. "I'm not the brightest man but I know when

204

somethin' is wrong when it shouldn't be. I know Ezekiel Clemens is a man of God because he has done so much for people over the years and across the globe. But I'm a bit confused by all this. The strange man, Pastor Clemens actin' out at me and everybody. The smoking? I just can't seem to get my head around it all. Has he been playin' everybody all this time?"

I stand straight with my arms folded and I can't help this feeling that my eyes are bulging with panic. I'm caught. No excuses left. The truth is inches away from bursting through the seams and flowing into the air, almost purifying it. Cole's words lingering, tearing the seam and letting it all loose. My fears, the conspiracy, the secrecy. I want to peel the layers back and expose the center. Conflict is the essence of life. Between shame, pride, and fear, I fumble the truth inside my head and I can feel my palms begin to sweat and that shake in my hand returns. Why am I so nervous around this young, naïve child who has his starry-eyed dreams before him? Who thinks the service of God is flawless and those who serve are empty of sin, torment and disbelief? In the mortal realm, perfection cannot exist. I am a man. Ezekiel Clemens is a man.

"I am a man." I say out loud. Surprised that I vocalized my thoughts. Surprised I said anything. For a brief second, I wonder if I said more of my mind.

"Excuse me?" Cole says.

"I mean...I was trying to...uhhh...," I trail off. A man twice Cole's age, reddening and shaking like a frightened animal before a predator. Life is a constant transition. The opportunity is here.

Should I? My mind is spinning like a carnival ride, around faster and faster until everything blurs into one multicolored haze and time and space are no longer dictates but ideas of a moment in time. I want to purge myself. To empty my guts of all the festering rust into the lap of a young man who I've only known for a few hours. Just a few heavy hours. Is this my hour of atonement? My moment of redemption from my warped life and the bondage of this religious ideal? Are You even there?

I think I'm having a heart attack. But it is the guilt talking, torturing me to the point that the only cure is to cut myself open and spill the contents before this child. Why him? Send an angel, Lord? Send someone above me. The taste in my mouth is bitter and metallic and, without regard for my appearance, I smack my lips, running my tongue around my mouth to try and scrape the flavor out. A voice in my head says one word over and over and over. I can't, God. I can't do it. What about Your ministry? I can't jeopardize our calling. Clemens is too public. I have to keep him clean for the sake of Your word. I have to...

And then it hits me.

I see Cole, as if for the first time, standing, a little puzzled and scared, in front of me. A little farther back than my memory recalls. He must think I was exorcising a demon. I know now what I have to do. Without Clemens or any help from anyone, I have to create a clean heart, my own self.

"Come with me," I say urgently to Cole, ushering him down the hallway and back outside. Out of the dark. He mumbles some words but I can't catch what they are. With my hand escorting him out, I feel slight resistance from him but, maybe out of intrigue, fear, or my vice-like grip, he comes along. I kick open the door and flinch at the light and there we are on the loading deck. Just us, illuminated and exposed for everyone who cares to see.

I pace, preparing my confession. I spy Bill still sleeping and look at the phone booth again. It's empty. I can hear the small crowd and the lone street preacher around the other side of the building faintly and it is only a matter of time before some zealots sneak around to try and enter through the back. We need to get some security out here soon. Focus.

"Jeremiah," I say. I run my hand across my bald head and try to control my shake, "Somewhere along the road, I...I got lost. This road I've travelled alongside with him has been a road paved with hypocrisy. And I am not blameless of any of it. I have been witness to some abhorrent sins and fallacies. I've seen Ezekiel drunk more than sober, I've closeted his sexual escapades and his lust and the money, Lord forgive me. I didn't commit these sins against God but I am more to blame than any other. I am the janitor. I am the cleaner. My inaction is my failure. I sweep these under the rug to trick, to lie, to con the fragile believers in Christ Jesus into thinking this man is filled with the power of God. But he's not, Cole. He's full of hurt and pain. No God could live inside that man. How could God live in *me* when I do nothing to stop it and everything to aid it? From the moment I was saved, I was a new creature. A new man with a new purpose. But what was my purpose? It certainly wasn't this. I want to be used by God but I've squandered my purpose. He saved me and I wanted to be a disciple. A Paul. In my desire, my sin of control, I became what I never wanted to. I became the devil's advocate all for a purpose. Thirty years of lies and hypocrisies all in the name of God and salvation. Fifteen years of hearing my family grow up but never watching it happen. Thirty years of disillusionment and misguided callings and what do I have to show for it?"

My heart racing, I feel something wet trickle down my cheek. I reach up and feel it and realize for the first time in years I can feel again. Cole stands there, taking all of this in. I know he's not a dumb kid and he probably followed his heart his entire life. I can't say the same. I feel the tears slide down my cheeks but they are foreign to me like they are a natural part of life but there is no emotion connected with them. They're just tears.

Cole, without saying a word, takes three slow steps toward me and, softly and tenderly, embraces me. Our roles reversed.

I feel it, the pressure and energy of his body next to mine and, without warning, the emotions come. The purification has begun and there is no damming this flood. My body a factory of shifts and shivers and leaks, grinding the lies and hurt and disappointment out my eyes. I groan into his shoulder and he holds me steadfast. Like a rock. I cry and cry with each sob and each tear, I feel my soul lightening as if the weight of my burden is hoisted by a heavenly crane, ready to be dumped into the deep sea of forgetfulness four hundred and ninety times. During all of this, I'm not thinking of Clemens or what has to be done for the meeting tonight or the ministry or my family or all the things I've done wrong in my life. I'm pondering the simple power of forgiveness and how great it is to finally feel alive. It's not like I imagined. It's so modest and intimate. Internal. There's no flash of light. Celestial voices or thunderous clapping. It's silent and still like a breeze. Only whispers across my ears. Nothing externally visible but wholly within.

Jeremiah holds me, his arms squeezing me tight and my emotions spew from my body like a fountain. I weep without fear, exposed for all to see. So foreign but undeniably cathartic. I don't care if Clemens comes out or if George arrives seeing me like this. I am absorbed in the reception of forgiveness. I have confessed it openly before someone. Before God. Before the heavens. Before man. And nothing feels more regenerating than the act of surrender. The process of losing control. Losing yourself. I want to burn down everything I've become to build it again.

1935

His legs could only take him so far and, though he knew not where he was going, he wanted to get nowhere faster than his legs could take him. This skill was not acquired quickly. He disliked horses and, once, had hitched a ride with an old Navajo on horseback across desert from Gallup to Winslow. After all those miles, he knew that horseback must be avoided at all costs. He preferred trucks and, if the owner proved charitable, he may get some food or lodgings. Trains were risky. He had witnessed a fellow hop-on being beaten with a pipe by one of the train's ticket checkers as he ran off with the others to safety. The crack of pipe on teeth a caveat he held tight.

He had arrived in two days prior, traversing the streets of the mining town at the foothills of the sierras, sleeping under overpasses and surrounding forests. He enjoyed the town, the people, despite the weather, and wondered how this could be the land of the antichrist his father had warned.

He exhausted his interest in the small town and chose to head westward to see what lay ahead along the highway that snaked through the mountains, inhabited by towers of pines and redwoods fed by a clear river that as cold as snow. He admired the beauty of creation. If there was a God, he enjoyed his handiwork. He walked with broken shoes and a new coat and skull cap he had found outside a church. His belongings the same as when he begun minus the can opener. Now he carried his father's Bible and the gold cross he kept in his pocket. As he walked, he rubbed the cross with his thumb, feeling the texture and design of it. He rubbed it for comfort at times but it never reciprocated.

The chilly, mountain air was sharp below the pines. A manifest between sun and shadow. He chose to walk between light and darkness where both extremes could find a middle ground. However, the middle was a precarious place on the road, either in the line of traffic, too close to an edge, or on pocked roads.

He walked in the omnipresence of foliage. The stillness eerie in its silence. Disrupting the natural sound, he heard the hum of an engine coming from behind. The morning sun shone bright in his face as he turned to view the approaching car. He shielded his eyes and gestured his thumb but the small car sped past. He followed its passing then raised a calloused hand to his face, twirling long sticky strands from his chin, raising the fingers to his nose before wincing and wiping his hand upon his pant leg.

He continued along the highway, powering a steep hill. His hands numb. His skin below his grime itching underneath. The muscles ached dully in his calves until he crested the hill. Below lay a vision of creation unparalleled. Atop this incline, he purveyed solemn, the clean air burning his lungs. The pit of his belly noisome like one who is drowning. In the distance lay a dead animal. The stench coming to him as he drew close. A dead doe; decomposed and half-masticated, fragments of furry, skin dangling. He stopped before the carcass and examined the decay. The black eyes blank, casting his own reflection mirroring in the darkness. Exposed bone visible at sporadic parts of the body. The delicate hind legs bent and the stomach distended. He crouched, staring, unable to turn away. The memory resurfaced, awaking from a cavernous slumber like some titan resurrected. Suppression heeding to the past's power.

As he crouched, another hum came from behind. He glanced over his shoulder, the sun blocked as it hid behind the steep hill. He waited till he could see the driver, an older man, about his father's age, and a young boy. He rose, gestured with his thumb, despite his doubts. The truck passed, then stopped quickly twenty feet ahead in the road skidding.

He put his hand down, standing over the carrion as the truck shifted into reverse so the passenger window was at his feet. The man drove a red truck, rusted on the door handles, the paint scratched and shaved. The body dented, giving it a crumpled appearance.

The window stuttered down and he could see the occupants well. The driver an older man with a smooth, chubby face above a checkered shirt. His overly inviting smile outlandish. In the passenger seat, the boy kept his face down, the area around his eyes bluish-black like he had not slept in days. He wore suspenders with no shirt underneath. The chill seen on his skin. Ezekiel looked left and then right along the road and saw no one around. Cautious, he stepped forward till the smell of the interior wafted. The chubby faced man smiled wide yellow teeth and spoke in a low voice that didn't seem fit, "Hello there."

"How do ya do?" Ezekiel responded warily. The inside of the truck immaculate and spotless. The young boy sat with hands in his lap, his right hand shaking. The chubby man leaned over to the window and looked Ezekiel up and down with his eyes, smiling a decrepit toothed grin.

"Where you headed?" he asked.

"Wherever you're willin' to take me," Ezekiel answered. The chubby man's green eyes glinted and Ezekiel regretted his phrasing. He pushed the boy back against the brown leather seat as he struggled to reach for the door handle.

"Sit back. Sit back, right now. You're in the way," he barked as the boy flinched. Ezekiel watched as his face agonized at the proximity of the man, the closeness. The man reached the door handle and it hissed open, swinging toward him.

"Hop in and I'll take you," the chubby man said, never taking his eyes off of the weary traveler. Ezekiel looked right and left again then at the doe behind him. Something about this animal struck him. Like an omen of the most beautiful of creatures capability of the ugliest demise.

Against his feeling, he tossed his sack holding his Bible, some bread, and a pack of cigarettes into the truck bed next to a rope coiled like a striking snake among the leaves, twigs and dirt that had piled around it. Tucked up against the cab, lay a deeply, stained square shovel. He hesitated, caught in a quandary of intuition and faith. The man's horn interrupted his dilemma. He scooted onto the leather seat next to the young boy, face down, shuffling next to the chubby man, a slight moue arising. Ezekiel noticed the boy's profile, witnessing an emptiness in the microcosms of his features. He shook ever so lightly, like a sturdy leaf in a breeze. Ezekiel reached and shut the door. The driver gave a contemptuous stare at the boy as he neared then smiled at Ezekiel before shifting the truck into gear and slowly climbing the steep hill westward. The engine whining its ascent.

The cab was uncomfortable but clean. The leather dashboard spotless and smooth, the seat and floor straight from the factory. The chubby man took his smooth hand and turned the radio volume up as the station played a nameless bluegrass song on fiddles and banjoes. The music so vociferous Ezekiel didn't realize the chubby man talking to him.

"What's that?"

"What's your name?" he shouted over the music, making no attempt to lower the volume.

Ezekiel hesitated before answering. "Jeremiah."

"You from here?" he asked, watching the road and licking dry lips.

"Far from it," Ezekiel shouted.

The chubby man nodded and asked, "You like it?"

Ezekiel looked down at the boy again. "It's alright. Mighty pretty," he said. The fiddles and banjoes created an audible cyclone in his ears. The chubby man nodded his head in an exaggerated fashion and said something that Ezekiel couldn't hear. The song ended abrupt and a slower song resumed.

They lingered speechless. The truck now descending.

"Is this yer son?" Ezekiel asked as they came around a corner. The view from the hill opened to a beautiful valley where the river funneled through. The chubby man looked at his new passenger uneasily then at the silent boy. The chubby man hesitated then answered, smiling, "Yeah. He's mine."

An unknown aura lurked between the three, a mute spirit that disrupted the natural harmony and normality of interaction. Ezekiel persevered with the small talk.

"What's his name?" he asked.

"Bud," the chubby man answered almost before he could finish the question. Ezekiel looked from the man to the boy then to the road. They had reached the top of another hill and began descending toward the valley, still clinging along the shadows of the towering pines and rocks. The minutes felt like hours. The palms of his hands had begun to moisten despite the cold air.

Ezekiel looked at the boy and asked, "You cold, Bud?"

The chubby man snapped his face toward him, darting his eyes from the boy to Ezekiel in a frantic manner.

"He don't talk much," he shouted in absolution. He stared ahead, wrapping and unwrapping his fingers around the wheel. He licked his lips over, pink tongue flicking in an out. Ezekiel saw a turnout ahead.

"Ya can stop at that turn out there and let me out, friend. I thank ya for the ride. I appreciate it much."

The chubby man gave no response. He passed the turn out, increasing his speed. Ezekiel watched the turn out pass and struggled to keep his wits about him.

"Sir, ya passed up the turn out back yonder. Ya can pull over here and let me out anytime."

The man remained reticent and kept ahead, dancing his fingers around the steering wheel. The speed caused the truck to start to bounce and shake, jostling the three passengers more than before. Ezekiel looked at the boy, eyes shut and terse. Ezekiel noticed that a wet stain had spread around the crotch of the boy's pants. His heart began to pound inside his rib cage. The chubby man said nothing more and drove on as the fiddles and banjoes picked a cacophony of intensity like some perverted march.

The road leveled as they drove speeding westward through the surrounding isolation. The sun crested the trees, prohibited from penetrating the shadows. Ezekiel thought of his mother and sister. He looked at the driver who kept an intense and determined countenance then to the silent boy. Ezekiel nudged him but the boy sat still. He waited and then tried once again to get his attention. On the third try, the boy finally lifted his gaze just enough to bare his pupils. Some event or events had sucked the innocence from those orbs and left a shell of a boy. Ezekiel tried to speak with only his eyes to tell Bud that he would help them get out of this.

"Where are we goin'?" Ezekiel asked but the driver gave no response. He swallowed, his senses ablaze in the stuffy cab that smelled of fear and waste. They drove a long distance until they turned down a dirt road that led into a thick segment of pines. The truck bounced along and the music played as any trace of sunlight became only a trace. The truck ascended up the long incline. Green and brown colors thickened to a dark shadow squelching their vision until it ended at a clearing where a small cabin sat windowless. The scenery now an accomplice as the truck's engine died close to the structure. The music continued swirling inside the cab. Ezekiel put his hand in his pocket and felt the gold cross. He saw the derelict cabin, covered by moss and mold, abandoned by all decency. He closed his eyes and offered a quick plea, if God was still listening. The music played a loud and frantic dueling of banjoes and fiddles.

The chubby man leaned forward with his hands evenly on the steering wheel and he smiled, watching the cabin as if he were reminiscing about some epoch of great joy. He turned his round face toward Ezekiel and shouted over the music, "Now, listen Jeremiah. I'm going to take you into this cabin. You're going to do something for me." His green, rapacious eyes peered from between his brown locks, lips moist from his constant wetting, smiling. Bud sat still. His eyes cinched tight as if such evil would disappear.

"I ain't goin in there," he tried to say sternly yet voice wavering.

The chubby man's smile faded. "You are," he commanded yet threatened simultaneously.

"Like hell," he declared, tensing, gripping his hand around the golden, metal cross in his pocket.

The chubby man's fat cheeks grew red. He huffed a growl violent like a possessed beast. He raged with his handle, kicked open the truck door, bending the hinges. Out of the truck, he reached into the back, cursing unintelligibly, and emerged with the shovel and rope in hand, proceeding around the back end. Ezekiel's muscles tightened at his stature. Fear settled upon him and a presence lurked behind that serpentine green.

Ezekiel grabbed for the door with his right hand but the door swung wildly open with a hiss. He kicked at the enraged man flailing. The man grasped at his legs, giving no heed to the sporadic blows. He caught hold of an ankle and pulled him out of the truck. Ezekiel thumped onto the thick layer of dirt and dead leaves, squirming to break free but the man's strength overpowered his slender frame. The strong scent of the forest filled his nostrils.

"Come on, Jeremiah. Settle down, now. You'll like it. I promise," the chubby man reassured between struggles and groans above the frenzied banjoes and fiddles. The man had fumbled a strong hold of Ezekiel's torso like a hug from behind. His elbows pinned, suspended in the air. Ezekiel continued his fight, losing strength. Bud sat in the truck, watching with sad eyes at the familiar spectacle before him.

Ezekiel grit his teeth as he kicked the air. The man placed his chubby face next to Ezekiel's and took in a deep whiff of his scent. Ezekiel's stomach fizzled. The impulse to cry hovering above his throat. Submitting to evil and facing the horrors that man is capable of. He swung his head right, left, then right, resting. With nothing else to rely on, he looked. Atop a small incline in an area empty of vegetation, he saw a slim tree grown straight with two branches jutting from the trunk. Ezekiel realized the God he had abandoned had answered his cry. He stopped struggling, breathing heavy and exhausted along with the man.

"That's it. That's it. Easy and calm now," the man whispered, close to Ezekiel's ear, as his hair obscured the tops of his eyes. "Nice and calm," he repeated. He tucked his smooth face close to Ezekiel's beard and sniffed again. Slowly and intimately, savoring the scent.

Ezekiel slid his hand into his pocket and grasped the gold cross. The cross that had found him so long ago. He held it tight in his fist, the end a tall shaft jutting forward. The man nestled his face close, placing his lips a breath away from Ezekiel's skin. He held the cross taut and swung his forearm straight back toward the side of his face. The cross collided with the cartilage. The man squeaked in painful surprise as the cross cut deep into his skin. He squeezed Ezekiel harder, clenching, pressing. Ezekiel plunged again at the man's face and felt the shaft of the cross sink in with a soggy sound. The man released, cupping his hands toward his face, crying atop the music in a shrill, "God! My eye! You took my damn eye!"

Ezekiel landed on his back, scrambling, and saw the man cradling his wounded face as it poured through his fingers. He watched the grotesque spectacle transfixed. Ezekiel, sucking in deep breaths of air, lay as the wounded man grabbed his foot, yanking frenetically. Ezekiel's instinct waned and he had lost energy to fight. The man groaned, spitting with anger and pain as he pulled Ezekiel closer. The spectacle an outlandish dance as the bluegrass cyclone scattered about in the air. Ezekiel could smell the man, the face saturated with red, and noises of pain above him. He closed his eyes, exhausted, ready to finish. A metallic thump resounded above him and then he lay still. Ezekiel opened his eyes and saw the man, as if unplugged, on the ground, motionless.

Ezekiel fell back, feeling the adrenaline subside in his veins. The unconscious body laid face down atop his legs, the hair smeared with blood and leaves. He looked around and saw a crow sit in the branches slightly ahead. It cawed just above the frenzied melody. The music abruptly ended and Ezekiel looked back to see Bud's hand on the ignition. The other holding the shovel. The two exchanged a relieved look. Ezekiel pushed the body off, exhausted, drifting into sleep, away from consciousness and death.

"Is h-he dead?"

Ezekiel looked up to see Bud, upright and shirtless, leaning on the door frame. His quiet voice meek and hopeful. The dark spot about his groin lightening. Ezekiel looked at the body and said, "I ain't waitin' to find out."

He stood up slowly and limped to the truck bed to grab his sack of belongings. The sensation of pain steadily coming to him as the excitement waned. He threw the sack over his shoulder and turned to Bud.

"You comin'?"

Bud nodded, shivering. Ezekiel, seeing the face clearly for the first time, took off his coat and gave it.

Bud took it absently and put the oversized coat on, losing his hands into the massive sleeves. Ezekiel put a hand on the boy's back and he flinched.

"I ain't gonna hurt ya," Ezekiel said.

Bud raised his sunken eyes to this new face, dropping the shovel at his feet.

They walked down the dirt road, in the shadows of the pines and the chill of the absence of light for what seemed miles. Both glancing back expecting to see the truck tumbling after them in a smoke of dust. They breathed a sigh when they reached the end of the road and came out upon the highway. The sun shone bright as the sun hung above them, casting its rejuvenation on creation. Ezekiel looked left then right, deciding to keep west on the road until a place to rest that was out of sight could be found. They walked in silence, propelled by fear and freedom, until they spotted a trail that lead into dense foliage. Pushing through brush until they came to a small opening. The sound of birds echoed throughout and they both collapsed, feet throbbing and hearts pounding. Ezekiel fell onto his back and lay supine and empty. Bud calm, staring into the lush greenery as if admiring its beauty for the first time.

Ezekiel closed his eyes and said, "God saved us back there, Bud."

There was no answer but Ezekiel kept talking.

"I turned my back on God but he ain't ever turn his back on me. Even after all these years, He was always watchin over me. I ain't ever felt this before. Like God was with me. But He is. No matter where ya are, God is there. That's how it's always been. I just been too blind to see it."

He opened his eyes then sat up and got on his knees, clasping his hands together. Bud watched disinterested as he prayed.

"Lord Jesus, forgive me of my sins. My ignorance. I want Ya to come into my life and save me. Take away all the pain and the filth. I promise that I will serve Ya all my days. I will proclaim Yer name to all the nations. I will be like the apostle Paul. I will spread Yer word and preach the name of Jesus Christ. Even in the face of certain death. I won't run no more."

Ezekiel began to weep. Bud, intrigued, watched his conviction. Ezekiel prayed and prayed repeating, "Forgive me, Lord."

Bud continued to watch until the moment had passed. Ezekiel, sniffling with a new joy and purpose in his life, lifted his gaze to heaven, saying, "Thank you." Bud watched, swimming in his massive coat. When he finished praying, he realized Bud had been watching yet he felt no shame.

"Bud, I've been saved by the power of Jesus Christ."

Bud wiped his nose with his sleeve and responded, "I-is he d-dead?"

"No, he's alive. Hallelujah!"

The memory of the last hour flooded back to Ezekiel, realizing that the man might be dead. He grew nauseous at the thought and vomited bile into the dirt. That expulsion so common to his spirit he felt near obligation to do it. He asked God for forgiveness once again. The boy sat with neither a whimper nor tear. Ezekiel looked up with moist eyes and asked, "Bud, I'm so sorry I hit yer Pa. I didn't mean to kill 'im. I swear."

Bud looked at Ezekiel, his back towards him and said, 'M-my name isn't B-Bud."

"Huh? But yer Pa said..." he asked, wiping his nose with his dirty hand and smearing a glistening streak across his thick beard. The boy looked straight ahead interrupting, "That m-man isn't my f-father."

Ezekiel scratched his scalp. The faint sting of his abrasions now noticeable. "What is it?"

The boy looked with those blank eyes. The eyes of someone forced to bite of the forbidden fruit without choice. He paused before answering, as if recalling information long in the past that he had been so disconnected from that it was almost part of another life.

"G-G-Gerald," he muttered.

Out of Darkness

In my selfish concentration, I never saw it but now, as I sit spent and lifted from my guilt, Jeremiah Cole by my side, I can see it now. The burden of lies no longer on me. Only the truth. It's riding the rays of sunlight. Lingering in the particles that hover and float upon the subtlest of winds. It holds this building together. It flows with the blood in our veins and prompts our heart to beat. It clings to decibels in the sound of car horns, laughter, sobbing, song, and thunder. It is there, invisible to all of us because we are distracted, focused on the role of man in it all. As God's representation.

I realize this in this moment of sincerity and weakness. What baffles me most is I never felt truth in the countless meetings of ours. Every church or tent was a show. The wailing, cries of woeful lament. The tongues like gunfire. The hands raised, the falling down, shaking. It is all so fake to me. I feel it when I least expect it. In silence and isolation. In bare naked humility, shed of everything I think I know.

Jeremiah smiles at me and helps me to my feet. His shirt is blotched with my tears and I apologize. He shrugs his shoulders and tells me, "These stains are the best stains I ever got."

"Thank you," I say to him. It's all I can say. I want to say more but what do you say when you've just emptied your soul into an unsuspecting man's lap? He smiles and says, "Yer the one who shared yer soul." I look down into his hopeful face. I feel light but completely responsible. I, in my own distorted way, am partly responsible for his disappointment in Clemens. Everyone is affected by other lives. Each individual imparting some essence or thought that is a catalyst, however small, into the life-path of another. When he spoke of Ezekiel's importance, he sounded so honest. So genuine.

"Cole," I begin, "About Clemens..."

He holds up a hand. "No, no, no. Forget it. Clemens is Clemens. He ain't God nor a good representation. You didn't make those choices, he did. Forget it now."

I admire this young man. In Cole, I see the man I always wanted to be. The man that God desired me to become. The man He wanted Clemens to become. Our lives the victims of our circumstance yet we don't have to be victims of our lives. It's simple but so complex. A process of changing that takes time, patience and grace. Takes time?

"What time is it?"

He looks at his watch. "Twenty to five."

"We gotta get Clemens dressed and ready for the pre-meeting prayer. The other ministerial members will be here in about twenty minutes. We should probably check on..."

"Mr. Lambough," Cole says interrupting. I snap out of a mode. I realize I've already fallen back into my old pattern and a sense of shame stings me. I look at him and we both have a common understanding of what needs to be done to help me break free of me.

I nod.

"That's a good idea. I'll take care of everything else."

I give him another hug now that we are beyond the handshake and enter through the doors once again. The door of a new belief and new purpose.

I walk down the dark hallways that now seem much darker and walk right into Clemens' room. My feet no longer hesitant ships. The vanity lights are bright and he is nearly dressed. One of the mirror's fragmented images reflects back the room.. The smell of alcohol still strong, now mingling with the musk of cologne. He stands in his undershirt and suit pants. The skin on his arms worn and leathery. It always surprises me how old he looks for a relatively young man. Middle age should not have so many lines. The gold cross tosses a sparkle from the lights.

"Ger, my friend," he says, gapped grinned, "I feel tonight is goin' to be filled with abundant blessings from the Lord above. Praise Jesus. Hallelujah." This is how it always starts. 'Hallelujahs' and 'Amens' abound when he gears up for these meetings. I know soon that he will ask about the miracles.

"I hope so." My voice sounds stronger to me. Like there is a new force driving the words. Words caged for so long now ready to be released.

He slips his arm through the sleeve of his white dress shirt, whistling an old hymn. I watch Ezekiel in the light of the mirror. In my throat, I feel the remnants of tears. I don't know why exactly. But it's there nonetheless. His image seems so sad to me. A broken, fragmented man who doesn't understand life, God, or himself. I never have seen Clemens in this light before. Even at his lowest, most bitter moments. The dark eyes, sagging cheeks, speckled hair. It all speaks despair to my spirit. A man with no home, no family. A binary faith. Two souls inhabited in the same body. Does he have an identity? Does he have an anchor? He puts his other arm into his sleeve and shrugs the shirt up on his shoulders and flicks his sleeves straight. He buttons the cuffs, slowly, whistling but his face a battlefield. A sad song in costume. I feel the lead again. A prompt that I know so well from fighting it for over a decade. My cowardice ironically defeating my courage. Or my fear. Both are synonymous, I guess.

"Ya ready tonight, Ger?" he asks me. The musky stench of his smoke adding another layer to the bizarre aromas of this once normal room. This room that has changed my life. Maybe both our lives. If there's ever a time to ask, I guess it is now.

"Boss," I say.

Clemens turns toward me as his whistle dwindles into a breath. He looks right at me. Right at my eyes. This is the moment where I always take flight but my feet are stones to-night.

I take a step closer to him. "We've been through a lot together right?"

He nods with a puzzled look on his face.

"So I could ask you anything?"

He shrugs. "I don't see why not, Ger?"

I play with my knuckles. My heart pounding despite my new strength. This is the moment. To find out the truth of this man.

"Do you believe in God?"

Clemens gives a puzzled look to me like I'm joking with him. He snorts and shakes his head.

"What kinda question is that, Ger? You pullin' my leg?" He adjusts his collar.

"It's a simple question," I ask directly with a sturdy tone. No stutters.

He tenses his brow at me with a hint of annoyance.

"I'm a preacher of the gospel of Jesus Christ and have been for most my life. What do ya think?"

"You haven't answered the question," I say.

He waves a dismissing hand at me and begins buttoning his shirt, starting from the top and working his way down. In the mirror, I can see his eyes.

I repeat the question slowly, each word deliberate. "Do you believe in God?"

He grimaces and doesn't answer. His face flushes to a deeper tone but he continues to grasp at buttons and loops as a distraction. The heat from the lights is getting more intense.

"Do you believe?"

His reflection frowns and begins to aggressively button his shirt, missing loops and fumbling. His brow tensing into a violent state. He mumbles, "Stop it. I need to get ready. No mor..."

"Do you believe?" I interrupt sharply. My nerves are solid and it feels so revitalizing. I feel like I am fulfilling a purpose. A surgeon's tool.

In a burst, he slams his hand on the vanity and faces me. "Damn it, Gerald, I said quit!" His face red and terse, eyes moist and red yet I stand firm. I feel a sense of affirmation in my spirit. Lord, do with me as You will.

"No more games, Clemens."

He throws his hands up, wiping his hand across his face, scowling with grit teeth. He lets loose an agonized growl and paces back and forth.

"I don't need this shi..."

He brushes past me but I push back. I feel his body retaliate and soon we tangle with each other, a short burst of arms shoving and flailing like two blind fighters. He looks at me wild eyed. I can see the surprise and anger in his black pupils. We stand in a brief pause as if neither of us quite understood the other's motive.

"What the hell is this? I am a prophet, you bastard! A prophet of God! Who are you to stop me?" He screams. My soul is steady and comforted for once. The days of intimidation are gone. I am reborn into the man I held off being for so long. Seeing Clemens react like this is both encouraging and agonizing.

"Ezekiel," I say, almost whispering, "do you believe in the God you have dedicated your life to?"

"I swear, Lambough. So help me God."

"Answer."

He stands, a hand clasped to his hair, inhaling and exhaling large huffs of air. His body begins to relax and I see his face drop down. Sweat trickles down my side and it suddenly dawns on me how warm it is in the room. I step closer to Clemens, the mirror reflects his eyes cinched shut, face contorting. The sides of his mouth drop, brow gathering in wrinkles. The resistance fading from him.

I place my hand on his shoulder. My new eyes perceiving a sympathy and care for him. When my hand makes contact with his damp shirt, he begins to sob in long laments. He grabs me so tight that my ribs begin to pulsate with pain. We stand together. His words and groans muffled by my shoulder. I begin to cry myself. An excess of tears and pain colliding as two men go through a process of purification.

Clemens begins to apologize through sucks of air. "I'm so sorry, Ger. So sorry. So sorry," he repeats over and over. I pat his back. He's so thin I can feel his ribs through his shirt. He squeezes me tighter and tighter, his gripping vicelike. Throughout all our years, the fear and the confusion, the infinite amount of hours spent in prayer and praise, I have never felt as connected and close with Ezekiel Clemens as I have now. The bitterness has dissolved. The burden of guilt has been cast into the tomb. We are new creatures and the process of redemption is happening right now. He continues to apologize, "I'm so sorry. So sorry, Jem, so sorry."

"Jem?" I exclaim, confused.

Clemens lets go of me quickly and stumbles over the couch and falls into it, laying down on his back with his arm over his eyes as he always does. His face glistening and red.

"Is this about your brother?" I ask.

Clemens doesn't answer.

I walk over and push the magazines off the coffee table and sit down, leaning forward on my knees. Clemens seems hesitant. Like he's still battling the truth. Fighting true healing.

I don't say anything. I wipe my nose and sit patiently. No regard for time or schedules or ministers or anything. Not anymore. Nothing human to interfere with this.

"I'm tired, Ger. Oh, God, I'm tired."

"Then let it out."

"No. I can't. I can't."

"You once said to me when we first started all this that God is the doctor of our souls. Do you remember that? Well, He's here, ready to cure you of your disease. You just have to sign the form." I had never said anything like this before. Never even thought something as inventive as that. Did he say that or did I read it somewhere?

He sits up, resting his face in his hands, elbows on his knees. He almost looks like he's about to throw up. I want to say something but this time nothing needs to be said by me. That need to say the right thing is gone. He sighs a deep, tragic sigh. Then he begins, "I ain't ever got over it all this time. It's been eatin' away at me since I can remember. And the worst part of it all is that I still blame God for it all. Me, a preacher? I can't seem to forgive God for what happened. I can't forgive myself. I can't let it go, Ger. I thought this would heal me, ya know. Take it all away. It started out alright but it keeps comin' back to haunt me so. Visit me in the night."

He pauses. His eyes obscured from me. I see his bottom lip quiver. He cringes, reliving some old pain he is still dealing with from his father.

"It's alright, Clemens. Just let it out," I assure.

"Forgive me, sweet Jesus. Oh, forgive me, Lord," he pleads through his sorrow. The words like arrows to my heart. An indescribable emotion that can only be felt, never explained.

"I will never see heaven for what I've done. "

"You are not your father, Clemens," I say to him. I feel sweat tumbling down my temple in the heat of the room.

"No, no, no..." he moans, trailing off.

"Yes, Clemens. You are not your father," I repeat with more force.

I know he's getting closer to complete submission of himself. It always hurts most before being set free. Every muscle in my body feels like piano wire. It's clear Clemens feels the same way. I decide to repeat it once again. Push him closer to the breaking point where the self is destroyed. "You are not your father."

"It's not about my father!" he screams, pounding his fists onto his knees. His face smeared with tears. "I mean, it is but it ain't..."

"Then what is it? What is it?!" I scream, giving to the heat of the moment. The words flying from my vocal chords violently. My gut is shaking inside me now. I can feel my pulse shooting through the veins in my head.

"I can't! I can't do it! You don't know anything! Leave me be!" he replies. His defense crumbling little by little, brick by brick. I have to say it again.

"You are not your father!" I yell, my voice burning with strain. The ground seems to move, shifting like an earthquake under my feet and my equilibrium spins around me. The moment feels surreal. In a fitful voice of rage yet still saturated in sorrow and sadness, he confesses, "I killed my brother!"

What? All I can hear is the buzzing of the lights. The world has stood still and the eye of the emotional hurricane has been reached. All this time, this is what he has kept hidden. The crux of his existence has been surfaced and we sit together in silence. The sentence lingering like a vapor in the air before us. This information hammers me and I sit up, my back slouched and shoulders hanging. The words traveling through my ears slow like thick syrup, absorbing. He killed his brother?

Clemens crumples onto his side, laying on the couch, fetal, emptied as if the words were connected to his strength. He weeps, spent and vulnerable. A boulder-like burden rolling off his shoulders into the sea. The weight of his secrecy and sin visibly no longer sinking him.

He lays still, mumbling brokenly in heaving sobs in a distant voice that seems to float on his breath as if the fact that he vocalized the act had brought on a new recognition of its severity. Resurrected from his mind and now out there for judgment.

"I killed my brother. I killed my brother. Oh, God, forgive me, I killed him."

1947

The metallic bus slowed near the end of the two blocks that made up the main street. Its brakes hissed and the doors collapsed open and the two filed down the steps into the dust, standing with their scant belongings in hand. Ezekiel turned to thank the driver but the door shut and the bus blew dust into the wind before he could even speak, expelling its gaseous waste into the air.

Ezekiel looked at Gerald and laughed. "They sure in a hurry," he commented. Gerald smiled and turned his gaze toward the town before him, empty and desolate. Mere stragglers appeared in windows while others walked the old road like gaunt apparitions. The distortions of childhood unnerving his return. He didn't believe his death would produce this type of communal mourning. A decade from his exodus, the ghosts of his past had not abandoned this place. It sat as he remembered it to be, souring his homecoming. The small main street where Bidley would sell him and his brother pop, the feed and grocery. The buildings aged like stepping into a portrait, some extinct past where dusty cowboys held shoot outs in saloons and equines were the automobile's ersatz.

"I never had a family. If you have one, you should call them," Gerald had commented on many occasions with Ezekiel's dismissal. While driving in Bismarck, Ezekiel stopped at a payphone and dialed home. Since his father had regarded electricity as "the devil's convention", he had no way of reaching them directly. He remembered the number of a friend and, through a series of sporadic phone calls, he received the news from an acquaintance of his death. The words became garbled inside his head to the point he had to ask again.

The sun shone hot and thick above them. The heat clinging to their skin as they walked through the lonesome streets. Ezekiel felt old, imbedded emotions bubbling inside with each step, trapped with surreal nostalgia that held nothing but pain and he wanted to run again. Movement was his anesthetic. Gerald walked by his side with chin up and back straight, a new man. He saw the uneasiness in Ezekiel's body.

"You alright, boss. Do you need to take a break?" he asked.

Ezekiel shook his head. "Nah, I'm good as I ever have been, praise the Lord."

"Alright," Gerald responded. They continued walking main street in silence, perspiring and tired. They reached the end and continued past the old, beaten house that had seemed on the verge of collapse fifteen years ago but still stood, untouched by time. Ezekiel gazed at the house as Gerald walked by. Every intricacy standing out in his mind. The sagging porch still sagged and the paint still chipped. Time gave no healing. He watched until it waned from view and blurred in the heat's haze.

When Ezekiel finally faced forward, Gerald was probing his face for answers. "You remember that house?" he asked.

"No," he answered curtly and marched forward.

They continued to pass old familiar places, landmarks, localities that Ezekiel knew vividly but never expatiated upon. Noiseless. Nothing but birds and the rattle of small creatures at the passing of their foot falls. Soon, they came upon a turn in the road, now heavily overgrown with tree limbs and brush but still wide enough to be considered a path. Ezekiel stopped and gazed heavily into the path leading into the foliage. The road foreign as if placed from a different location and a hollow into a more sinister world where light cannot reach.

Gerald walked ten feet before realizing Ezekiel had stopped. He turned and saw his profile leering into the dense limbs. His eyes dark and wide, a lucid terror mounting inside. Gerald was bothered by how he looked. He knew because he had frequently, until recently, been possessed by that terror. An unexpected haunt that gives no warning.

"Ezekiel!" he hollered, surprised at his own initiative. His voice echoed across the flat, dry land, heart beating faster than it should.

Ezekiel startled and shot his face into Gerald's and the look was receding. He gave one last glimpse down the path then walked forward quickly, head down, past Gerald. Gerald looked down the path and felt nothing. He turned and followed.

They walked on in slow time. Gerald's gait slowing as the alk lingered on. His head saturated with perspiration. His clothes clung to his damp skin as waves of heat radiated up and down his covered body. Ezekiel turned to see his lumbering friend.

"Are we close, boss? I can't take this much longer," Gerald pleaded through his parched, white lips.

Ezekiel didn't answer.

"Boss?" Gerald asked again.

"Uhh...almost there," he answered as if returning from some mental conference. "Almost there."

"Thank the Lord, I can't take much more of this heat. Who would of thought God could make a place so warm? Makes me glad to be a believer." His attempt at conversation fell on his ears only as they crested a small hill.

"Isn't there a short cut we could take? How about through that grassy area?" Gerald suggested, pointing toward a more direct path with foot-high yellow grass and Tupelo gum.

"Nope," Ezekiel responded without a look.

"Why not?"

"Coppers and rattlers like that grass."

Gerald stopped and looked around his feet as Ezekiel continued to walk on, becoming more cautious as he trailed behind.

They halted at the meager peak. The small cabin stood amongst yellow, dead grass. A rickety fence poorly made encircled the structure. Both men peered downward to the land. Ezekiel gazed solemnly, taking all of the memories at once. His eyes glistened as a warm breeze blew.

"That it?" Gerald asked.

Ezekiel said nothing.

"Boss?" Gerald asked again.

Ezekiel continued to stare. There before him lay the testament of his broken vow to never return here. At first to run and then to serve the call of God. Both equal in their purpose. The weight of déjà vu crippled him and he sat down on the dead grass. His elbows on his knees and his head hanging between them.

Gerald said nothing but sat down as well, tucking his feet underneath him and leaning forward relieved. They sat, partially shaded by a small oak above them. Gerald couldn't help but be grateful for the mild relief. He looked down toward the cabin and examined the area. Nothing stirred within or outside. Exhaustion settled in on Gerald and, in the cooler shadows, he felt sleep creeping onto him. Ezekiel's voice brought him back, startling him, "It's all the same. Ain't nothin' changed," he remarked forlorn. He lifted his head and stared forward.

"You come back to a place ya tried to forget and, no matter how hard ya try, it still sticks with ya. Like it ain't ever left. Nothing has changed. Time didn't help it. Neither did runnin'. It's the fact that the past don't fade that bothers me so. I remember all these awful things and things that shouldn't be awful but have become it. I can still hear the songs on the phonograph. Everything else is like an old dream I had but all foggy."

He shook his head, biting his lip to the point of drawing blood. Gerald watched, listening.

"I guess we remember what we want to," Gerald said aloud, though meaning to only think the words. Ezekiel looked over at Gerald and smiled a subtle grin.

"Yeah, maybe so." He stood and walked in necessary stomps down the hilly incline. As he always did, Gerald followed.

They came to the old, wooden gate that surrounded the house. The chickens scampering and pecking around the yard now absent. He opened the gate and it spoke the same awful noise.

When they reached the doorstep, Ezekiel stood, letting a deep sigh and stepped up the tilted porch as it creaked memory. The screen door still there, the old hinge broken, now remedied, affixing the flimsy door to the frame. He seemed to shrink to the power of the building. Like it held dominion over all who should enter. With trepidation, he gave three soft knocks that rattled the silence. He remembered the golden cross in his shirt pocket and felt for it quickly, to feel its presence. It's metal burning his palm.

They waited with held breath but no answer came. Ezekiel felt his legs begin to quiver and he feared he may fall. He turned to Gerald and shrugged a response, Gerald's hand beginning to shake.

"You alright?" Ezekiel asked. Gerald nodded.

Ezekiel looked right and then left, trying to peer through the cloudy windows. The cabin robbed of life, decency. A structure known by its dereliction. Ezekiel raised his hand and startled when the door slipped open, revealing the face of a young woman. Ezekiel scrunched, perplexed.

"Can I help you?" she said in a high tone Ezekiel recognized her but his tongue hung paralyzed in his mouth. His mind's eye failing to comprehend her transformation.

She eyed him curiously then spoke again.

"Do you need somethin', mister?"

He stumbled over his words. "I-It's me, Abby." His guts fluttered awaiting her response.

She held her puzzled gaze until the warmth of recognition thawed her defenses. She slowly opened the door, her eyes wide. She shook her head slightly then threw her hands over her lips as her eyes moistened. Ezekiel cracked an awkward smile. Banging, she kicked open the door faster than its creak could follow, flinging her arms around his neck, embracing him with such vice he nearly fell. He stood with coat and bag in his hands at his side, paralyzed, as she sobbed into his shoulder. He dropped his belongings to the dirty porch and put his weary arms around her. His embrace cumbersome, never fitting where they should.

Gerald sat quiet a few feet away, watching warmly. Sweat poured and his head pounded with the heat yet he endured.

When the shock faded, the siblings detached and stood apart. A subtle comforting embarrassment passed between both as she wiped her cheeks. Ezekiel looked much older like ten years separated them.

"Come in," she said, heading through the door into the house with a gesture. "Mama's restin' in her room."

Ezekiel stepped forward as if he traveled alone until he recalled Gerald.

"Oh," he exclaimed, turning around. "Abby, this is Gerald."

Gerald gave a friendly nod. "It's nice to finally meet you, ma'am."

She creased a smile as he entered the house. Ezekiel picked up his things and Gerald followed.

The interior set unchanged to his memory. The chairs, worn smooth, made by the hands of his father in their identical positions he had left them. The iron cross hung near the phonograph in its designated location. The portrait of Jesus still remained, futile eyes and ears. A spectator to a show preconceived. The eyes conveying a deep sorrow witnessed this life.

"You two want somethin' to drink?" she asked from the kitchen.

Ezekiel looked to Gerald who sat down in the closest chair, panting like a hound, head low and darkened shirt.

"Make it two," he answered.

She returned holding two, foggy glasses with no ice. Ezekiel took both and handed one to Gerald who proceeded to guzzle the liquid voraciously. Ezekiel looked down to the glass.

"He never gave in?" he asked, examining the glass.

She shrugged. "You knew daddy."

She wore a modest yellow dress, her hair long and smooth atop her shoulders. Her body had grown curves despite her slender frame and the thought of his sister flashing into an adult woman terrified him. She resembled her mother and little of her father and this pleased him. He drank till his throat slaked. She played with her fingernails, swaying.

"You've grown up," he said.

"Yeah. Time does that."

He scratched his arm though it did not itch. They looked at each other, searching. Ezekiel scanned the room, adjusting his footing, crossing and uncrossing legs like some man with feet afire.

"So yer a preacher now?" she asked. A slight smirk revealing on her lips.

"Yeah, who would of thought it, huh?"

"I sure didn't."

"Me too." They both smiled.

"A preacher," she exclaimed. "Just like daddy."

His smile faded and his eyes lingered everywhere but in front. Ezekiel turned to Gerald, who had closed his eyes to fade into unconsciousness.

"I guess I better take care of him," Ezekiel said, "Is my room still open?"

She nodded. Ezekiel helped Gerald to the back of the house. Their weight croaking the floorboards as if the flooring exploded with the remnants of some biblical plague. As he passed his parent's old room, he stole a glance and saw a figure in the darkly lit room, a sheet blanketing the lone window. Her back to him as she lay on her side. He wished to shut the door but there were none and the sermons came to him on secrets and how doors "were a festering place for sin." It was hard to imagine he was dead.

He ushered Gerald into the dim bedroom. He stopped. The room as it had been left ten years ago save the sole window had since been boarded. His brother's belongings as if he still lived. Undisturbed; the bed, the dresser with his Gideon tract Bible, his shoes, even the clothes he had laid in random parts of the room. Great care had been taken to not disrupt the memory. He turned. His side held nothing but floorboards and empty walls.

Gerald moaned and Ezekiel shuffled his tall, sagging limbs over to the bedside and flopped him like some bag of clothes. Gerald slipped into unconsciousness during the fall. Ezekiel straightened, breathing the familiar musk, rubbing his hand along his lower back. He noticed the stain left by gutting a rabbit in his room. He spied Jeremiah's dresser. The scratch he had made in spite when a boy still streaked the top drawer. He ran his finger through the groove, methodical. He opened the top drawer, smelling that familial odor and choking back it all, slamming the dresser shut.

He entered the kitchen to see Abigail seated at the pine dining table, cupping her glass of water. She raised her eyes at his entrance and smiled and Ezekiel reciprocated. He pulled out a chair across her.

"He can't take the heat. He's a California boy," Ezekiel remarked with a tincture of humor. She chuckled then fell into a thick silence. Both their thoughts near audible in the volatile air.

"How did you find out?" Abigail's voice echoed in his ears. Her voice seeming loud in the moment.

"I felt the Lord urging me to call home. I don't know why now but all things work together for the glory of God."

She nodded, listening, disinterested. Her wide eyes perpetually displaying a sense of intrigue.

"Well, it must be the Lord for ya to be here three days after he passed. The timing is a miracle, it is."

"Yeah, I guess so." He looked toward the small kitchen window and envisioned his mother standing there washing dishes, humming. Then a cracking dish. "When's the funeral?"

"Tomorrow at the church. S'posed to be a good turnout for it. Everybody loved Daddy."

Ezekiel took a drink.

"Ya should have let me know ya were comin'."

He put the glass down hard. "Where's the body at?" he asked blankly, the words coarse.

Her brow narrowed, mouth slightly agape, then answered waving her hand in a disinterested tone. "At the church, I think. The casket is there anyway. Why?"

He nodded and stared at his glass. The question faded. The burden of conversation ever present.

"It's good to see you again," she stated. Reaching a hand forward across the table, touching his as he grasped the glass.

Ezekiel looked at their hands. "You too, Abby."

She stared at him, round empty eyes, mouthing words to her thoughts. "Ezekiel..." she began before he cut her words off.

"How ya been?" he asked, ignoring her, though he felt the question too formal.

She paused. "Good as can be expected. Mama isn't doin well. It's harder on her than I thought it would be." She averted her eyes to the tabletop. Her face grave and worrisome.

Ezekiel began to scan the home again, lost in a painful nostalgia he had submerged himself into. "Everythin' is the same as I remember it. The buildings, the smell, this place. It's like I never left." He spoke this more to himself than to his sister. She shifted in her chair, returning her hand to her side, now placing her smooth chin into the palm.

"How'd he die?" he asked.

"Ya didn't hear?" she asked surprised.

"Hear what?"

She looked to her other hand, biting her lip. "It's not important."

"Come on, now, tell me."

She gazed long into his eyes now forward for the observation. Satisfied, she said, "He done it himself."

"How?" he asked flatly.

Her body tensed at the memory. She wiped the corner of her eyes. Composed, she said, "He went out to where they found Jeremiah and he took..."

She paused. Her face cringed and she turned away.

"Yer rifle."

He cupped one hand around his fist and placed his chin atop it and looked absently through the cloudy kitchen window. The afternoon sun sank in the west, blood red and violent. Abby rose and went to the cupboard, retrieving a lamp and matches. She sniffed and then sighed as she opened the top.

"Zeke," she said. He turned his attention to her. She shot short glances to his eyes than to the lamp as she struck a long match, the fire igniting in a flash of flame.

"If there's somethin' ya wanna ask, ask it."

She fixed her gaze on him and asked, "What happened?"

He hesitated. His slight mannerisms halted, survival instincts revving.

"I mean...after the funeral, ya disappeared. Without a note, without a reason, without a goodbye. We didn't know if ya was dead or alive?"

The emotion he had been expecting from her slowly began to crack the moral shell. The shell and discipline of God's request of us could only hold the carnal and instilled emotions that inhabited all creation for so long.

"I mean...ya weren't the only one hurtin', Zeke. Not just from Jeremiah but from daddy as well."

Her melodious voice began to tremble and she faded. Her delicate features infected with repressed anger.

Ezekiel held his head down. No words could express the truth. The horrific and devastating truth. It was a bulbous mass ever increasing inside him that only grew when confronted. It proved far better to absolve the truth.

"Ezekiel?" she asked annoyed. Her eyebrows undulating.

He looked at her, eyes sagging.

"Answer me."

"I just had to go," he said, hands raised. "I had to leave."

"But why? Why didn't ya stay with me and Ma? We needed ya, Ezekiel. It was hard enough with ya here but when ya left, things weren't the same." She was showing the signs of battle again.

"I couldn't take it all anymore. I couldn't face it." He was amazed at his own loss of words. Behind the pulpit, he was a master of speech but, when placed before his bare essential being, he was as lapidary as an idiot.

"It. It. It. What is 'it'? All ya keep givin' me is 'it'. I deserve more than that. As yer own flesh and blood, I deserve more. Jeremiah wouldn't have left us."

He slammed his glass down, kicking his chair back and pacing. "What can I say? What can I possibly say that would fix all the mess I've done?" His voice retaliated. "I made a selfish choice for my own reasons to leave. They are my reasons that ya would never understand. Never. So jus-"

"Try me! While ya were off free from 'it', me and Ma were livin' in a hell. Ya probably didn't know that he would blame Mama for yer leavin' and he would strangle her sometimes till her face turned so purple she saw white spots of light while I beat him tryin' to make him stop. Did ya know that?"

Ezekiel shook his head and said just above a dejected, near inaudible whisper, "I didn't know.'

"That's right ya didn't know!" She harshly concurred into the cramped air of their once communal home. "Ya got some nerve comin' back here tryin' to fix everythin' that can't be fixed. I don't know why..."

"Abby?" a frail voice came from behind them. "Who's there?"

Ezekiel whirled around to see his mother, gaunt and weak, leaning on the nearest wall that entered into the kitchen. She squinted her eyes in his direction.

"Is that Jeremiah?" she asked hopefully.

Abigail answered routinely. "No, Mama, it's Abby."

Clementine Clemens's hopeful face deflated and she shuffled forward. Her once white sun dress dragging on the old floorboards, a mess of mysterious stains and smears clung to the fringe at her feet.

She felt along the wall with her skeletal fingers, bumping and jostling various odds and ends until she reached the kitchen sink and looked out the square, dingy window into the waning sunlight. Ezekiel unable to take his eyes off the remnants of his mother.

She turned her face toward the two. The face of his mother gothic in its depiction. The eyes hung low in the skull, the bluish bags supported those eyes and her once round, supple cheeks had stretched and ebbed into her mouth. The eyes glazed and Ezekiel could not confront them. Red rings encircled her neck like brandings.

Abigail, now somber and calm, watched Ezekiel. Their mother began to hum an old hymn she had played on those rare Saturdays in a haunting tone and bizarre smile. The world now a place devoid of feeling or reality.

Ezekiel asked Abby, never taking his eyes off of his mother. "What happened?"

Abby looked at her mother sadly. "She quit."

He listened to her humming a moment. "Can she see?"

"No."

"What happened?"

"Mama was late with supper. Daddy had been out." She looked at him. "She woke up two days later and couldn't remember a thing. Couldn't see a thing either." Her lips pursed at the memory. "She got it in her head that Jeremiah was still alive somewhere, hopin' he would come home any day."

"Does she know about him?" Ezekiel asked.

"She doesn't know about anything."

Ezekiel placed a clammy hand to his forehead. She hummed in another, naïve world where no one could visit her. In his escape, he had lost her.

"All she does now is wait for Jeremiah at the window, humming the same song over and over." Her words full of spite. Her real colors showed bright and blinding.

He walked over slowly, eyes fixed, carefully, his hovering steps came closer toward her. Her back to him, humming. He reached her and could smell the familiar scent of her perfume. He breathed it in, absorbed it.

She paused in her humming. "Who's there? Jeremiah? Are you come home?" she asked in anticipation.

"Yes, Mama. I've come home."

She turned quickly toward the voice and put her hands to her face. Such joy overcame her she began to cry and she reached her hands out wildly toward him until she grappled at his clothes to pull him close. She tightly clasped him yet, though he wanted to, he could not embrace her in return.

"Oh, Jeremiah, my son, I've been waiting so long for you to come home. I've missed you so much. So much has happened since you've been gone. Oh, thank the Lord Jesus, my son has come home, my precious son has returned to me."

Her body so thin and fragile. Her embrace weak. He thought she would crumble to ashes if he were to hold her. Her lips close to his ear as she spoke just above a whisper, cheek to cheek, "Oh, Lord, I've prayed for this day. I never stopped praying for you to come home. So much has happened while you've been gone. Abby is walking now. She's growing up so fast. You should see her walk. Your father is such a lovely man. He takes care of us so much. He's going to build us a bigger house with doors and electricity and maybe, we'll even get one of those cars too. Oh, praise Lord Jesus, my dearest child has come home. A boy can never sever the love of his mother. Never. Never. Never. Let me feel your face, darling."

She placed her frigid hands on his face, gently caressing, squeezing, prodding his features with diligence. Ezekiel thought of Jacob and Isaac. He was Jacob. He had wrestled with the angel with the life he'd been given. And lost.

"What about Ezekiel?" he asked her.

She furrowed her brow. "Who, dear?"

His stomach fluttered like a wounded bird. "Ezekiel."

She laughed. "Whoever are you talkin about?"

Ezekiel felt his life slipping away. "Yer son."

"You're the only son I have."

She embraced him again, holding tighter than before and humming the old hymn again. The sadness overwhelmed him, the isolation more lugubrious than that which he knew on the road. He raised his arms, taking her in, feeling the brittle bones of her torso, and he wept.

Broken Spirit

I have this reoccurring dream. I'm standing in a cemetery and before me is an open grave and beside it a shovel. Next to the shovel is a box that is locked and in my hand is the key. I don't know what is inside but I feel compelled to do something. To open it, destroy it, I don't know. I pick up the shovel and then the box and I know I am supposed to put the box, the chest, in the open grave and bury it but I can't do it. I try and try to force myself to do it but I can't. Suddenly, the sky becomes dark and the earth begins to shake and I shake, not from the earth but from fear, and begin to feel the burden of some weight upon me. I open my mouth to cry out but nothing comes and soon I feel hands grasping me, trying to pull me into the open grave. I struggle and fall into the grave. Into darkness. And then I wake up. I've been thinking about that dream lately but I don't understand it.

Almost three decades and thousands of miles, six continents, hundreds of countries, thousands of services and millions upon millions of souls saved, it's amazing that after all this, two men connected for years, near inseparable could know so little about each other. "I killed my brother." The words seem out of some movie I watched long ago. An old memory though I just heard the words.

Clemens sits. His face, its sallow slopes and weakened veins, drained of feeling. All his being releasing the stress and tension accumulating over all these years. Over all his life. The one defining moment that no one besides God himself knew is now shared with me. I am both honored and devastated to know this information. I feel a responsibility, a privilege in being his confidant. But I can't help but wonder if anyone would have served this purpose. I am just here. Ezekiel Clemens? A murderer?

He lays on his side on the couch, knees tucked up to his waist. I sit across from him, watching him breathe. They are long breaths. Years riding the gusts in and out. I don't say anything because I am not the one who has to say anything now.

It's hot. The lights blaring on us from the vanity, illuminating, revealing every imperfection. Our faces and bodies open for examination. My heart beats fast and I inhale and exhale easy breaths to calm myself down. On my bald scalp, I can feel drops of sweat forming. I glance at the clock and it is quarter past five. The time is drawing near for prayer and preaching. But right now, I don't care.

"How did it happen?" I ask.

"It was an accident," he whispers. "I didn't mean it."

He wipes his face streaked with tears and blushed skin. A faint wheezing in the back of his throat. My guess would be all those cigarettes doing what they do.

"We were just kids. That's all," he says.

"Did your parents know?"

"I told 'em he did it himself, cleanin' his gun. They didn't know we was hunting. But he knew. I could see it in his eyes at the funeral." He coughs a burst of noise.

His voice. Something about his voice. It's real. After all this time, I am hearing the true Ezekiel Clemens. Not the preacher, not the entertainer, nor the bitter son. All the personalities and facades he has kept up all these years are laid aside. I should be surprised by this but something tells me that I have always known this. Known that who we really are is buried deep inside us, concealed by skilled actors that we placate before different people.

He sits up quickly and runs his hands down in his face, slow as if to wipe the pain away.

"What have I done with my life, Gerald?"

I walk over and sit next to him. He leans into his hands, covering his face. Next to him, I see closely now. The agony of his guilt visible throughout his posture. I raise my hand and place it gently onto his back, rubbing soft circles. What guilt he has held inside! Such a burden to carry for forty years upon your back without the courage to release it. He hiccups his sorrow into his hands and I simply keep a comforting hand upon his back.

"So long. So long I been carrying this," he moans when the weeping subsides. "And God has been my drug. But He don't work no more."

He stands, pacing slowly back and forth in front of the door, his eyes ponderous and deep in thought. He looks ragged, both in his eyes and in his body. The episode we just experienced draining life out of his body. Both inside and out. Between the lie, the secret, the smoke, the drink and the road, Ezekiel Clemens is withering away. He is simply taking the long road to dust.

"Do you feel you have used God to gain what you want?" I ask him. He looks at me with dark, black eyes. His face growing longer and longer. He looks down to the floor.

"I've perfected it."

There is a long pause and the thick air is still. I spy the clock and it is now five thirty. There's not much time. His hair and once nicely pressed shirt now disheveled. Slumped about on his frame like blankets. The look of a man who has never forgiven and may die that way.

I stand up and head over to Clemens and face him, his body pulled by invisible weights, dragging all of him down into the Valley.

"Clemens, do you want to cancel tonight?" I try to sound as gentle as I can. Personally, I would much rather end all this. Stop now, abandon everything. Leave without a trace to go home.

He contemplates a moment, turns his pale face to mine and says, "I'm as broke inside as a yard dog." He chews his bottom lip in deep contemplation as if he's deliberating some unseen dilemma that he cannot escape. He decides and says, "We need to get ready"

I feel sad at this response. Though he opened up, though he poured his honesty and sins and secret into my lap for me to examine, I expected more. A dramatic change to a dramatic life. I expected a declaration of repentance. A proclamation. I expected knees and gravelling, profuse apologies, embrace, hands and tears in desperation for deliverance. I expected our arms to be around one another's necks as we boldly marched from this room into the world to live a new life. I expected to call my wife and tell her I'm coming home and to hear my children's voices say how glad they are to know that daddy will be there soon. Angel's voices. I expected change in every sense of the word. I expected something. Anything.

He begins to get ready in no rush, methodically smoothing his shirt and pants. He walks to the vanity mirror and combs his hair back, a determination in his eyes and lips. I don't want to think this but I fear there is no change in his confession. A confession for confession's sake. More for my own well being than for his own salvation. Does he have conviction for anything? I feel diseased around him for feeling. I don't want to think these things but he leaves me no other possible path.

"End it tonight. No more games, Clemens. Let's leave now."

"Ger, ya remember that meeting we held over in India with all them Muslims and Hindus?"

I nod.

"Must have been over a million people at that meeting. They all come to hear me, me, preach the word of the Lord. And instead of being excited to lead these sinners to the cross, I felt terrified. I had this awful sensation that I was really a wolf in wool. Before that meetin' I prayed for the first time in a long, long time for God's help. But the one thing I couldn't ask for was forgiveness. Never could do it."

I'm confused and there's a knock at the door. I ignore it and go to Clemens.

"End it, Clemens. Walk away."

The knock returns, louder this time and I hear a muffled voice through the door. By the tone, I can tell that it is an agitated Sonny. I ignore it again. "You don't have to run anymore."

He looks at me and smiles, the wide gap staring me directly in the face. "Ger, yer a good friend. My only friend. But the Lord's work is never done."

His words are gentle, meant for reassurance but I get no comfort. I feel angry, the blood rushing to my cheeks but I know that, despite my constant companionship, there is nothing that can change him. Not even God. A long battle has finally ended and I have neither the strength nor the motivation to go on.

The loud knock rattles the door again and I wait for something, though I don't really know what. A look. A word. A gesture. Anything to give me hope of leaving all this. But he is a stone.

Frustrated, I turn and stomp toward the door opening it faster and more aggressive than I intentioned.

Sonny and Lyle stand before me. Lyle smiling dim-wittedly and Sonny with the same scowl he held when we first met. They are both dressed well for the night's meeting and it brings my attention to how casual I must look to them right now. In all this excitement, I forgot to get dressed for tonight. Strangely, I don't care. I don't feel like this. Any of this.

When I speak, I try to sound as cheerful as I can manage despite how difficult it is. "Sonny, Lyle," I say, nodding in turn to each man. "Is everything alright?"

Lyle nods, as if conditioned to answer every response this way. Sonny rolls his eyes and looks me straight in the eye.

"Look here, Lambough, I've been patient this entire day with all of this...this circus show around us. But, by God, I ain't gonna sit around doin' nothin'. I just can't bear it any longer. It ain't Christian."

He waves an accusatory finger at me as spit lightly sprays off the end of his bottom lip, catching my shirt front. He is actually pretty funny when he is trying to be serious which makes it even more difficult to keep a straight face. I don't have time for this.

"What are you talking about?" I say phlegmatically.

He huffs his cheeks and shoots glances from Lyle, pitiful Lyle, back to me. His voice raised and ignited.

"What am I talking about? Dear Lord in Heaven, I'm talking about everything. This whole ministry is corrupt. The church could never approve of this! Never! Lord, save us. It's of the devil! Ya hear? Of the devil himself!"

He is getting so flustered his scant hair begins to unravel and the shoulder pads of his suit gather round his neck, making his face seem even more red like some suffocating turtle. A large thick vein bulges down the center of his forehead. It pulses with every word. I feel like I am smiling but if I am he doesn't notice.

"Sonny, I've had a hard day and...."

"It's a sin is what it is, Lambough! Ya can't call yerself ministers of the Christian God and have musicians with that long hair like that. This ain't California! If Jesus Christ were to walk through that door, he would smite us all for blasphemy. Yer breakin' the first and foremost commandment. I can't even begin about the songs, Lord in Heaven. Ya call that music for the Savior? It's that devil music those long-haired hippies do those drugs and lustful sins to. It's a sin. A downright sin. In my day..."

I watch him, as meek Lyle stands as told next to him. He flails his arms about, pointing and jabbing at invisible adversaries in an attempt to hang on to his religious traditions. The God he so desperately clings to an afterthought to his tradition. He continues ranting on and on and on near the brink of chaos. Doesn't this man know that Christ was a liberal? I am too tired to fight anymore. This is God's battle now.

I look at Clemens but he has disappeared into another world in his mind and nothing would distract him from his mission. Frankly, I don't care about any of it. The songs, the lights, the church, the people, him. I have become desensitized to God. I turn back to Sonny who never lost a second in his tirade. The red, vein-swollen and outraged face. The crackling voice. Lyle. Me. The entire scene. Something hits me.

Out of nowhere, I begin to laugh. Not just any laugh but a hysterical, tear jerking, loud, uncontrollable, truly humorous laugh. As if I am being tickled by a thousand hands and I have no way of ending it. Sonny pauses, breathing heavy.

He says something but I can't hear over my own laughter. He keeps saying something but it is lost in the wall of sound coming from my mouth. He looks at Lyle, who begins to chuckle himself, and then at me. Sometime during my episode, he leaves along with Lyle, who has now become hysterical as I am, and I laugh so hard my knees become weak and I end up sitting on the floor against the door frame, clutching my side, feeling it all escape. Maybe God's sense of humor finally makes sense to me.

I don't know how long it lasts but when it ends, I wipe the tears from my eyes and see Clemens, dressed, crouching next to me. He watches me a moment. Examining or waiting, I don't know. Who cares? He smiles and stands, extending his hand. I take it and he pulls me in then hugs me, patting my back warmly. My head feels like it is full of cotton. He holds me out before him with both his hands on my shoulders and smiles. Almost like a father.

"I'll see ya for prayer in a few minutes."

He gives my shoulder a pat and then disappears down the hallway with his Bible in hand and I am left standing alone. I feel sleepy. I close the door to get dressed and pick up my suit off the rack and head over to the vanity mirror. The lights shine on me and I glance at my reflection in the mirror. I am an old man now. Bald, belly paunch, deep creases in my face. My eyes red from the day. It dawns on me that I never really look in the mirror. I examine myself for the first time in I don't know when and I resolve that I am content. A man but a man saved. That's all one can ask of their life.

Redemption. And in this redemption, I have found what I must do. I place my suit back on the hanger.

I glance at the clock and it is almost six. It dawns on me that George and the other ministers are waiting. Normally I would be in a panic over this, afraid of things falling apart. But it is not my job anymore to worry. Everything is orchestrated outside of my hands. Either of my own volition or not.

I head out the door, turning to look back at this room that has changed my life. Our lives. Smelling the aftermath of this cataclysm. I close the door and make my way through the labyrinthine hallways until I come to one of the larger back rooms of the convention center. I see Jeremiah Cole standing outside, leaning against the wall calmly waiting. I stroll up casually and he stands straight and shakes my hand. I smile at him and he in return.

"Is he here?" I ask, peering through the partly open door. A hum of voices seeps through the crack.

"Not yet. Should we get started? We're already behind schedule."

The exchange has no urgency. As if it is just a suggestion rather than a need for action. The fact that the meeting starts in less than an hour is of no consequence to either of us.

"We'll wait. Whatever happens happens."

We walk through the door into the large room. All the ministers as well as some unknown faces are standing around in semi-circles, segregated groups chatting about various topics. The noise is loud and chaotic. A room of ministers. Some are ancient in age, others similar to mine and some as young as Cole. It all sounds like a frenzy in my head. There is a massive table filled with various snack foods, cheeses, ham with toothpicks, and coffee. Sonny and Lyle are nowhere to be seen. I spy George and I catch his attention. I faintly hear a joke about Baptists drinking "spirit-free" drinks and then uproarious laughter. He laughs with them, excusing himself from his conversation and walks over to me with that steady, hunched shuffle.

"Ger, my friend, I did as you asked. We were here right on time."

"I know, George, thank you. Thank you for everything. You're a good man."

He smiles modestly and takes a sip of his coffee. "I just try to live a good life." His white, thinning hair, growing ears and sagging eyelids are full of sincerity and wisdom.

"Is Ezekiel here?" he asks.

"Not yet."

"Well, we should start. The auditorium is full already."

"Is it?" I ask.

"Honest truth. They are scramblin' to try and find places for the extras to sit or stand. It seems they oversold the place."

I nod, amazed. Last year, at this same building, the turnout was rather low for what we expected. In the short lapse in conversation, Jeremiah joins us. I didn't notice how short he really is until now, situated between me and George. He adds to the conversation as if he had been there the whole time.

"The network team is gonna try and set up a screen outside for those who can't find seats so they can still watch the service. It's gonna be quite a night." He flashes a smile, raising his eyebrows up and down as if nudging me.

I hear the voices begin to lessen and I turn to face the door to see Ezekiel coming through. His presence seems commanding of attention. A new inexplicable aura about him. A rebirth. Maybe his corpse-like appearance has shocked everyone silent. He enters the room holding his father's Bible in his hands, stands as the voices hush. He peruses the room, the faces.

"Let's circle up and join hands tonight, gentleman."

Each one of us extends hands out to the other and reposition ourselves to create a circle about the room. The men clasp hands like a fence around the perimeter in a rustle of shuffling shoes. When everyone is settled, all eyes are on him.

I watch him, head high, visibly gaunt and sickly, yet exuding a power, a presence of supremacy. Metaphysical. He bows his head and all others follow suit. A lingering silence follows as everyone meditates for intense prayer as is tradition. I open my eyes and look around the room at all the solemn faces. Each person having their own tick and prayer movements. Some raise their heads heavenward; others bow theirs low. Leg shakes or jitters, shifting weight from sole to sole, rocking on heels, whispering their own prayers in hushed fervency. Before Clemens even starts praying, half the men have already begun to pray in hushed tones.

I glance over at Clemens, head bowed and eyes open, staring into the carpeted floor. He closes his eyes as if he knew I was watching him and begins.

"Lord, in our lives we have all fallen short. In our minds, in our hearts, we have blackened Yer name and I am no exception. I am Yer greatest sinner in desperate need of Yer forgiveness. I have eaten of the fruit and I enjoyed it too much. Too much. How can I speak Yer words to those gatherin' tonight if I can't follow Yer will? How can I be a light in the darkness if I put my cornerstone on sand? Lord, my prayer is a plea. A plea for change, for hope, for salvation. Lord, I come tonight a broken, shell of a man, on my knees, beggin' for Yer blood to wash over me and cleanse me. I am not fit for Yer ministry, Yer love, and I am askin', pleadin', cryin' for redemption. Accept me. I pray for these men in this room. Let them not fall as I have fallen. Let them rise up on wings of eagles as promised us in Yer Holy Word. Now, I pray for these righteous men. Save them, heal them, do whatever is necessary for them to be men of true faith. Not of the church, not of the tithe, but men of true, honest faith. Let Yer will be done in their life, as it is in heaven. Amen."

The circle gives a habitual amen. The whirlpool of laments and decrees of praise morph into song as everyone begins to sing in one choral voice the doxology. I don't sing. I only watch. I watch Clemens as the torment and anxiety of the night becomes a more serious reality. I feel it too, whatever this impression is saying. I don't know. I just don't know.

Praise God from whom all blessings flow...
The song is a wall of sound. A permeating presence in the room and in every face, it can be felt. An invisible force

expanding and seeping through the molecules, sinking in and moving the souls of man.

Praise Him all creatures here below...

Ezekiel has changed or is changing. A man in process. Layer by layer peeling back the filthy skin and hate he has harbored his entire life. That he has medicated with liquor and women and religion with each progressive year. The layers of secrets, one by one. The layers of hate. Layers of doubt.

Praise Him above the heavenly hosts...

The layers of hypocrisy. The layers of blame. The layers of guilt.

Praise father, Son, and Holy Ghost...

The layers of pain. The layers of fear. The layers of himself.

Amen.

The sound lingers, a faint echo in the room as if churning around us. Something riding the wave of sound, going in and out of each and every one of us. It is a moment of unforgettable serenity. In the presence of something awe inspiring and indescribable. The naked presence of the divine. But of what divinity? I thought I knew but now it has all changed. The new Ezekiel raises his face, dark eyes mournful and long. He smiles lazily and says, "I want to thank you for being with me this long. May God bless ya'll abundantly. I love each and every one of you."

He sounds meek, empty. The words having a finality about them. The group is touched by this gesture. By the sincerity in the words. Right now is not a show. Now is a genuine, naked surrender to everything other than himself.

The group disbands and files out of the room toward the auditorium much quieter than before. I check my watch. Sonny gives me a dirty look as he files out with the group. Lyle, on the other hand, waves genially and I wave back before Sonny smacks him in the arm.

Soon, everyone is gone but me, Jeremiah, and Ezekiel. We stand silently in the now vast and empty room. The faint hint of the song still dwelling in the air. Ezekiel, grave and focused, looks me hard in the face and then powerfully embraces me with a hard grip, squeezing with a strength, based on his current physical state, that seem impossible. The musk of smoke, sweat and cologne fill my nostrils. Yet the smell carries with it a torpid hope. He doesn't say anything because there is nothing to be said. Our lives are a testament enough that no words are necessary. The rescue, the tears, the fights, the miles, oh Lord, the miles. Sermons, worship, praise, readings, tongues, miracles. Journeys to the past, journeys into darkness and now journeys into light.

He releases me and turns to Jeremiah. Jeremiah extends his hand only to be engulfed by Ezekiel. An embrace part fatherly, part apologetic. Why does this moment seem so final? Such a sad and permanent parting?

He releases Jeremiah and stands back, smiling a soft, anguished smile. As if he is Christ being led away by the Romans to be tried before his enemies. A penance for his hypocrisy. Whatever the reason, it unsettles me. How it all came to this. He leaves and walks toward the door. I call after him and he stops. I walk up to him and stand before him. Our eyes meet and I say, "This is my last night." The words are harder to say than I expected. I am relinquishing my wasted life yet it is difficult and painful to say goodbye. He nods. Accepting this resignation of mine as if he knew it all along.

He exits through the door, away from the brilliant lights, fading into the darkness of the hallway. Embarking on some mission alone to purge himself, a battle into the past for the future. The words of the song echoing, reverberating, speaking in my ear. Over and over. And in my heart, the redemption I so believed in, the God I had dedicated my life to, feels like a hoax and I've been swindled over and over my whole life.

1947

Black as pitch and warm was the night. A sliver of moon glowed above as he stole out of the cabin into the wilderness, careful not to wake the others. To wake Gerald for fear of his prying.

The house had not changed and he remembered vividly every step that would produce a creak or whine of the old wood, surprised he recalled so much of so little. The screen door proved more difficult but he managed to slip through without stressing the hinges where they would speak his departure. He still thought the house alive. A malevolent beast that watched patiently any movement or action. Ready to bellow in warning.

He had to see him. He had to see, personally, that face as cold in death as it was in life. Once on the natural floor, he could quicken his pace and head the few miles to the old church. The door held no locks and, even if it possessed them, no one would put them to use. The inhabitants of small towns viewed locks as accessories of doors like a knocker or doorbell.

He walked brisk, stumbling periodically over rocks, roots and other natural traps with no moon to guide him. Nothing but his compulsion. He reveled over the meeting with his sister and mother. Emotions swirling, pulsing thunderous through his veins like floodwater. Had He called him home or was it his own perverse curiosity. The body, the reactions, the smell. A form of vicarious atonement. Whatever his reason, he regretted coming. His sister's words lingered like a short, open wound. Stinging continuously yet almost a hum in his head.

He spotted two small orbital glows bustle across the road in front of him, hissing, and he stopped. He watched as they glistened in the scant moonlight then disappeared. He continued. His feet making soft footfalls on the thick dust. The warm air scent of wilderness and isolation. An organic, nostalgic aroma. He felt eyes watching him in the dark but dismissed it.

He heard the chants and calls of the wilderness as he walked. Above, the soft hoot of the owls. Bushes shuddered like dry hands on dry paper. A land at once foreign and familiar, tracking him.

Reality is worse than dreams. In nightmares, there is no control, mere players in a horrid, unpredictable play without the ability to walk off stage. Unlike nightmares, it is choice that creates these atrocities. It is choice that creates the pain endured.

He walked further, lost in thought. He passed the shadows of houses from his youth. He knew he was close. His mind began to play tricks on him, manipulating the murkiness of the night. A simple tree warped, grew horns and fangs. The chameleonic shapes shifted into horrendous images in his eyes, some moving, scowling, moaning, snarling. This place the origin of himself and omniscient of him. He quickened his step, short bursts surging through his veins, increasing his heart, his fear.

He shot quick glances behind and to the sides. These protean devils becoming alive around him. Soon, he was jogging. No longer focused but desperate. He spied the faint outline of the church in the distance roughly a quarter mile away, standing alone on its vacant lot, surrounded by feathered trees. His mind became wet with relief.

He continued his pace no longer seized with panic. Yet as he took each step closer toward the building, his mind rushed to the conclusion of devils but he fought the urge to fall prey to that idea.

The church was close now. Its details beginning to come to fruition in the faint candescence of the house lights. The words, or wind, became stronger, more distinct. He ran. The breath pounding out of him. His heart beating, beating faster. Still the voices came. Speaking in serpentine staccato, words familial, his brother, his own poisoned thoughts. A cavalcade of ghosts chasing him, surrounding him.

In this imbroglio, he had reached the front door of the church. He grabbed the massive handle and pulled. The voices raised now, shouting, calling for him as if the inhabitants of death exhorted his presence. The doors swung open to the dark church's hollow sanctuary before him. The culling voices now a fever pitch. He flung himself inside, shutting the door with a thunderous clap. The sound echoed through the building as he stood, breathing heavy breaths. His heart slowly began to return to its usual rhythm. The soft glow came through the streaked and cracked window panes, accenting the make-shift pews, the walls, the musk. Reverent phantoms facing the cross in shadow.

His eyes adjusted to the darkness. He was back in his father's realm, transported to his old station at the rear of the church suffering from severe boredom. His father's church. Through the glow, the shapes came into view. He saw the piano. The center.

He needed light. He was certain no electricity flowed through the walls. He felt his way along the back wall toward the furnace. He hit his knee cap on a bench and exclaimed in pain, grabbing his clutching the pain as the other hand felt without a misstep. He heard tiny feet scurry past in the dark, startling him. In what seemed several minutes, he reached the box that held the matches and the oil lamps. He rummaged through the wooden box, feeling each object delicately until he felt the familiar paper of the matchbox. He fumbled, opening, nearly losing the matches onto the floor before finally producing light. With a hiss the fire gleamed in his hand and the portion of the building became illuminated.

The wall was dusty and cracked. As he scanned upward, the brownish water stains of the leaking roof had swollen like engorged puddles. He wiped his forehead, returning to the box, easily finding the lamp. Quickly, he lit the lamp and the wick burned brightly.

With the lamp's yellow glow, he arose and held it out before him. The small sanctuary alive. The rays bouncing off the corners, benches, and angles of the architecture. Everything inside the building as he imagined. The old piano more weathered than he remembered. He wondered if the keys even made a sound. The sanctuary appeared asleep, resting, torpid. Yet he felt the life of the place. The energy coursing through the cracks, just below the surfaces, inside the grooves. He wondered whether God cared for church buildings.

The spirit of this church was one of solemn despair. A heavy clear fog that crept and lulled in voluminous churns.

He walked down the aisle, rubbing his free hand along the smooth, pine benches. His other hand held the light aloft. He could see the faces, the bodies of those old, banal souls that sat here Sunday after Sunday, bored but determined to come. These apparitions yawning, stretching, scribbling, and teasing. The transparent, smoky images part present, part past, part future. The souls of the church that had never left. Faith without works. Sunday after Sunday.

It lay ahead. He walked trepid forward. He felt an anxiety he had not expected. Half believing he was not dead and would open the casket to find a soft, plush lining and stale air. Or maybe he had died but not died and would arise as he neared, walking toward him laughing robust, nefarious, as he stared into those black eyes. He placed his hand on the piano. The flame dancing in the dark. The casket more ornate and illustrious than his brother's.

He sidled by the coffin. It had a latch that opened the first half of the top of the coffin so as to reveal his torso alone.

The subtle smell of preservatives emanated. Even in death, he trembled. Even his meager attempts at valor and justice as a child seemed sad little plays. He wanted to believe he was strong but before his father, he was a lamb. Bleating for mercy.

He placed the lamp near the foot of the coffin then ran his fingers across the wood, caressing. He had seen this all before. It was practice to leave the body in the church the night before the funeral. Someone had told him it was so God would see how devoted they were, even in death, but he never believed that.

He had arrived, standing before his adversary now passed on. He stood still before the head of the coffin, staring at the latch in the glow. He felt a compulsion to leave. To let his demons lie with this man and walk but he had to know. He had to see. Faith would not do in this moment. He tensed, his heart steadily beating faster, as he placed his hand on the latch. He took a few deep breaths, in and out, in and out, and flung the coffin lid up, clanging and echoing into the darkness.

It was him. The drawn back, lifeless face sat peaceful in the light. He sucked in breaths until the intensity of the moment waned. His features so different from what Ezekiel remembered. The mustache turned a whitish grey, his lips thinned into skin. His skin fake, leathery, the complexion waxy. It looked a replica had been made. Yet the face was at peace. The hate and pain and volatile conflict omnipresent in the minutiae of his features had gone with him into death. Ezekiel reached in, slow and hesitant, placing a single finger light upon the cheek. The cold skin a sensation new, not just cold but void.

His mother's face came to him, reaching out supine, swollen, red. He took his hand away. He wanted to see suffering and misery. Such cowardice of the suicidal. He didn't know what he wanted to see but not this. Not this placid, serene scene into the next life. He needed demons dancing in laudation, summoning the devil to drag his soul to the depths for the pain and destruction he had caused. He needed to chastise God for this travesty. It was injustice at its finest.

A progeny cheated and vindicated at once of the sins of his father. His father now dead. That should be the end of it. Never would he have imagined the spectrum of emotions he would experience on this day.

Under the chin, he could see the small puncture the round made. The small hole that his life exploded out of and into the ethereal realm to be caught by angels or demons. The song Jeremiah loved so much came to him in this moment.

He looked down into the still face, the lamp flickering. Though he cared nothing for this man he shared blood with, he wanted to weep. For reasons that came and went with each flicker of light. He wanted to cry because he should. It was his father. Because the man who had beaten his family into fragments was now dead by the work of his own hands. Because he loved him. Because he hated him. He felt nauseous. He grabbed the lid of the coffin and slammed it down, clenched hands into fists, pounding them on the wood.

"Heaven ain't big enough to share with you, ya bastard!" he screamed, his eyes squeezing out restrained sorrow. He banged his fists harder, the wood making sharp splintered cracks. The lamp falling to the floor and shattering. No longer burning but merely a dying ember that would fade into the powerful darkness in time.

"Heaven ain't big enough," he repeated as he turned from the body and walked into the darkness, wiping his eyes. He felt the pain and anger punishing his heart, the suppressed emotions he had kept at bay since his fleeing moment. His hands began to ache and he couldn't stand it. His mother, his father, God, all of it. God wasn't enough.

The sound of the church door clapped in the night as he exited the building, standing outside in the wild darkness. His chest thick and it suffocated him. All the wounds were open again and he had no gauze to seal them as the thoughts clashed, surged through his mind.

He walked aimless, knowing not where his feet took him. No heed to the night. The landmarks passed unnoticed. Something dark scurried in front of him and he wished to kick it but was gone before his foot could reach it. He cursed and blotted God out of his mind. He wished to erase this false healing God promised but couldn't.

He saw a light in the distance glowing yellow. He wandered forward, cautious, hearing the light conversation travel toward him, joyous, uninhibited. He knew the place. He loitered outside the closed door before stepping forward, passing the bench, and entered.

The door opened and the swell of noise suddenly grew louder. The stench of spirits, musk, and smoke filled his sinus. It looked the same as it had always been except Bidley was not behind the counter, but a young man his age hunched over, serving some whiskey to a couple of old farmers Ezekiel didn't know.

The occupants didn't notice him enter and if they did, hid their indifference well. Ezekiel scanned the room, taking in the memories. He imagined his father sitting with those here, drinking over his Bible and preaching his insincere sermons. He wanted to turn and run but he was transfixed in his body.

"I'll be damned!" a loud, familiar voice exclaimed from the three drinkers.

He, startled, looked toward the bar where three sets of eyes were watching him. Standing behind the bar was the scarified face of Freckles.

Ezekiel felt a dread, a stone in his stomach, at seeing him but responded as if he shared his enthusiasm for their reunion. Ezekiel waved a hand, dazed, and wandered over to the bar, coming close enough to smell the two old farmers on their thrones.

"Git, git out the way. Make room," Freckles ordered the two with a wave of his hand who reluctantly shifted to the right, nearly toppling off their stools.

"We's all thoughts you was dead and now, in my estabishment is the prod'gl son. This is some world, it is."

Ezekiel questioned whether this was Freckles or not. He had never heard him talk before and here, before him, rambled on the reticent boy from his past.

"It's good to be back," Ezekiel lied. The low light from the bar cast shadows upon Freckles face, faintly diminishing the severity of his man-made imperfections but Ezekiel knew they were there. Freckles skin was porous and oily, glistening in the light. He held a naïve grin and revealed dark patches where his teeth were beginning to decay.

"Ezekiel Clemens. It sure is hard to believe ya's is here. I was but sixteen las time I's seen ya. And now here's he is. Where the hell ya been all this time?"

Ezekiel looked into the face of his past, remembering the fights, mischief, rebellion.

"I've been travelin' and seein' the country," Ezekiel responded. "What happened to ol' Bidley?"

"He gone up and died. Not too long ago, neither."

"How'd ya come about ownin' the place?"

Freckles hiked up his pants slightly and smiled a prideful grin. "He handed it on over to me when I was jus' cleanin' the floors here. He knews I was cut to keep up his place when he died, I would believe." He patted his slight belly twice and then rubbed his hand along the material of his shirt.

Ezekiel was still standing. His demeanor one of anticipatory flight. He looked at the bar and the army of bottles along the back wall behind the Freckles and he could smell the bitter odor they emitted.

"Set down, set down." Freckles said with humility, frantically gesturing toward the bar stools then remarked, "Hey, sorry about your daddy. He done died and all. It's a damn shame is what it is." Freckles shook his head as Ezekiel slipped his slim frame onto the stool.

"Thanks," Ezekiel said. His memory came back and he could see Bidley standing behind the counter, smiling that empathetic, guilty smile at him and Jeremiah. Now, he could see his father walk in and stagger out.

"I bet I knows what yer thinkin'," Freckles informed Ezekiel, staring at him in the low light. Ezekiel looked at Freckles querulously.

"I bet yer thinkins where's John Jakes and Petey at, ain't ya?" He grinned as if he had predicted his thoughts, even without validation.

Ezekiel leaned on the counter. "Yeah, it may have crossed my mind."

Freckles straightened with a sense of confidence before he continued. "I knews it. I knews it, sure as hell." He crossed his arms across his flabby chest. "Well, Petey done gone to the war and such. He come back with no legs and such and he ain't the same Petey we's used ta know. He moved on outta town to somes place. Don't know where. Din't walk there, that's for sure."

He paused to grab a couple of glasses and filled them with a dark drink. "Now, ol' Johnny Jakes. I knows you and Johnny's had some fights and such 'cause he had a worse temper than you, sure as hell. But anyways, this was bout...mmmmmmmm...five years ago when this happened. Well, anyways, John was real sweet on this young girl from heres. What's her name? Uhhhhh...Emma. That's it. She walk around with that fat lady that talks a lot. Pretty, nice girl all the boys done want ta...ya know. Get ta know her and such. Anyways, John was real sweet on her and gots ta datin' her for a little whiles. I mean, everyone could tells he was mean to her but everone just kept ta themselves and let em be..."

Freckles downed one of the glasses before continuing on, refilling what he had taken. Ezekiel looked down to see a glass with the same drink before him and he felt cold all over. He stared at the rapacious potion with fear and desire as Freckles wiped his mouth and continued.

"So, anyways, I hears one day that Emma don't wanna be with Johnny no more so she decides to leave him and such. Says she gonna run on up the state and hide away from him cause she don't wanna get hit no more. Well, Johnny hears about this and he turn red and angry all over. Hootin' and yellin' that he gonna find her and cut her head off and other horrible things. Now, I wasn't with John no more cause he was always getting' in trouble, startin' fights, and makin' things hard for me so I stops hangin' round him. Ya know he done robbed the corner store affer ya left? Rambunctious fella, he was. Best thing I ever done leavin' him, sure as hell."

Freckles stopped and began filling another two glasses with some bourbon and walked over to the two older men. He handed them the drinks and they nod. He returned, polishing a glass with a towel whose original color was a mystery.

Ezekiel alternated his glance from the drink to Freckles in a nervous frenzy. The cool, dark drink beckoning to him, begging for his participation. Promising freedom. Happiness and escape. Ezekiel began to feel sweat bubble upon his skin. He sought distraction.

"Well, what happened with the girl and Jakes?" Ezekiel asked, thankful that Freckles had allowed him to break away. Freckles looked at him a moment puzzled before the epiphany of his fragmented story arrived.

"Oh yeah. What was I thinks? Yeah, anyways, John was real mad. Real mad. He decides to go after poor Emma and make her comes back, ya know. So he steals a pick-up, I think it was ol' Mr. Mayhew's. Damn, was he pissed. Hehehe. Anyway, Jakes heads up the state and disappears. Come the next mornin', I reads in the paper that Johnny found poor Emma and done stabbed her ta death for leavins him. Stabs her thirty three times! I thoughts ta myself how smarts I was ta not be hangin' round with that looney. Read in the papers that he's on death row up in the state. Jury done found him guilty and set to shock the life outta him for what he done. I agrees with em on that part of it. Good thing you ran aways when ya did."

An image of Emma's timid face popped up in front of him from the recesses of his mind and he pitied her then as he did now. He felt sick, staring at Freckles homely features as his thoughts weighed on his mind.

"Makes ya wonder why God allows such things," Freckles commented. Ezekiel focused his eyes, pondering the words.

"Ain't ya gonna drink up?" he heard Freckles say.

Ezekiel looked down at the drink. His mouth began to salivate and he wished to forget but the curiosity crept in, beckoning. His father's lifeless face looked to him and spoke but silent. He looked at Freckles, grabbed the drink and

poured the poison past his lips and into his soul, burning
down his virgin throat.

Akeldama

My watch indicates that it is nearly seven. The events of the day have left me shaken and it doesn't bother me that we are a half-hour late. It's been an emotional and spiritual roller coaster. It is as if I have lived my life in one day and now it is ending. An ending I accept with open arms.

Cole and I walk through the hallways toward the back stage entrance. Through the walls we can feel the energy and hear the restless voices of the congregation. Why is tonight different? I have stood in this moment thousands of times and nerves have never been an issue.

We don't speak as we walk the gauntlet. Normally, talk of lighting, sound, capacity, timing, aesthetics, security, music, camera set-up would be fluttering about our lips but a communal assurance is among us. The building feels alive, circulating within the walls, pipes, wires and cracks. It doesn't feel like the same building. Or have I changed?

I see Ezekiel with his head bowed near the entrance to the stage. The spotlights are shining on his profile, the Bible held against his chest, near his heart. His eyes are closed and he seems so serene. Something he has never, in my years with him, ever given the aura of.

The music begins through the thick walls and the powerful words are clear above the drone of the instruments. Sung with a humble and faithful melody steeped in an undeniably modern rhythm. The new and the old collide and mesh. It is beautiful to my ears. Cole looks at me and smiles. The unmistakable power of the drums kicks in with force, elevating the song into a new dimension and the elation continues to lift us.

I watch Clemens in the glow of the spotlight. This eerie scene gives me a hesitant feeling. His countenance so grim and focused as if there is something he knows that all of us do not. Like how Abraham must have seemed when Isaac gathered wood for the fire.

I tell Cole I'll meet him onstage and he nods as we part. I walk to Ezekiel's side. He remains in prayer, head bowed, eyes closed. The open door makes the voices clear and differed. Through the doorway, I can see an immense mass gently swaying and lulling in the darkness beyond the stage. Thousands of bodies with hands raised in fervent worship. Each soul a broken jar of clay in need of repair. Aren't we all jars of clay? So fragile as to what is put in us, how we are handled. It's a miracle we even last.

I stare mesmerized at this sight. I see the ministers near the outer edges of the flat, wide stage. Both arms high with hands fetching the air, the sway on the sides of the feet, the clean, sharp suits and the rapid-fire tongues. This I have seen many times before. It is how the world sees ministers, preachers and evangelists. Fanatical, dedicated, flawless. So iconic.

The lights above the stage are bright, forcing me to squint as I leer into the crowd. The long-haired band plays on, the rush of the rhythm trembling the building. In the back of my mind, I know we will be condemned for allowing this. Especially in our allegiance to the Assemblies of God. Ezekiel decided to televise the meetings a few years back and the only way to do that was by directing our meetings to a more Pentecostal audience. This meant speaking in tongues and slaying people in the spirit. What did it matter? I never cared much for classification of faith. It is all the same God, just under different labels. Like soap or toilet tissue. That's all denominations are. Labels. Just as the drunk said.

Out of the corner of my eye, I notice Clemens now looking forward, peering through the doorway with me. I turn my head to look at him and his placid face has a readiness to it. Without turning his eyes to mine, he says, "It's about time."

"I'd say so." The wall of sound continues, now switching to a new song. I don't know the words, nor the melody but I let it wash over me none the less. I've never been this content with my life at this moment. I've made a decision I know is right. All the tension of this ministry has been lifted from my shoulders by the utterance of the truth. My truth. My decision to leave behind it all.

We stand, side by side, listening together. No words, no cigarettes, no drinks and no clean up. Two men who have shared a lifetime together comfortable in the silence between them. I have never considered it fully, but he is my friend. My closest and most intimate friend.

"Life is funny," he says, interrupting our moment of silence.

"How so?"

"Ya spend yer whole life searchin' for somethin', not knowin' it's right before ya, ready for the findin'."

I don't know what he means sometimes but I act as if I do. I feel a hand on my shoulder and I look at Clemens as his red eyes gaze into mine.

"You are the man I should have been."

He says these words with such conviction and sincerity that it moves me deeply and I try not to cry. His old face, illuminated, sagging and etched with the effects of one who tried to outrun the life he had. He looks much older than he is and I feel the same way. He squeezes my shoulder tight and says, "Now it's my turn."

He steps through the door onto the stage. I watch the silhouette of his slender, battered frame walk away from me to stand before the mighty sea of believers. They cheer at his sight, forgetting God in the process. Creation before the creator.

I watch him because I can't help it. Unlike before, he keeps his hands and Bible by his side and his head low, almost as if he is too ashamed to raise it. Normally, the show starts with a bang but there will be no show tonight.

It is a confusing world, complex and full of all that is good, evil and the grayness between. A world where God is both present and absent. Where the devil roams as if in his own kingdom but held in check by the idea of accountability. A world where faith, to most, is simply a word and religion is the reason for that faith. All these intricate and paradoxical webs of humanity, divinity and morality. Who can fully understand these things?

I walk through the door and onto the stage, assaulted with the stimulation of sound and light and I blend in with the others. I don't bow my head. I do not raise my hands. I watch the crowd and the man who leads them. The volume decreases to a soft swaying melody and Clemens raises his head and walks toward the pulpit. He places his Bible on the stand and leans in to the microphone. The crowd is hushed, listening. The cameras zoom in on Ezekiel, the large flat projector screens showing his ragged face magnified.

He looks with those blackish, dark eyes into the faces of the crowd. A slow, morose pan as if each face held a sorrow too much to bear. Soon, Ezekiel begins to pray:

"In this dreadful hour, we come. Life, in all its twists and turns, has run us ragged through the pins and pricks of evil. Some out of our control and others of our own accord. So tonight, Father, I ask for Yer forgiveness and Yer wisdom in speakin' the words that You have tonight. No flash, no shouts, no tongues. Only Yer holy presence in our hearts tonight. I am a sinner as we all are and Yer salvation and precious blood are the only things we can hope for. Amen."

The crowd agrees and settles into their seats with a loud rustle as the music ends. I notice some people sit on the floor and I wonder how far over capacity we are. I hope there isn't a fire. The two camera men are talking into their radios with concerned looks on their faces and shrugging in puzzlement. I smile at this because it is none of my concern. My concern lies a plane ride away. I imagine myself walking through the doors, my doors, and seeing their faces, feeling their little hands around my legs.

Ezekiel opens his Bible and peruses it a moment, lazily flipping the pages. He picks up the black Bible in hand and holds it over his head, looking from one side of the crowd to the other.

"Does anyone know what this is?" he asks. The majority clap their hands and shout out of conditioning. Some clap because they don't know why and others sit silent with furrowed brows.

"Does anyone in this building read this book?"

He waits for an answer but this time the responses are sparse and flailing.

"How many of you self-professed believers who would call yerselfs Christians have ever opened yer Bibles and read the words printed on the page?" He waits a short second before beginning again.

"That's what I thought. In my years of traveling over this earth and all the believers I have encountered, I found one common factor. None of ya do. Yes, ya may say, 'Pastor, I believe that Jesus Christ died for my sins and rose again' but the fact is, ya don't...read...yer...Bibles. Now brothers and sisters, I am just as much at fault for this as you. I am a minister of the Lord, in a leader position, and I am like you. I can't remember the last time I opened this damn thing. And frankly, I never had a good reason to open it anyway."

Wow. There's a bustle of murmurs about the crowd. Ezekiel sticks his hands in a halting position and interrupts, "Wait, wait now, listen. I ain't sayin' the Bible is not the word of God. I ain't sayin' that. I'm sayin' that I never had a good reason to read it. Ya want to know the reason? Because I never fully believed in God."

This last statement shocked me and every person in the crowd. Is he really doing this? He could have just said he was sleeping with hookers or gambling or something. Is he opening up fully before his fellow ministers, his followers, the world? The camera men are livid now. They throw their hands in the air and make cutting motions that Clemens ignores, looking to me but I just shrug. The crowd gasps and is restless.

"Now, now, listen! Listen!" he yells in the microphone. Everyone settles down slightly and he begins despite their clamor.

"Now, why do ya'll act as if ya have never had these same thoughts? That ya have never doubted that God is even up there or, if He is, that He has simply ignored ya all this time? It's a natural thought to have. I have doubted and doubted. Do ya think that if ya go to church or if ya are a pastor ya are exempt from havin' these thoughts? Everyone has these thoughts. Thoughts of if what they believe is really the truth. Christ in the garden had doubts about what He was doin' so what makes us, His believers, different? Nothin'. We are all liars. Isn't that what humanity is all about? And if ya think that if ya go to church every Sunday means yer a good Christian then yer blind. What is it about church that somehow makes ya a perfect person? I have travelled the world and preached at hundreds of so-called "Christian" churches and most the people I seen are as black inside as the night. I met preachers screwin' their choir girls and boys. Look at me, I am that black inside yet ya trust me to be yer connection to God."

He chuckles to himself and shakes his head. He picks up the microphone from its stand on the pulpit and begins to pace back and forth under the spotlights. I spy Sonny on the far side of the stage, his face replicating the flustered, red face I had evoked in him earlier. I chuckle and the minister next to me eyes me. The crowd sits silent, listening, steaming.

"I am not yer connection to God. Just because I say I am a preacher does not make me the better man. Just cuz I come in the name of God does not mean I am of God. I am a fake. A hypocrite. A lion among lambs. I have stolen money. I have been a slave to alcohol. I have given my body to whores all in the name of God and you have picked up the bill. Your tithe has funded my hypocrisy. No, no, no I am not...I am not yer connection to God. There is no connection to God to be found down here."

He walks back and forth, looking at his feet. The crowd is agitated and rumbling. The ministers are looking at each other in denial of what the most beloved evangelist in history is saying. They look at me and I shrug it off. His words are cutting through the façade like a knife. As for me, I understand what he's doing and I lean back and listen happily.

"And if ya are lookin for God in a minister or a building or a religion, ya are in for a rude awakenin'. Don't ya know that religion is an excuse to do man's work in the name of God? It was religion that put Christ on the cross. Wars are started in the name of God. I am a minister and many of ya have been followin' me thinkin' I am the prophet ya want me to be but I am nothin' but a man. Some of ya look to the church for God but it's just a building. Wood and nails and concrete and roofing made by man, inhabited by man. God does not live only in the church. He is everywhere. Inside us, around us, in all creation. If ya want to meet God, isolate yerself and call to him. He'll answer. Now some of ya are hung up on religion. Religion? God never speaks of religion or dogma. In fact, God hates religion. I hate religion. My father was religious. All religion is a political idea that uses the power and comfort of God to gain worldly desires. Manifest destiny? Hell, that was in the name of religion. The crusades were in the name of religion. Lucifer is the father of religion."

All hell was about to break loose. The crowd throws hateful glances and hollers at Clemens for these so-called blasphemies. Sonny, from across the stage, eyes me with disdain. He gives me a look like I should intervene and stop this attack but I stay where I am. His face becomes inflamed with anger and he stomps over to George and begins yelling for him to stop this, flailing his arms about like a wild man. The roar of the crowd is bordering on riotous. Clemens stands before the crowd, looking into them, listening to the insults and threats fly toward him like martyr's arrows. Does the truth really set you free? I see Sonny and George charging over to Clemens who yells through the monitors, "God is not religion! Man is not God! Have simple faith in whatever faith you may have!"

As George and Sonny grab a hold of Clemens jacket, he retaliates and fights back. Loud thuds pounding through the monitors mixing with the restless, oceanic roar of the hostile crowd. The rustle of clothes comes through the speakers. I hear Clemens tell the two ministers to let him go and soon they are tussling and snapping at each other. The air is frenzied and chaotic. The other ministers seem frozen in disbelief, watching a complete dismantling of what they had dedicated their lives to.

I head over to break up the fight and get Clemens off the stage before a riot breaks out. The band starts playing a song to try and distract the crowd but only adds more confusion. A soundtrack to a brawl. Unexpectedly, Cole is at my side when I reach the scuffling men and I grab Clemens to try and pull him away from the other two while Cole and Lyle grab the more volatile Sonny who is screaming at Clemens, spit spraying off his lips. George is caught up, scared and panting and confused.

There's a swirl of noise everywhere. A wall of sound that has taken on its own life. My head is spinning and I am there but not there at once. My last meeting! Simultaneously gripping Clemens and pulling him while watching it happen outside myself.

The understaffed security is acting as a pathetic blockade between the stage and the crowd. Some disgruntled believers approach the stage, waving fanatical hands and screaming how we are all going to hell for this. God's judgment is upon us. Right now, I don't doubt them. Could this be our time of atonement? The security guards struggle to keep this group of warriors away from everyone. The music plays loudly through the chaotic swell of noise. The struggle on stage continues. The idea of faith and religion colliding with violent consequences. Whatever happened to turning the other cheek?

Everything is in blurs and glimpses. Clemens shirt, Sonny's snarl, the flash of angry faces, the spotlights. It is all a dream like trying to move but unable to. I get a good grip on Clemens and begin to pull him away, his old anger surfacing in the heated moment. Sonny, with his suit jacket around his shoulders and his red, flushed face, is finally at a distance away by short Jeremiah Cole whose surprising strength in the moment goes unnoticed. Everything is so comically terrifying. Poor George stands between the two, now alone, looking flustered and baffled. His face begging answers as his white hair is a mess.

The two are still fighting as the crowd steadily becomes more and more agitated, small fights breaking out among members of the audience. Between the fight on stage and Clemens's words, the police may be arriving any minute. Who would have thought a meeting of Christians would climax with the police?

I say to Clemens, "You need to leave this stage or this might be the end of you."

"Then let it be!" He screams at me above the frenzy. His eyes are wild, hair flung above his forehead. He looks like a caged beast desperate for freedom. "I won't run no more! Come home, Come home..." He screams echoing the words of the song over and over.

I succeed in pulling him toward the edge of the stage. Hoping the violence is over. Out of the corner of my eye, I see a figure standing near George. I glance over, expecting to see another minister or security guard but I see a man instead. I know this man. The old, tattered and dusty clothes and the deep brown skin. My mind flashes back and I see him standing on the street corner with the same stance. The same vacant gaze in his eyes. The only difference I see is that he is holding a black object now and he is shaking it in my direction, finger ready.

"Hold on, a second, sir..."

I say this much before I hear a loud, unnatural clap that makes me flinch. Am I hit? The crowd is aflame with gasps and screams. The music stops as the sea of faces is in motion now, moving in sporadic directions. The cramped building now a mess of ants running for cover. Behind me, I feel my arm drop and turn quickly to see Clemens crumple to the floor, his hand clutching his stomach. His white shirt begins to spread and dampen with red. I drop to my knees beside him, feverishly glancing back and forth between the gunman and Ezekiel. Lord, save us. The man shakily holds the gun out in front of him and he starts blubbering. The tears pouring from his eyes as he mumbles garbled words in Spanish and broken English. The other ministers stand in a semi-circle around him but none dare to try and take the weapon. All we can do is watch. Where are the police? Where is help? The security guards are lost in a maze of a fleeing congregation. Helpless.

Clemens is laying on his back, cringing and clutching in shock at his stomach, moaning. Oh my God, he's been shot. He writhes, curling and uncurling like a wounded snake. I look back to the man muttering the same phrase over and over. I try to make it out. I hear one of the other ministers say, "Son, you can't blame the pastor for that." I ask the man directly, though beside myself, what he means and he says in a tremor of broken English and gasps of sorrow, "My son, he die...You no heal him...You no heal him....now look what you make me do. Mirame! Ayudame, Dios, ayudame."

He takes his free hand and clasps it to his forehead in torment, swaying, sucking in breaths, and Clemens groans in pain behind me. Not like this, please. Not this way. I attend to Clemens, forgetting the man, forgetting myself, and put pressure on his stomach. Blood seeps out from between my fingers as a steadily growing red pool gathers underneath him. Can this really be happening? Am I dreaming?

"Someone get help! Get help! Now!" I scream above the chaos of the stage. My voice stinging. I feel like I am in the midst of a battle from which there is no escape. The man is mumbling "que he hecho" over and over as the ministers try to coerce for the gun. I look to Clemens and his frail, thin frame seems to be vanishing before me and I can't stop it. Somehow, I feel guilt for all of this. I shouldn't leave. I should have stayed. His eyes are so fearful.

I hear a sudden clap and it startles me. A thud and cries of horror from the restless crowd and stage behind me. I snap my head back to the man to find him lying flat on his side with his face toward me. The eyes affixed in their sorrow. Blood pumping from the back of his head to a puddle on the floor. My stomach churns and I choke back vomit.

The other ministers are frozen in shock, jaws open, hands to lips.

Clemens continues to groan and writhe. He is bleeding badly and I wonder if he is going to die right here, in my arms, killed by his ministry. Is this how it ends? Like this?

"It's alright. You'll be alright," I say though I know it won't be. Nothing will be alright. Nothing will be the same. I keep pressure on the wound trying to stop the bleeding. He's so helpless. So scared.

"Is any help coming?!!" I scream. I feel alone amidst everyone. The roaring sound of the building fades into white noise behind me and it is just me and Clemens. Everything is ending and fading. Ezekiel's eyes stare upward, large black pupils, frightened and waning. The smell of sweat and cologne and death all around us. I look into his eyes and see a recognition come over them. A peace. An acceptance. He grabs my bloody hand on his stomach with his red hands and lifts his head as if to speak. He tries to speak but only a choking, gurgle comes out as blood dribbles from the corners of his lips. I look up and swivel my head around me, looking for someone, something to stop all this. To step out laughing saying it is all a big gaff. An ill-mannered practical joke.

"Clemens, sit back. Help's comin'. It's comin'," I say to reassure myself more than him. Am I doing all I can? Something else must be done. I think of God and wonder if this is it. "I won't leave."

I look up for help and then I see him. Standing among the panic and frenzy of moving people, peaceful and still as the bodies dart, trip and scatter around him. Those eyes;

they're so blue. The khakis, the shirt. I freeze and those magnetic eyes paralyze me once again and then the knowledge comes to me. The man, the being, nods at me, as if reading my epiphany and I understand his purpose. His paleness and serenity unnerve me. I hear a voice in my head tell me that we will meet again, but not today. I begin to shake. Why? Next to him, his hair matted with black, stands the Mexican man with calm eyes. A grotesque vision and I shake my head to make it leave me. I hate this. I hate all this. I look behind me and see the body of the Mexican man laying as I found him. But how...? George and Jeremiah are at his side, praying furiously. I shoot my gaze back to the vision and they are gone.

I feel a weak grasp at my arm and return my attention to Clemens. He takes one of his red hands and fumbles into his breast pocket. His hand shakes uncontrollably. The last tremors of life. I look into his agonized and weathered face and I know. He knows it too. The spotlights shine down on us and I wonder if Clemens thinks that he is seeing the mythic white light. I don't know why I think this. The warm fluid is flowing less through my fingers but the puddle has gathered around my knees into a large expanse of life force. Lord, is he ready? Am I ready?

Clemens removes his shaky hand from his pocket and drops his hand onto mine and wriggles whatever he has into mine. I feel the hard object and look down to see the golden cross, chain and all, resting in the palm of my bloody hand. Through the fog of sorrow, I see him mouth the word 'brother' to me.

I feel the tears blur my eyes and then fall and I begin weeping mournfully. I clasp the bloody cross in my hand and hold it close to my body. I look into Ezekiel's face and he looks into mine with eyes of one who is ready. We always wonder what our last moments will be like. Will there be fear or peace or tears or anger? In Ezekiel Clemens eyes, there is a peace he has never known. I see in those eyes of my friend, my family, my brother, the face of a man who is ready to meet God for the first time. To ask the questions with no answers. To experience what the living can never comprehend. He smiles ever so slightly. Just enough to reveal that gap-toothed grin. My head is beginning to hurt with the violence of my sorrow. Of what is to come.

I want to say something important to him. Something meaningful. Something to sum up our complex relationship. A final phrase to make sense of it all and part him with a word that tells him his life was not just another life. That he meant something. If not to the world, then to me. I think but nothing sounds right and as I ponder what to say, wracking my mind for the right words, his eyes glaze over, the muscles relax and his face sinks in ever so slightly as his spirit lifts from him and vanishes.

1932

The lake pulled the mist to it as a blanket. The sun's face barely peaking over the hills as the two young men walked surreptitious across the natural debris. Chattering of squirrels rattled overhead in the brown and dying leaves. They descended between a group of new trees, walking parallel to the lake and mist.

The older paused, looked to his younger, then pointed with two fingers from his eyes to the shoreline at the water's edge. The younger followed his brother's fingers to a buck drinking from the lake. On the other side of his, a head, antlerless, inched just ahead. The black nose close, pink tongue lapping water gracefully.

They stood concealed behind two oaks whose gap proved enough shelter of their presence. They crouched silent, watching. The deer both drank, peaceful, unaware. The fog lumbered slow, obscuring the opposite shoreline. Ezekiel looked to his brother, who steadied himself on one knee in a kingly position like some honored statue he'd seen in magazines.

"I can do it," he muttered under his breath but loud enough so he would here. Jeremiah glanced over at his brother than back at the deer. "No, you can't," he remarked in a whisper.

"Yes, I can," he insisted.

Jeremiah took a thin flank of dried meat from his shirt pocket and tore a sliver with his teeth, wiping his mouth with his sleeve. He lifted his ball cap on his brow and surveyed the area, assessing. Ezekiel watched him for an answer. The buck raised his head and looked in their direction motionless. Almost lifeless. His massive, web-like antlers protruding erratic into the fog.

"He spotted us," Ezekiel fretted. "Let me take the shot."

"No, be patient," Jeremiah urged. They waited, crouched, silent. Ezekiel's calves began to surge with burning. He could smell the humidity creeping in. The buck turned his head and took two slow steps forward before dropping his head to drink again.

"Listen," Jeremiah said, "We want the best shot possible. Straight through the neck. We want as much meat as we can get. If we're gonna take a life then it better be for a good reason."

Ezekiel became restless. "Look, would ya let me take the shot? I swears I can hit him clean. Swears to God."

Jeremiah looked into his brother's face. "You mean that?"

Ezekiel nodded. Jeremiah looked back at the buck's raised head again, facing the opposite direction. The doe raised her head as well and he could feel they might know something was coming.

"Alright," he said.

Ezekiel smiled before focusing the task at hand. He carefully lifted his rifle and placed the butt snugly against his shoulder. Nice and tight. Placing the barrel gently atop a small, thin branch jutting from the trunk of the oak and following the sight of the black barrel until it landed on the delicate animal. The cool air still as ice. All four beings trapped in this moment. Ezekiel's heart began to beat in his ears, the pulse in his neck bouncing. He wrapped his finger around the trigger. The buck kept still as the doe drank.

The branch snapped and the barrel dropped. Ezekiel's finger snapped the trigger back and discharged the shot into the dirt like a earthen puff, erupting fear throughout creation. The buck and doe bounded without hesitation, leaping fast and frantic in jumps until they disappeared from sight into the coming fog.

The scene resumed its natural peace as if no disturbance occurred. Ezekiel stood upright and kicked some leaves and rocks, cursing himself for his stupidity. Jeremiah began laughing. "Shut up. Just shut the hell up!" he barked but Jeremiah kept chuckling. The rifle slung across his back comfortably with his ball cap resting on his scalp.

"How was I s'pose to know the branch was dead?" he argued. "Ya didn't know it either." Jeremiah strolled ahead, content in his amusement. Ezekiel grabbed his cap from the ground with an angry swipe and stomped after his brother. "It ain't that funny."

"Yes it was," he replied.

The fog was thickening and the shoreline of the lake waned invisible. The habitual bird noises had ceased and the area settled quiet. The fog sucking the sound from life. Jeremiah stopped and looked around. Ezekiel caught up.

"Let's head back," Jeremiah exclaimed.

"What? No, we can't head back now. We ain't got anythin' yet," Ezekiel protested.

"The fog's too thick. We ain't gonna see what we're shootin' anyway."

"Ah, come one, Jem. Will try for a little longer and then we'll head back. Deal?"

"We're liable to shoot somethin' we don't wanna shoot."

"Please?"

Jeremiah thought a moment, keeping watch on the fog spread across the water, and then conceded. Ezekiel smiled. They continued to walk softly in pursuit, vigilant eyes prying.

They walked along the shoreline with no luck. They turned more inland into thicker brush to try their chances. After seeing nothing along this way, they stopped to reevaluate.

"Well?" Jeremiah asked.

Ezekiel looked around. "I bet there's a buck still around here."

"Not after that shot."

Ezekiel shot him a contemptuous look. He noticed his pointed nose, speckled chin, the scar under his right eye in the shape of a scythe he had given him. Jeremiah knocked his cap down over his brother's eyes playfully. Ezekiel adjusted the bill.

"A little longer."

"Alright. A little," Jeremiah agreed reluctant.

"Let's split up. I'll go around this bush that way and ya the other. We'll meet up on the other side and if we ain't seen nothin', we'll call it quits."

Jeremiah nodded. "And then that's it?"

"Yep."

They parted opposite ways around a large thicket embedded in the fog. Ezekiel walked with eyes and ears alert, hoping to spy a buck or rabbit or something to kill, something to impress. He stepped careful through the fallen leaves. The place reticent, still and grey. He peered meticulous around every bush, hedge, tree, his rifle ready in grip.

He longed for these moments by the lake. He longed to be here for as long as it took. Since Jeremiah had taken that job driving a delivery truck for the lumberyard out in Canton, he was rarely seen at home. Ezekiel wondered why he even worked out there. It was an hour bus ride one way and sometimes he wouldn't even come home. Ezekiel was envious of him for that luxury.

He crept on, hunched and ready. The thicket tall and wide. He could see neither over or around. Inside dense, nearly black, regardless of the increasing fog. He listened for anything but it was still and empty. He felt restless. A dreadful feeling inside yet he didn't know why. Pausing, he listened for any rustle. He heard nothing and continued skulking along the perimeter.

The fog thickened so he could hardly see within ten feet. He wondered if maybe Jeremiah had been right. Something snapped in the thicket. A short snap of deadness that left as it came. He froze and scanned the thicket. He could feel his heart beating in his ears again. A primal instinct to hunt. Among the twine of branches, he peered intently for any movement, not so much as twitching. He waited for the first time today, his finger on the trigger, hammer cocked.

Then he saw it. Still, almost imperceptible, the animal stood within the dense thicket. The long face, pointy ears and slender legs nearly extensions of the brush. He watched. His heart a muted thumping inside his veins. They waited as if in anticipation of the other's next move. A standoff of in-action. He could see the black eye hovering inside the heavy foliage. The world vanished, predator and prey reliant on the other's decision.

Ezekiel licked his lips, raised the barrel, inch by inch, re-peating in his head to be slow and steady, slow and steady. In what seemed an eternity, he had successfully rested the butt against his shoulder and the barrel near parallel to the earth. The reality of a decent shot trembled inside his gut. The fog all around, encapsulating him in this epoch. He inched the gun upward. Without warning the doe erupted into motion, loud and terrified, crashing through brush and foliage in its frantic state. Ezekiel lifted his gun and fired a quick, sloppy shot. The echo ringing in his ears and bounc-ing in and out of the opaque air.

He heard the doe fleeing and followed along the perime-ter, catching fleeting glances as she ran in front of him, weav-ing in and out of the thicket's edge. He raised his rifle run-ning, aimed, and then dropped the barrel. The breath pour-ing in and out of him, the chase compulsory. He needed to hold this animal's head between his legs and proudly display his conquest. Jeremiah would be proud of him. Father would be proud of him.

The path led around the thicket held overhanging and protruding branches that scratched and whipped his body as he pursued. He paid no mind to these in his determination. The doe continued to weave in and out, almost drunken with fright. He ran full speed, closing in then losing sight. The dreaded fog blinding with no definitive way of knowing what lay before him. He ran, stumbling over rocks and discarding any chance of concealment, rabid with bloodlust.

He caught a quick glimpse of the animal as it darted deep into the brush, crunching and snapping wood and plant as it dove. He could hear her fighting inside. He grit his teeth and went after her. Fighting nature to overcome nature. The branches scratched and broke his skin. He could not see far within and he wondered if he had lost her. If she had won the battle. He did not know how far he had gone. He saw glimpses of grayness through the mesh-like cave. He stopped to listen, panting and sucking in breaths. The wounds stung his cheeks and hands as he crouched enclosed. He made a circular turn of his head and then he saw her. The faintest shadow of her blocking the gray light at the edge of the thicket. The fog so thick her silhouette a mere shadow.

His black eyes widened. He raised the gun quickly and sighted the target. He inhaled and exhaled, his nerves crackling through his body. The shadow moved and, from the center of his fortress, he pulled the trigger. The shot was sucked from the air inside. She fell instantly with a soft thud. Ezekiel felt exhilarated. He had done it. He had won the hunt.

"Woo-hoo! Jem! I got 'em. Come on!" he yelled as he headed toward the fallen animal, pushing and forcing his way with wounded hands, not giving heed to anything to witness his kill. In a short time, he broke free at the edge and stood in the grayness of the fog on the path encircling the thicket. It surprised him that he could hardly see anything outside the bush. It was a good decision for him to escape the fog and hunt where the fog could not penetrate. He estimated where he had emerged and where the shot had taken place and he headed to his right.

"Jem!" he hollered again, echoing as he walked toward the kill. He could see the shadowy, translucent mass laying on the earth just ahead. Excited, he walked brisk. The fog's cover began to wane, the deer morphed into another, more tragic outline.

Slumped and crumpled on his side facing away from him, lay a human body. The grass around a dark stain resembling a black hole ready to swallow him into the earth. Ezekiel's knees began to quiver and his head seemed to spin on his shoulders.

"Jem? Oh, God, Oh God, no, no," he mumbled. He dropped the rifle and fell to his knees beside Jeremiah. His hands palsied as he placed them on the body, pulling toward to roll the body over.

The limp body turned and flopped onto its back. The face absent of life, smeared with blood and dust. Ezekiel leaned over him and felt frantic and panicky. His reactions colliding inside him, creating a concoction of terror, sadness and anger. He shook the body, trying to awaken the soul from within.

"No, no, no. I didn't mean it. I swears I didn't mean it," he said to his brother in some vain attempt at consolation. The eyes did not stare back. They held love nor faith any longer. Ezekiel looked around but saw nothing but fog. He felt suffocated, alone before God and creation as they lay witness to his mortal mistake.

He searched the body. The bullet entered the chest, tunneling through his heart and emptying his life onto the earth to return to dust. Ezekiel put his hands on the soaked coat, putting pressure on the wound but there was no blood to stop.

"No, no, no. Not now. Not here. God, not here, this way. Why him here?" he asked to the silence, praying God would answer him for once. He grew enraged and beat his brother's chest screaming, "Why didn't ya say somethin', damn it?!! Why didn't ya speak?!!" He collapsed onto his brother's body and held him as the tears now came, torrents of loss spilling, mixing with blood. In the fog, they laid like this. A final embrace, a hastened goodbye.

Ezekiel's breath came in quick bursts. He had to hide it, get rid of it. Tell them he ran away. He met a girl. He looked over the body and then around again, help absent as God. He wiped his face, feeling his brother's blood smear. He slung his rifle over his shoulder and leaned down, cupped his arms under the armpits and hoisted. Steadily, he shuffled and shimmied the body down the path toward the water, leaving a tragic wake in the dust and leaves.

He periodically stopped, dropping the body with a grotesque thud. The distance to the lake seemed further on the
way back though his thoughts wove between lucidity and
nightmare. The questions came to him, first thoughts then
audible, inquiring voices of where his brother lay, what became of him.

At the water, he laid the body down on the embankment
and phlegmatically sat next to it. The closeness to a dead
body unnerved him. He looked at his brother, at the cooling
body, beholding an expression bereft of tranquility. The severity of his actions became heavy on him, a burden too
much to bear. He felt abandoned by God. Judged from on
high with disapproving shakes. Another father to disappoint.
He thought to run. To abandon everything as is and flee,
retreat from family, God, his life. Everything.

The fog began to lighten, revealing the still lake before
him. Impatient and nervy, he hoisted the body and stepped
to the water's edge, the legs dragging and thumping till he
stopped. In a half-hearted swinging motion, he tossed his
brother into the water. The splash seemed loud in the stillness. A plunge into dark waters. The body became fluid
again, floating on the surface in the shallows face down like
hollow wood. The pale skin and blood dissipating in the
gray-black water.

Ezekiel watched his brother floating like driftwood. No
longer human but an object, an ignored part of nature returning to the place all life returns. He stood at the water's
edge and crouched to wash his hands of their stain. He
rubbed yet it would not come off. He then scrubbed

vigorous, frantic, the water frolicking in front of him until the death overwhelmed his senses and he fell on his hands and knees into the water and purged himself. He wiped his lips of bile and stench and wept until he could weep no longer.

The open air confined in his lungs. He felt no possibility of escape and, in his heart, he felt an unmanageable pressure in his chest, as if it may burst from his chest. The fog crept into his brain, causing thoughts and images to infect his spirit. He mourned his lament so vociferous, he felt life unworthy of him.

Beside him lay his rifle, black and caustic, inviting. Without knowing how, the cold metal was in his hands, heavier than before. He examined the barrel, the brown stock, the trigger. His face raised and he saw the body of his brother floating aimless across the waters. His stomach cringed, tightening within. The barrel of the rifle now under his chin. The cold bore digging into soft flesh. He felt sweat seeping from his pores and he wondered what hell would be like. Death was all he had now.

He fumbled down the stock and found the cold trigger. He licked his lips quickly, tasting the salt and blood, then a deep breath. He wrapped his finger around the metal and pulled the trigger with an empty click that rang in his lugubrious ears, denying him escape from the life he had created. A life he would have to face. A life of permanent haunts.

This Side of Heaven

Last night I had my dream. But it was different. I stood before the open grave, the shovel and box in their places. I felt the need to do something and I picked up the shovel and box as I have always done and I feel the same need to bury the box. I hold onto it and the sky begins to darken and I feel the tremble come but this time, instead of doing nothing, I place the box down into the grave and the oppressive hands and sky become still. I take up the shovel and begin to pile dirt upon the small chest in heavy scoops, higher and higher until the grave is full. Nothing above ground. Upon the last shovel full of dirt and earth, I see the bud of a plant begin to grow and, in rapid time, a mighty tree grows tall before me, covering me in shade and yielding fruit that I pull and taste and it is good. It is very good. And then I woke up.

It's a cloudy, misty day in the cemetery. I'm told it is quite unusual weather for this time of year in this part of

Mississippi and I can only take their word for it. Regardless, I still think it is a beautiful day.

The rectangular grave is open and the cheap casket sits on the floor of the hole. A mound of dirt next to it ready to be put back. Ezekiel would have wanted a cheap casket. He probably felt unworthy of a coffin but I think he deserves one. I found this spot between his brother and father. There's something sadly comforting seeing a family of tomb-stones. In a way, they are together and I think that comforts us more than it would the dead.

My wife stands next to me, holding my arm as we gaze at the box. She doesn't weep and I can't fault her for it. She knew the man I allowed her to know and now she knows the truth. The real man is no longer in that box but somewhere above us, walking in his heaven, I hope. Maybe embracing his brother. Maybe looking up. I don't know the limits of grace.

After that fatal meeting, I went home and poured my se-crets into my wife's lap. The final step of my purge. She was as precious as she has always been to me. Forgiving and com-forting just as her constancy has proven over the years. Yes, she was shocked, as was the nation. How could I blame her?

The attendees of the grave-side funeral are much less than I thought. I shouldn't be surprised considering the news of the final sermon spread through the media like a fire in a drought. Since then, the ministry was divided between be-lievers and skeptics. The IRS audited the financial records. I had calls every day from newspapers and other interested media outlets. The church denied anything he said and the ministry of Ezekiel Clemens was all but gone, a pariah for the hypocrites. George and the others were gone too and I have yet to speak with them. If they ever want to speak to me. A penance for my involvement, I guess. It was a short-lived grieving period and then life went on. By this moment, Ezekiel Clemens was yesterday's news and another had taken his place.

Jeremiah Cole came to pay respects but was busy doing interviews and working on his book to stay for the entire ceremony. Even a good man like that can't fight the temptations that come our way. Especially green temptations. I gave him the black Bible. I figured he needed it more than me. Hopefully, he can put good use to it. I hope I made the right choice in giving it to him. Maybe I have. Maybe I haven't. There is no family unless you consider me family. His mother had passed away and Abigail could not be found. I tried to find her but she had simply vanished. A pudgy man who owned a bar told me she left town sometime after her daddy's funeral and was never seen again. That's too bad. I had hoped she could have been here. I wanted to tell her the truth of it all. The truth of his life and the shadows he lived under. Maybe it would have redeemed him somehow. Made clear some obscure thoughts she had. To help her understand. But she's not here. I kept the letter I had written for her in my breast-pocket in case she showed up. Maybe it would have opened her eyes to the man her brother truly was, behind the show of it all. Opened her eyes to the demons that plagued him.

It was difficult to find a preacher willing to do his memorial. He was the church's figure for sin now. An example of how not to serve God. I think Clemens probably would have liked it this way. A rattling of the cages of faith. A revival, so to speak. He was a great man afflicted by demons. Great or not, what man isn't?

The preacher gave a modest eulogy, said a few prayers, and then we sang an old hymn. He's a younger man. Probably fresh out of Bible college. He must be. Otherwise, he wouldn't have even accepted the task. He'll learn.

The headstone is just a cross made out of stone. I had it made in the shape of a tree because I thought he would like that. I like it anyway. It doesn't fit in with the rest of the headstones though. His brother's grave next to him is more traditional. I guess it doesn't really matter in the long run. We all end up in the hands of God at some point.

I've thought a lot about my faith since that night. About God, man, the church. I tried to grasp how life works out and what's the purpose of it all. But I know that will never happen. It just doesn't turn out that way. Despite these questions, I still believe I am being looked after. And in return I live my life according to His codes. Otherwise, what is the purpose of it all? What is life but a waiting room to die if man has no purpose.

The attendees have all left, leaving my wife and I to stand before the open grave. She rests her head on my shoulder and I rest mine on her head. Her hair smells fruity and I take it in because I can. Because I am here, next to her. She dabs her eyes with a lacy rag and says, "It's hard to think he's gone."

I squeeze her tight, watching the clouds roll slowly across the hidden blue sky. There is no breeze. Everything is just plain. No ray of sunshine to shine hope upon us. Nothing so romantic. Simply nothing but the sound of the dead.

"He is in a better place now."

I look at the grave and it reminds me of my dream. I see the few flowers that had been tossed in, mixed with the dirt. I can still see his eyes the moment he died. So pure and peaceful in that one brief moment. I wonder what my time will be like. Will I beg for my life or will I accept it as he did? Will there be peace or fear? Only God knows and that's good enough for me.

"Dear, you mind if I have a moment alone?" I ask her.

She looks at me with that beautiful face, smiles softly, and gives my arm another squeeze as she leaves. I watch her leave, glad beyond words that she is in my life. Bill holds the door open for her and I nod my appreciation for him. The kids are in the backseat, fighting it seems. I turn back to the grave. Death is so glamorous in our minds but, in this moment, as his body sits concealed behind wood, about to be covered with tons of dirt, it is a rather pathetic, sad scene. So lonesome and absolute. I'm going to miss him. I sigh and I reach into my pocket. I hold the cross in my hand and I feel it with my fingers. He is my brother, despite what blood says. I kiss it, taking a last long look at the shimmering gold then toss it into the grave, to bury the past and the pain. Both for Ezekiel and for myself.

I watch it fall in slow motion, turning and tumbling, until it lands on the coffin and bounces to rest. The mixed blood of the cross at rest finally, left to lay with the life it attached itself to.

A song comes over me and I can't help but sing it. Sing it fully in my flat, toneless voice. I know it well and it brings me to a point of brokenness before life's fragility and I sing from within a hollowness inside my heart the same song of my now departed friend.

As my broken voice sings those words, I envision before me two young men embracing, their bodies restored, as if from a long absence. My heart is glad at this sight and I sing more, wondering if we really ever will meet again this side of heaven.

I picture another scene. An older man, slender frame and dark eyes, his left hand missing a finger that grows back miraculously before me. The young men see him and embrace him without trepidation. Without regret and pain and memory.

The song stops from my lips and I stand before the open grave, listening to the silence. Whether these are visions of mine or visions above, I don't know. Maybe just visions I want to see. The silent and final moment. I watch as the three gravediggers grab their shovels and return the earth back to where it came. Return to dust, where we all shall stand before our maker and speak of what we have done. And what we have not. Maybe we will and maybe we won't. It all comes down to faith.

I watch the shovelfuls of dirt wash the casket, the cross slowly disappearing into the earth. I keep watching until it is all gone beneath me and I know that I am a man with no past but a man with a future and I will wait for that day to see those paralyzing eyes and when it comes, I will have no fear.

Smiling, I turn to head home.

ACKNOWLEDGMENTS

I wrote this book, my first book, a long time ago and have learned much since then. So, there are plenty of people to thank for their help. First, my wife, who reads all my manuscripts and doesn't hold back on what she thinks. My family who read and promoted the first printing and also gave feedback.

A thank you goes out to those who have helped shaped my writing, directly or indirectly, and a thank you must go out to Doug Rice and Joshua McKinney who both helped guide me in craft and purpose. Also, thanks to Ron Hansen, Flannery O'Connor, John Gardner, and Robert Olen Butler for creating invaluable essays and guides on the art of fiction.

In an odd way, I want to thank all of those wayward preachers out there. The ones I know and the ones everyone knows. Their stories, good or bad, inspired this book and   Ezekiel is more of an amalgamation of those fallen leaders throughout history.

As celebrities often say, I want to thank my Lord and savior Jesus Christ. Not for publicity, but because this faith is the cornerstone I live my life on.

ABOUT THE AUTHOR

N.T. McQueen is a writer and professor in Kona, Hawai'i. He earned his MA in Fiction from CSU-Sacramento and his fiction, essays, and reviews have been featured in issues of the *North American Review, Fiction Southeast, Entropy, Sunlight Press, Spillwords, Litro Magazine, Camas: Nature of the West, Stereo Stories*, and others. He has done humanitarian work in Cambodia, Haiti and Mexico and teaches writing at Hawai'i Community College.

For more info and events, visit www.ntmcqueen.com
or follow him on social media

As an independent author, reader support is essential in helping indie artists create and share their work. Please help support independent authors like me by writing a review, posting on social media, recommending to a friend, or requesting a copy at your local library.

THE CRY OF DRY BONES

By N.T. McQueen

The boy's name is Tesfahun.

Nestled in the vastness of Ethiopia, he lives among the Akara, an ancient tribe untouched by modern civilization. His people live an isolated life where revenge killings are common and life is ruled by superstitions where cursed babies are thrown into the river for the sake of the tribe. As friends are forced to avenge the tribe and children disappear in the night, Tesfahun begins to question the beliefs of his grief stricken mother and hardened father. After his initiation into manhood, Tesfahun discovers a dark secret that pushes him to flee across the Omo River and into the territory of his people's enemies. In this new harsh land, he crashes into his deepest fears and must decide if he will resist the violence around him or be consumed by it.

Based on current tribal practices, *The Cry of Dry Bones* is a mythic coming-of-age story that takes readers into the untouched regions of the Omo Valley to examine the meaning of belonging, identity, and sacrifice.

www.ingramcontent.com/pod-product-compliance
Lightning Source LLC
Chambersburg PA
CBHW010440100726

47904CB00008B/2414